MW01595406

For Addison, who taught me how to love

CHAPTER ONE

In spite of her many flaws, she never thought she would be the type of person to commit murder, and yet right now it was the only thing that she could think about.

Stepping slowly into the room, she stopped for a moment in the doorway, holding out a trembling arm to steady herself against a tall dresser. Closing her eyes, she could feel the smooth but slightly sticky bumps of duct tape and remembered the weekend her sister insisted that they all help wrap the entire surface of this dresser in hot pink duct tape, changing it from a dull brown to a pink that could be seen from outer space. "Why don't you just paint it?" they all asked. But sister refused to change her mind, pushing the project stubbornly forward no matter the opinions from the people that she referred to as "the peanut gallery".

She could hear the whirling of the ceiling fan adding its voice to the almost silent air conditioner, attempting to ward off the intense heat that she had been almost oblivious to this week. All winter long she looked forward to this heat. She longed for the days that her body would immediately bead up with sweat just going from the car into the house. She lived for the long days, the bright sunshine, the picnics, the beach trips. The sticky, don't-turn-on-the-oven, blasting heat of July seemed to take forever to get here this year. She had been counting down, and for a while there between March and April she could have sworn that time stood still. It's as if nature knew what would be coming her way and wanted to delay the inevitable as long as possible. If only she had known, she would have thanked that blessed clock for its speed of mercy.

A crack of thunder interrupted her musings and the pattering of the rain on the roof picked up speed. Even the storm wasn't breaking the muggy heat of today.

Forcing herself to keep going, she lifted her bare foot to take a heavy step forward, feeling almost as if there were duct tape on the floor as well, giving just enough resistance to make her question what she was about to do. Looking down at her feet, she saw another painful reminder. The room was dark, but the light filtering in from the hallway allowed her to see her brilliantly painted dark red toenails. Remembering her excitement at that pedicure appointment, she felt herself whispering, *"Why, God why? Why are you doing this to me?"*

A soft gray cat brushed against her leg, whining for attention. She ignored it.

Dragging one beautifully pedicured foot forward at a time, her body moved more slowly than she wanted it to due to this week's events. She wanted to do this quickly— to get it over with, but just like everything else in her life right now, her legs refused to cooperate.

Only a few steps away now. She tried not to think about what she was about to do. Nestled in the blue pack 'n play in front of her lay the baby. Up and down his tiny chest fell, no effort given to drawing each breath. His cheeks were flushed in sleep. Perfectly shaped eyes lined with long eyelashes were closed for now, but she knew all too well the look of intelligence this baby had thanks to the new album on Facebook proclaiming his arrival. His entire body, down to the little fingers balled up into tiny fists, was plump and strong— just like a baby should be.

She picked up the baby's blue blanket carelessly thrown on the bed with the comforter that matched the hot pink duct taped dresser.

Staring at the almost unrecognizable arm holding the fleece blanket with satin edging, she felt the oddest sensation of floating out of her body to watch this all from above.

Aghast, she couldn't believe what she was seeing let alone comprehend that she was capable of this. But it was happening, right before her eyes. A distraught woman stood weeping over the baby while moving his blanket. Moving it so slowly and yet deliberately. Moving it, over his head.

CHAPTER TWO
(Six weeks earlier)
Claire

Claire Rose Bailey rested a hand on her rounded belly dancing with movement while trying not to wince at the pain in her back. How was she going to take another four weeks of this?

Standing in front of Claire were eleven five-year-olds each with a tiny violin tucked neatly under a tiny chin.

"Isaiah— plop all three fingers on the A string at once." She said, gliding toward him to adjust his bow hold. "Curl your pinky. Yes! Good job!"

Tiny violins scratched out the tune, *"Miss-is-si-ppi Hot Dog. Miss-is-si-ppi Hot Dog."* In unison, Claire's students worked the variation of *Twinkle Twinkle Little Star* precisely as they had been taught through repetition, ear training, and a world of patience. Claire felt a headache coming on, but she smiled encouragingly.

"Bridget, make sure your bow arm is making a square." She gently corrected while rushing to the next student in line to fix the placement of her violin under her chin. "Point your nose toward the fingerboard. Good. Just like that!"

Lily gave her a wink and a grin from behind her violin. Claire winked and smiled back while quietly adjusting the little girl's fingers more exactly on her brightly colored left hand tapes. "I wuv you." Lily whispered with a look of adoration in her clear gray eyes. "Love you too." Claire whispered back with a grin before moving on to the next student.

"Down-bow! Don't forget, we always start down-bow! There you go! Push your hand away from you. *Away*." She fixed three errant bows around her. "Great job. Perfect."

Threading herself through the room with as much grace as possible, she was intent on the position of every single five-year-old in the room. This was her job, and as a self-proclaimed perfectionist, she took it seriously. She knew better than anyone that one small mistake with bow hold or violin placement may seem like a little thing now, but down the road it can present huge problems in technique.

"Miss-is-si-pi Hot Dog." She clapped loudly along, attempting to keep their racing tempo on track.

Walking quickly over to the piano, she sat down and started accompanying her students from memory.

"One more time from the top! One, two, three, FOUR!"

Claire remembered all too well being the nervous five-year-old learning a new, terribly exciting thing. She remembered her teacher Miss Megan always smelling like flowers and having a cool but strong grasp as she would come by to help Claire with her left hand position. When Miss Megan would flash her a smile of the I-know-you-can-do-this variety, Claire would furrow her eyebrows and try again. And again. And again. She would keep trying as many times as it took for her to get the finger pattern right. Looking back, Claire realized now that Miss Megan inspired her career choice with that patient smile.

Remembering this now, she pushed the corners of her mouth up into her most sincere smile while playing her heart out on this week's variation of the theme even though in this moment she really just wanted to ignore them all and curl up on the floor for just a few minutes— or hours.

The afternoon class drew to a close as eleven excited five-year-olds unleashed an avalanche of wiggles that had been mildly tamed the past half hour for group lesson time. Parents surged toward her with questions. Tiny violins were packed into tiny hardshell cases that were excitedly carried by tiny hands out the door to another week of practice. They all held tightly to a chosen treat from Claire's treat basket for a job well done: erasers, stickers, bouncy balls, and plastic rings.

With several gushed comments such as, "Thank you so much! You are my child's favorite teacher!" and "See you next week, Mrs. Bailey!" still ringing in her ears, Claire shut the heavy door behind the last student and sank down in her soft teaching chair in the front of the room, surveying the damage of the afternoon on her shared teaching space. Three chairs knocked over, some paper trash in the corner, a small yellow rain jacket, a *Suzuki Book 2* left on one of the stands, and what appeared to be a crushed muffin next to the door— pretty typical group lesson road kill.

With an expert swipe of her hand, her low bun tumbled into a sheet of bouncing dark curls down her back. Pulling off her shoes, she awkwardly pulled a foot up onto her knee in an attempt to rub some feeling back into the numb appendage all the while rolling her long neck in a half circle to stretch out some stiffness.

Usually after the last class was done for the day she would tidy up her small classroom, but right now she couldn't imagine moving one more muscle— except of course for those muscles in her hand kneading her feet. Her shiny black clogs had never failed her before, but for some reason they hadn't been fitting well lately. Her mother suggested that maybe her feet had grown, but Claire gave her the death glare reserved for only the naughtiest of students

8

before stiffly assuring her that no, her petite feet never ever swelled above a size six-and-a-half.

Frowning at the sweaty, puffy stubs that she used to call feet, she grudgingly admitted that her mother had been right.

She paused in her foot rubbing and smiled. This pain was worth it. She couldn't help but think of her hallway encounter last Sunday, right after she taught her Sunday School class that week's lesson on trusting God. Notebook, Bible, and highlighter in hand, she rounded the corner at the end of the long church hallway to see Susanna with her brand new baby girl Emily tightly swaddled like a burrito against her shoulder in a pretty pink wrap. Sweet little Emily had rosy cheeks, sparkling eyes, and perfectly flat ears adorned with a large bow tied atop a hairless head.

"Ohhhhhhhh," Claire squealed as she stopped to admire the sleeping girl who maxed out the word *adorable*.

"It's amazing how anyone can look at a beautiful baby and not believe in a sovereign Creator," Claire murmured, reaching out to brush Emily's soft cheek with her finger. Emily's perfect lips curved into a smile in response.

"I know, right? Babies are such a miracle. I love being a mommy. It's your turn next!" Susanna proclaimed, tucking the blanket back under Emily's chin as it started to ride up over her mouth.

Claire beamed, and she swore that the baby did a cartwheel in her uterus. *It was her turn next.* She could do this. She was so close. The sacrifice of puffy feet was nothing compared to the goodness that was coming her way.

Looking around her office now, her swollen and aching body stood back up in spite of itself to tidy up and leave everything prepped and ready for next week's lessons. Glancing at the clock above the piano, she saw that it was 3:05. Let the weekend begin.

Claire promised herself a hot sudsy bath (at precisely 99 degrees F since 100 is the suggested limit for pregnant women)—okay, so warm sudsy bath with lots of scented candles and soft music before settling down for her own evening practice time. Tomorrow morning was a big Charlotte Symphony rehearsal. On Sunday her orchestra would be performing a Leonard Bernstein concert. As a member of the second violin section, she had a couple of passages to perfect before she was ready for the weekend's rehearsals and performance. Perfect was the key— it had to be perfect. Definitely a bath was required first, though. She had plenty of time for both.

And of course time for a large vegetable omelet with lots of spinach and cheese. She could picture the cheddar now— hot, melted, and delectably stringy folded in with plentiful layers of spinach to pack an iron punch. The good kind of iron punch. She was taking iron supplements in addition to her prenatal vitamin regimen, but frequent appearances of iron in her diet seemed to help keep the dizzy spells away. Her stomach growled out a surprisingly accurate rendition of Handel's "Halleluiah Chorus" just thinking about her omelet.

Trevor didn't like omelets, so this would be the perfect opportunity for her to give in to her latest egg craving. He wouldn't need dinner tonight because he had a youth group activity at church. If she remembered correctly, she thought that maybe tonight was a scavenger hunt and pizza dinner?

Quickly running through her end-of-the-day cleaning system, she motivated herself by visualizing that bath at home. Pick up, file, straighten, wipe, line up all the music stands against the wall, and dust. The weekend janitor would vacuum for her.

Dedicated to the arts, Edgewood Charter School K-12, had six music teachers— four of them full time. Claire, one of the part-time teachers, taught mostly group and private Suzuki lessons to prepare students for the larger orchestra ensembles led by her office mate, Carl Jones. She would substitute for Mr. Jones if the need arose, but she preferred to work with the students in a smaller setting. Teaching a large orchestra class gave her nightmares about keeping that many kids in line at the same time. Not to mention it was much more difficult to isolate and perfect problem spots when there were thirty other kids waiting around because their problem spots were in entirely different places of the music.

Claire loved her time at Edgewood, and was more than a little sad that she would stop teaching as part of the music staff here once the baby arrived. She loved her students. She loved her colleagues. She loved that her husband was (in her completely unbiased opinion) the smokin' hot Vice Principal working only a hallway away. She and Trevor had decided that she would continue performing with the symphony, especially since the orchestra was about to take their usual two month summer break, but she wanted— no, needed— to take at least the first year off of teaching. If this pregnancy had taught her anything, it was that juggling too many responsibilities while being exhausted was not her strong suit.

Finishing up her tidying with only some dusting left to do, she reached down to put her snack bag of organic carrots into her bag, but instead fell back into the chair with a small cry. Braxton Hicks contractions. Again. This was getting old. Was this the real thing? No. Maybe? No. But that felt like— "ARGH. Leave me alone!" she sputtered aloud as the tightening across her abdomen gripped her in its annoying intensity. Not so intense that she would call Trevor, but just intense enough to take her whole attention and exhaust her that much more.

It's not that she didn't appreciate being pregnant. And of course it wasn't that she didn't appreciate the gift of approaching motherhood. It's just that— *this was hard*; gritty, sweaty, entire-body-fallin'-apart hard. Because pregnancy took its sweet time happening for her, Claire assumed that once she had a viable pregnancy everything else would be easy— perhaps even apologetically beautiful to make up for the long wait. Before this pregnancy, she endured five and a half years with a negative for no apparent reason and more tears and frustration than she cared to remember. That was supposed to be the hard part. The positive test, strong heartbeat at each ultrasound, cute maternity clothes, popping out an Anne Geddes model— this was supposed to be the fun part. Right?

Wrong. Oh so wrong. Twenty weeks of almost constant vomiting, hip pain, a weird ringing in her ears when she tried to practice for long periods of time, inability to sleep, aches and pains in places she never knew existed, her feet exploding into something that might be found on an elephant— sometimes she felt like pregnancy was just a giant joke on her. *Giant*— a word that described her now. It was just another thing about pregnancy that made her anxious for it to be over. She was anxious to move to the next part— to being the new mother, hearing the soft baby coos, and figuring out how to dress him in those super tiny onesies. She couldn't wait to be the mother in the hallway of church carrying the cutest swaddled baby of all time while everyone that passed by squealed at the cuteness that was her baby.

It was her turn.

Staying in the chair and allowing herself to slouch just a touch in an attempt to stretch out the spot in her lower back screaming for attention, she reached for her violin which she had left resting on top of her case. She usually put it away last just in case a student came back in and needed help with something. *Suzuki Book 5* was on top of the stack of music in front of her on her music stand. She randomly opened the book to Vivaldi, tucked the familiar curve of wood under her chin, drew her bow across the strings, and let the weight of her arm pull the richest sound possible from her violin. Her long, slim fingers danced their way across the strings of her beloved instrument. Her bow floated almost effortlessly above the strings. Something about the music connected with her in a way nothing else ever did. Leaning into each note, she felt as though they were bonded even though it was for only a fraction of a second until it handed her off to the next note. The lovingly caressed notes rose and fell, freeing something inside of her. The tension began to leave her shoulders and neck. Her feet seemed to regain feeling. Something about the logical order of the notes and rhythm relaxed and healed her. Baroque music has always been her favorite. Add a violin and she could unwind from the most stressful of days. Well, as long as it was not being screeched out by a violin the size of her hand. That's usually what caused her tension in the first place.

As she continued to play, sighing with enjoyment at every nuance of the music, the hopeful mother thought— *I hope my little bub loves violin as much as I do.* She grinned as a hearty kick chose that moment to perform some musical taps of its own. If kicks were any indication, he loved it when she played her violin.

Just then, someone pounded loudly on her office door, startling her out of the web of magic that she had woven around herself. Annoyed at the intrusion, she was even more annoyed when she saw who it was.

She knew that she was the youth pastor's wife. She knew that she was supposed to love the entire youth group unconditionally. She knew all of this, and yet—

"Hey Felicity, come on in," she said with forced enthusiasm, pushing aside her immediate need to snap off someone's head while gesturing entrance to the girl standing outside the door. Why was she even at school today? Wasn't she on break?

Shuffling into her office with a downcast gaze was a girl with long, startlingly red hair. This girl wasn't skinny or fat, but lately she had worn nothing but dirty sweatshirts and baggy jean shorts in spite of the intense June heat. Here she was— the fifteen-year-old who was intent on turning the entire youth group against Claire.

"If she really loved us, she would come to our activities. I mean, is she saying that a silly orchestra is more important than *ministry?*" Claire overhead Felicity sarcastically saying to a large group of teens after church one week.

Surprised that Felicity would deign to grace her office with her royal highness' presence, Claire wondered if they were going to start right back up with the fight they had had the last time they spoke two weeks ago.

"He's not good for you."

"It's none of your business who I date!"

"But look at who you're becoming. Is this who you want to be?"

"SHUT UP. Just because I'm different from you doesn't mean that you're right and I'm wrong. Not everyone wants to be a plastic statue of virtue."

Raising a carefully sculpted eyebrow at that comment, Claire wanted to whip back "A plastic statue? I think you are confused about the concept of actually *having* a backbone, dear—which if you were passing your biology class, you would learn is definitely NOT made of plastic." But she forced herself to swallow it back. She was the older one. She was more mature than this. She would not allow these ridiculous digs to drag her down to Felicity's fifteen-year-old level. Not this time.

Plus, as she told Trevor later, she was fairly certain that Felicity had been drinking some form of alcohol before their confrontation. Her breath smelled questionable, her cheeks were extra flushed, and her eyes were more than slightly bloodshot. Jumping all over Claire's innocent comments about Elliot in an overly aggressive manner was just another sign that Felicity was probably into some stuff that she wasn't supposed to be. Trevor, wearing his side gig hat of Youth Pastor, said that he knew that a certain sector of the youth group was dabbling where they shouldn't, and that he was working on identifying those responsible so that he could provide counseling.

Now dreading whatever Felicity wanted to discuss, Claire was surprised to see swollen, red eyes on the usually cocky teenager's face. Steeling herself, Claire tried to summon some energy for the fight that was sure to come.

"What's wrong?" she asked, curiously. If there was something Felicity was not, it was a crier. She always resorted to anger and witty comments that cut just enough to leave an impression. Never tears. Felicity once said that tears of the weak watered the resolve of the strong. Whatever that meant.

Felicity swallowed, picked at a crusty spot on her black sweatshirt, and whispered

"Sis?"

"Yes?" *Sister.* A term they hadn't used for each other in quite some time due to a dramatic fight in which Felicity screamed "I'd rather have Hitler as a sister than you!" —because that made so much sense. But if Felicity was in a familiar mood and wanted to toss labels around, maybe this is what being a youth pastor's wife meant. Zipping her lips shut and allowing herself to be associated with the girl wearing the filthy sweatshirt who hated her. Sister. Okay.

"I think I'm dying."

CHAPTER THREE
Felicity

Felicity Sarah Reagan settled into the passenger seat of her sister's Honda Odyssey minivan. Silver and shiny on the outside, spotlessly clean on the inside— Felicity sometimes wanted to drop crumbs in random places just to make it look like humans actually lived on this planet.

Her thighs burned as they rested on the hot leather, but she didn't give her sister the satisfaction of hearing her cry out in pain. She issued a silent apology to the bacon she so gleefully watched sizzle on a no doubt similarly heated surface just this morning. Quickly placing her hands between her sensitive thighs and the seat trying to burn her alive, she couldn't remember why she always claimed summer as her favorite season. Every winter she counted down to the heat and beach weather, complaining about the harshness of the winds and chill that cuts to her bones, but then when the heat of the summer was here, she longed for cooler days in which she could climb into a car without getting a second degree burn on her legs.

Looking over at her sister's curly brown hair brushing past slender shoulders, dark brown eyes framed by thick lashes, and small frame defied only by a very large baby bump, Felicity wondered, not for the first time, how it was possible that they were even related. Her bright red hair along with her taller stature and decidedly unslenderness rendered them polar opposites. Like the warm friendliness of a polar bear and the cold steel-like qualities of an actual pole. Wait, is that not what that phrase meant? Felicity grinned at her own cleverness, tucking errant, brightly-colored side bangs back into her hood that she had pulled up over her head— not because she was cold or wanted a hat. No, she wore the hood to set Claire off. She could see Claire's nervous tick coming into play when her neurotic sister spotted the large splotch of jelly stained on the back of the hood and seeing Claire off her game made Felicity feel more at ease. Much more at ease. Breakfast jelly fiasco? Worth it.

The sisters were silent as the van hummed along to the Emergency Room. Felicity was still celebrating her brilliantly timed, "How are those cankles workin' out for you?" comment while Claire was no doubt still stewing over it. Or maybe she was still trying to dream up a quick comeback. Felicity relished in winning the conversation wars. The next thing to say always came to her with lightening speed while it seemed that Claire's lightening bolt was always at least thirty seconds behind the crack of thunder.

Claire had been surprisingly cool about the whole dying announcement, calling up Trevor to let him know that she was leaving and then packing up to leave immediately— well almost immediately. Apparently dusting was more important than her sister's emergent need for medical attention. Hopefully that regret would be included in her eulogy, delivered by a sobbing, oh-so-sorry Claire. Perhaps the eulogy could read something along the lines of "I will regret forever my selfish, selfish choice of putting ridiculous chores before the life of my amazingly talented sister. She was Queen of the World! And beautiful! Way more beautiful

17

than me. (wail) What a waste of a life! And I can't believe that it's all my fault!" Felicity made a mental note to write this down in a document titled "Talking points for Claire at my funeral".

Felicity figured she had interrupted some sort of end-of-the-day dusting ritual and actually expected more resistance from her older sis. Claire called them "systems," but Felicity knew a ritual bordering on witchcraft when she saw one. Perhaps Claire was afraid of angering the gods with dust on her desk. Or maybe she was risking the wrath of fallen saints if that notebook was left at anything other than a perfectly centered position. Well, that's what Felicity would have said while she had to stand there and wait for Claire to finish if she hadn't needed her help so badly. All things considered, Felicity knew that she got let off easy by Claire's quiet, but slightly delayed rush to give her a ride.

Felicity remembered screaming at her only a week or so ago "MAYBE IF YOU WEREN'T SO FAT NOW YOU WOULD UNDERSTAND."

Claire had flinched as if in physical pain at the mention of her weight. Felicity brought it up on purpose, knowing that it was a sore subject for the eleven-billion-month pregnant lady. The comment didn't even make sense or even really have a purpose in their fight, but Felicity relished being able to hurt Claire. Just a little. An opportunity for a jab that close to home came around so rarely. When you have a sister who constantly glided so close to perfection, Felicity had found that sometimes you hurl any insult you can, not because it makes sense or even really fits into the conversation, but just because you can. The more random the better. So when Claire said, "Does mother know that you're here?"— shouting loud insults about her weight suited that moment to perfection.

Truth be told, Felicity was sensitive about her weight too. Mostly because where Claire was small, Felicity was broad. Where Claire looked carved out of a delicate hardwood, Felicity looked cut out of a puffy down winter coat. Whereas they both came from the same genes, Claire seemed to get all the luck, and Felicity was determined to never let her forget it. Twelve years between babies seemed to have changed the entire gene pool for their parents. The "if only I looked like Claire" comparisons started at the moment of her conception and seemed to let up only when she went for a completely different look— disheveled tomboy. The more splotches she allowed on her clothes and the more she threatened to dye her hair colors like purple or green, the more it distracted from the fundamental issue. She was not, and would never be— *Claire.*

Feeling another wave of exhaustion railroad her out of nowhere, Felicity rummaged through her backpack until she found her favorite— a large can of Red Bull. It wasn't cold, but the caffeine and sugar kick would keep her going until the doctors could figure out what was wrong with her and load her up with some drugs— hopefully some good stuff. Maybe she could just stretch out on a hospital bed hooked up to some sweet juice that will let her escape from all the nagging that seemed to surround her these days. "Why didn't you make it home by your curfew, Felicity?" "Stop rolling your eyes at me, Felicity." "You know, doing laundry really isn't rocket science, Felicity." "Why don't you try to be sweeter, Felicity? Like Claire."

She cracked her temporary drug open with a satisfying pop, fizz, and dramatic "ahhhhh" before she saw Claire frown in disapproval. Whoops. Someone forgot the "No drinking or eating in the car" rule. Well, hopefully the dying card would help cut her some slack because she wasn't going to make it without a little liquid consciousness.

She chugged half of the can before stopping, gulping it down as loudly as possible, and then wiping her mouth on the sleeve of her sweatshirt. When Claire visibly squirmed, Felicity smirked. The fun of this car ride was making her feel better already.

It was then that Claire decided to put on her "youth pastor's wife" hat. If there was anything worse than an uptight older sister, it was an uptight older sister who was married to the youth pastor.

19

"Oh holy rule abider, cuttest thou us some slack— we beseech thee." Her smirk widened and she opened her mouth to quip it out, but for once Claire beat her to the punch.

"So if you are indeed dying, why didn't you tell anyone you've been feeling so bad? I talked to mother at length this morning, and she didn't mention any complaints or problems."

Craps. Was this conversation really necessary? Couldn't this be a *quiet* good deed? Maybe if she offered to sign something that promised cooperation for silence during the life saving ride? She did say please.

"I dunno. Just didn't seem worth mentioning." A few more gulps of lukewarm Red Bull were really starting to do the trick. This pounding headache was even fading away. Maybe she could just request this be put into her IV? Bless the creator of Red Bull. There. And mother said she needed to pray more. Ha.

"Did you tell mother?"

Speak of the devil.

"Mother? Are you kidding?"

They both fell silent, no doubt picturing their mother who would grab onto the drama and run with it before they even knew anything for real. Best to confirm a diagnosis, life expectancy, and some preferred funeral home brochures before involving her. Felicity knew she made the right choice going to Claire— as humiliating as it was asking for The Queen Of Nosey's help. As annoying as Claire was, at least she wasn't Mother. The lesser of the evils.

"So what do you think is wrong with you?"

"Maybe cancer?" Gulp gulp ahhhh sugar, dear friend. "Or I read an article online of a teenager dying from being just too awesome. There was even a YouTube video of proof. Who can argue with the facts?"

"Come on. Take this seriously. Do you really need to go to the Emergency Room or are you just playing one of your games?

20

I'm really not in the mood for your— um— your nonsense." A vein in Claire's forehead was beginning to pulse.

"Your *crap*? You were going to say crap!!! Admit it. Admit it!"

The vein stood out and entered a new zip code. Her sister's long fingers wrapped around the wheel as if strangling a leather bar, precisely on ten and two. Poor van. Then again, who buys a mini van before her child is even born? What are all of the extra seats used for? Felicity peeked back and saw— oh yup. Very large expectations and rules were overflowing in those bucket seats. Forget poor van— poor baby! Felicity would have to be an extra cool, fun aunt to make up for the suffocating life that he was no doubt in for.

Claire cleared her throat and reached for her phone as if to make an important call. Oooh was she going to tell mom on her now? "I'm so scared"— she almost mocked with pretend eyes of horror, but then thought better of it when she realized that she didn't have another fight left in her today.

Felicity put her mostly empty can on her torn shorts and wiped the smirk off her face.

"I don't know— okay. I just feel— weird. Something is wrong."

"Can you tell me any specifics? What exactly feels weird. Your heart? Foot? Your hair? Give me something to work with here."

"I'm sorry. I didn't realize that a music degree came with a certificate to practice medicine." Oh puleeeze like she would discuss this with her. Not on a flea's life would she open up about the very sensitive specifics here.

Claire opened her mouth to reply and then bit her lip instead. That's gotta hurt. Life is so much freer when you just let it all out. Felicity felt that she had learned this the hard way. But she was glad Claire just let it go with a toss of that too-perfect hair and quiet exhale that sounded a lot like their mother. Note to self: bring

21

up "you are becoming just like Mother!" during their next argument no matter the subject of the argument.

Felicity *wanted* to tell Claire. Well, she wanted to tell someone, but Claire was definitely not her first choice. Maybe the doctor administering her drugs would have a less judgmental evil eye.

Hanging out at Elliot's house, having a great time with her friends, laughing hysterically at the SNL bit that they had all been talking about all week (Jim Carrey is seriously the funniest!), wanting some pizza but afraid she would come across like a greedy pig if she suggested it, snuggling up to Elliot's side, loving his hands caressing her hair, laughing at Stephanie's ridiculous story about her parents "grounding" her, taking selfies (minus the red solo cups full of the forbidden), competing for the most likes on Instagram, arguing who won when Ashlee got twenty likes but Jason got fifteen AND a comment when all of a sudden the grip of death grabbed her entire body and squeezed— over and over again. Acting cool, with a pale face and clenched teeth, Claire told Elliot that she just remembered that her stupid history teacher told her she needed to come in for a makeup quiz before he'll give her a semester grade and would he give her a ride to school? Elliot wasn't able to drive her because he had too much to do before going to work in a few hours, but Stephanie happily volunteered— flashing the stolen car keys while laughing hysterically that her parents had no clue that her "grounded" week was far less horrible than they had planned.

The freakishly shiny alien vehicle pulled into the parking lot for the Emergency Room, and Felicity almost felt bad. Almost. Claire was being nice to help her out of a crummy situation. But not bad enough to actually fess up to being a brat. Being a brat comes with the territory when you are dying. Everyone knows this.

Dying. The word sounded dramatic, and yet Felicity couldn't envision any other way to describe the feeling of yuck that had pervaded her lately. She kind of hoped that she was dying, but she couldn't handle feeling like this for another seventy years.

Would she be missed? Most likely not. Claire and Trevor would go on living their perfect life with their perfect baby who no doubt would come out pooping sparkles in alphabetical order and actually love the Expectations and Rules waiting for him in the backseat next to his car seat. Mother could stop her "We're so worried about you" lectures and get an extra ten years of her life back from the stress that would then be magically out of her life. Her classmates who ignored her anyway could start ignoring someone else. Elliot? Would her sixteen-year-old heartthrob miss her? In spite of herself she smiled. Elliot. She hoped he would. She would like to think that she would be a girlfriend that was hard to forget.

They got out of the car. One sister gracefully descended holding an almost empty can of Red Bull. The other waddled out like she was holding an entire continent between those legs.

"Do you need me to get you a wheel chair or should we go straight to a gurney?" Claire's normally smooth tone was clipped and tense.

"Well, grab a spoon and welcome to the Dish of Sarcasm. Doesn't it taste GOOD? My work here is done." Felicity purred back, forcing herself to run up ahead even though she was pretty sure it would cut another couple of weeks off of her life.

She'd rather be dead than let Miss Uptight get to that receptionist first.

CHAPTER FOUR
Claire

Claire perched on the edge of the only unstained chair in the waiting room, anxious to be done with waiting so that she could get home to that bath that she promised herself before practice.

Sinking low into warm water, surrounding herself with thousands of bubbles, feeling aches and pains disappear, taking deep breaths, smelling fragrant candles, listening to her CD of choice— mentally she was already there.

Stretching out her leg to ease a sudden muscle spasm in her right calf, she accidentally kicked the padded rectangle black thing sitting in front of her— her violin case. It was too hot to leave her violin in the car because of the risk to the wood in intense heat. It fell quietly and lay on its side on the floor, looking dejected and lonely.

One, two, three— okay spasm gone. Claire sighed; folding her leg once more under her chair and wishing that she was already home where she could dive into a bowl full of bananas that would provide her usual afternoon potassium boost.

24

Placing her violin case upright once again, she softly patted it as if saying sorry to her dearest friend.

It was now 5 p.m. She should have already completed her eleven-minute ride home, had her bath half-filled up, and had a delicious omelet sliding down her throat to her cavernous middle right now. Hungry. *So hungry.* The last of her carrots disappeared forty-five minutes ago. She put two fingers up to her temple and slowly massaged. A throbbing headache was focusing there and wrapping itself all the way around her head. If she had known that she would be taking an after-school field trip, she would have packed extra snacks to keep her going. But no. No warning, no chance to prepare. Just when she needed to eat every hour in order to maintain her blood sugar level— not to mention the necessary steps she still needed to take tonight to prepare for rehearsal tomorrow— she *would* have to end up in a long Emergency Room wait.

Felicity picked a lousy day to demand the bond of sisterhood. Typical Felicity. Everything was always about her— never asking how Claire was feeling or if she even had time to drive her to the hospital. Just the demand and expectation that Claire would jump and ask how high. Felicity turned fifteen last month. When was she going to start thinking of anyone but herself?

With her sister's snappy "Not even a little bit" still ringing in her ears when she asked Felicity if she wanted Claire to go back with her after their wait in icy silence, Claire stilled her mind and tried to focus on getting out of here as quickly as possible. Her bath and omelet were singing her name in unison— in a *G Major Theme and Variations* style.

What was going on with Felicity? What did she really need, and why did she come to her now— today? Pulling out her phone, she typed a text to Mother. If anyone knew, she would.

"Hey, everything OK with Felicity?"

The reply back, as usual, was immediate.

"The usual drama. Why?"

25

Claire started to craft a response when she thought better of it. If she tried to explain a "feeling" over text to her highly imaginative mother, no doubt a huge misunderstanding would grow and mother would come storming down to the ER with a cross stitch project in tow with demands to speak to the doctor in charge. That would push out omelet/bath time even further. No, best to wait this one out and only report actual news.

"No reason. Just checking in. Hope the rest of your day is going well! I enjoyed our chat this morning."

"Me too. I love you!"

Placing her black cased iPhone back into the side pocket of her shiny red teaching bag, Claire closed her eyes and tried to will the headache away.

Mother was right. Most likely Felicity was just exercising the usual drama that she came by quite honestly. She pictured Felicity coming back out with a sheepish grin and a quip about a killer cold that almost took her down except for these magic aspirin pills that the hospital so graciously provided her for the bargain deal of trading one vital organ. Maybe the doctor would write an official diagnosis for "sarcasm overdose" or explain to Felicity that "weird" is just an ordinary headache and she needed to just suck it up and endure it like the rest of the population.

Whenever Claire voiced quips toward Felicity that were less than her usual kind demeanor, Trevor softly chided her. Apparently they were not very "youth pastory" comments although he phrased it differently. "You need to love your sister, not bait her. She's searching for something and egging her on does nothing to help her find it," he would remind her gently. So she stopped biting retorts at her sister. But nothing could stop her from thinking them. As a soft-spoken, gentle person, sometimes the edgy side that her sister brought out of her surprised her. What is it about family that brings out the worst in her? With the rest of the world she was the sweet symphony player who loved to teach small children to play the violin.

26

Why was this taking so long? If she just left, would Felicity be able to hitch a ride home? Perhaps she wanted to give those non-cankled ankles that she was so proud of a little workout with a long walk home?

Taking her hand sanitizer out of her purse, she scrubbed her hands for the third time since arriving. The very air in this place was loaded with disease. She could practically see the germs doing a happy dance. What she wouldn't give for a can of sanitizing wipes right about now. Exposed to an entire city's worth of illness— just what she needed before bringing a newborn home. The things you do for family.

Shaking her head and sighing, Claire wished that Felicity had at least been nice to Claire for helping her. It would have been nice for her to use those long-forgotten words—"thank you"— perhaps instead of insulting Claire at every turn.

I don't have cankles! Claire thought stubbornly.

(Well, she was pretty sure she didn't. It had been a few weeks since she had been able to really see her ankles for herself.)

But then again, Felicity was just fifteen and an immature fifteen-year old at that. Because of the large age gap between them, Felicity had been basically raised as an only child, and she was spoiled. When Claire was fifteen, she was already on a self-regimented practice schedule with youth orchestra concerts and weekly lessons faithfully balanced with her 4.0 GPA at school. Apparently Felicity was skipping out on half her classes to go who knows where, and she hadn't bothered to keep her nightly curfew in months. What happened to the strict Mother who insisted on increased practice hours during summer break?

Just then a pajama-wearing mom with three young children hacking out their lungs walked into the waiting room. Of course. There was no way to make her sleeveless black shirt into a breathing mask without appearing rude. But then again, maybe a lifted shirt bare-belly would be worth it to stay healthy for her baby's sake.

27

This black knee-length skirt that flared and swirled when she walked and this tighter fitting black knit sleeveless shirt were the only things that still fit halfway comfortably. As a frequently performing classical musician, she was used to wearing black 90% of the time since that was the performance dress requirement, but now she felt herself getting weird glances because she was dressed so morbidly with no obvious reason. She wished she could at least wear a colorful necklace or something to help break up the black, but chunky jewelry unfortunately interfered with the placement of her violin on her chin. She lifted her bare left hand and looked longingly where her wedding rings were supposed to be. She couldn't even wear those as they stopped fitting three weeks ago. At least she was wearing dark red ballet flats— or at least she thought she put them on. She couldn't see her feet to see if she actually remembered to wear them or if she was even wearing two of the same shoe. Yesterday she got home and discovered that she had worn one brown shoe and one black shoe all day. She wasn't counting on both of the red shoes actually being down there. So here she was, a black ball of— no that was it. She was a black ball. A black ball who was about to catch three different kinds of infectious diseases. Thanks a lot, Felicity.

"Claire Bailey?" A frowning nurse holding a clipboard called from the door where Felicity had disappeared almost an hour ago.

"Yes?" Claire responded instantly. She half stood, struck mid-stand by another leg cramp, but then pushed through it and continued to rise as the nurse gestured her forward. Slinging her violin case over her shoulder while stuffing her hand sanitizer back into her bag, she waddled stiffly toward the nurse.

"Is everything okay?" Claire asked. She felt some genuine concern tap her frustration on the shoulder. The nurse looked rather stern. Maybe something really was wrong. After all, Felicity had to be feeling pretty bad to actually ask for help. Maybe—

"How are you related to the patient?"

28

"Sister. I'm her sister." They were walking quite quickly toward a back exam room, and Claire found herself panting a bit trying to keep up, talk, and breathe at the same time.

"Well then, you need to ask your sister."

Claire followed the nurse into a tiny exam room with curtains for walls. Felicity sat in a chair to the side of the hospital bed, slumped over and crying. Twice in one day? No sarcastic greeting? Fear joined concern in overcoming her earlier frustration as she immediately regretted the hard time she had given her sister, and she even felt bad for taking the extra thirty seconds she took to run a dust rag across her desk before getting her here.

"Felicity? What's wrong? What did the doctor say?"

Felicity lifted her head out of her hands, blinked surprisingly beautiful green eyes when they weren't glaring at someone, and confessed— "apparently I'm..." she paused to swallow and then sobbed out the most surprising word of all

"I'm...*pregnant.*"

CHAPTER FIVE
Felicity

The drive home started out in scary, deep, dark silence that Felicity thought would swallow her whole if she dared to break it. Hiding in the silence was a friction between the sisters that was higher than perhaps ever before. Even higher than the time that thirteen-year-old Felicity spilled a large cup of red punch all over Claire's white couch at a bridal shower that she was hosting. Why would you even serve red punch if you had a white couch?

One wrong move and a spark would appear, bursting into flames that would no doubt consume them both. Since she really didn't feel well, Felicity didn't want a fiery shouting match. Although she would much prefer the reason she wasn't feeling well to be described by the word *dying* instead of the one the doctor used— *contractions.* What a horrible, dirty word.

"Are you going to tell Mother?" She opened the discussion hesitantly, braving the silence because she was starting to become more afraid of the unspoken than anything else.

"Of *course* I'm going to tell Mother. Don't you think she'll notice when there's two of you sassing back at her?"

"Maybe the doctor was wrong. Maybe we should go get a second opinion. What do ER doctors really know, anyway?"

"When."

"What?" Felicity was startled by the random question that was asked calmly with no hint of the scream she was expecting.

"*When*. When did you start having sex?"

Felicity blushed— a rarity for her. She would never forget visiting Elliot at his dad's garage that warm fall afternoon. She could remember his dad leaving for an appointment, an empty couch in the waiting room, drawn blinds, being touched— *there*, being loved. Undoubtedly things beyond what she planned, but Elliot assured her that no one ever had to know and that if she really loved him, she would show him. Part of her becoming *his*. Loving the feeling of putting that happy look on Elliot's face, but feeling incredibly awkward because the entire encounter seemed short, weird, and nothing at all like the scenes in the movies promised it would be. It was the strangest thirty seconds of her life to date.

Elliot. She had to tell Elliot. Her cheeks went from blush to deathly pale faster than you could say "angry boyfriend". What would Elliot say? If zero was how much she wanted a baby then he was in the negative numbers. This could get tricky. Would he leave her? Would he still want to snuggle on the couch watching TV and teasing second base into third if there was a baby in the next room?

The whole thing just didn't feel real. This couldn't possibly be her life now. How could she possibly be thirty-three weeks pregnant? Sure, she had gained a little chub the past few months, but mostly because she had been extra happy, spending many date nights eating more junk food than she ever had before. She had felt weird sensations in her stomach but always passed it off as gas because of the unhealthy junk food. Her periods had always been on again off again, so she didn't think too much of a few missed ones.

Felicity should have known. After all, she had spent long hours obsessing over the extra oiliness on her face that seemed responsible for more pimples than she felt were her fair share. Not to mention, she felt weird about her boobs ballooning out so much this past year that she got catcall whistles from boys at school if she didn't drape the ladies with a large sweatshirt. She felt increasingly awkward in the proportions of her body, and always wondered why she felt so different than the other girls in her class who always seemed so petite and lip glossed to perfection. This eighth-grade year had been tough. Felicity just assumed this was puberty. Who knew that she was experiencing a different "p" word altogether— *pregnancy*? Not cool, body. Not cool.

She didn't want to remember, didn't want to feel, and didn't want to process this nightmare. If she ignored it— maybe it would all go away. A nice nap would cure her ills. Maybe she was dreaming?

Wake up, Felicity. Wake up!

Finally ready to answer Claire's rude question with an answer, Felicity quipped dryly, "I'm pretty sure this was an immaculate conception."

Claire rolled her eyes and gripped the steering wheel a little tighter. Felicity wanted to reach over and apologize to the nice steering wheel with some gentle pats. This was the second time today it was getting strangled because of her.

"I don't think you are grasping how serious this is." Claire sputtered. "This is *not* a laughing matter. You're going to have a BABY. In....um seven weeks. SEVEN. Are you going to be ready for motherhood in seven weeks?"

"Maybe my baby will be like the Twilight baby and will come out ready to save the world. *Super* baby." A dramatic fist pump up into the air seemed appropriate for the moment.

Claire ignored her and continued.

"Have you been taking prenatal vitamins? Have you been seeing a doctor regularly? Have you been eating healthy foods?

How many Red Bulls have you been putting back a day? Or anything— ahem— stronger than a Red Bull? This could be serious. You could have really hurt your baby by not taking care of yourself." The judgment on Claire's face with that "ahem" could have resentenced an entire death row.

"Please. Spare me the guilt trip. We're not all as hyper paranoid as you are," Felicity retorted. Youth pastor's wife again. Ick. Claire had made a big show of cutting out her coffee, processed sugars, and anything that could POSSIBLY harm her perfect little baby. Big whoop. Felicity had done almost the same amount of pregnancy and had complained far less. So there. Guess everyone knows who's the tougher sister now.

"And Elliot. Is he ready to be a father?"

"You leave him out of this. You have no business bringing him up again." Felicity could hear the harsh disapproval in Claire's voice. Claire and Trevor never liked Elliot. Claire snorted at the thought. Like it was *their* place to approve of her boyfriend. Felicity didn't realize that her flower girl performance at their wedding was permission for them to have a say about *her* future wedding. Jerks.

"Um— pretty sure I do have every right to bring him up since he has now *impregnated* you."

Felicity now had a new word to replace her all time most-disliked word of "moist". *Impregnated?* GROSS. Pretty sure her ears were now bleeding. What kind of terrorist comes up with these words?

The minivan rolled into the long driveway of their childhood home. The old Victorian house was surrounded on either side by beautifully maintained shrubs and a rolling lawn covered in a lush greenness that was a product of the tender loving care of a Mother who was good at everything. Felicity left here this morning worried only about her favorite pink shirt somehow shrinking and shrinking until no matter how much she pulled, it would not meet her belt line. Annoyed, she had grabbed a sweatshirt on her way out even though it was a million degrees outside. She knew girls at school who were fine with showing their belly buttons, but she was not one of them. She just wasn't comfortable enough with her body for it not to be completely covered. She had spent the morning silently stewing at mother because it was *her* fault for being so bad at laundry and somehow shrinking everything (was it *that* hard to keep her shirts long enough to meet her belt line?). Felicity now regretted her words of anger along the lines of "Why are you determined to screw up everything in my life? Why can't you just get one thing right?" before storming out to meet her friends.

Felicity felt a cold chill slide down her back. She would have to tell her Mother. What would she say? Would she kick her out? Would she ground her forever? How many weeks of Friday night movies was she going to have to miss for this one?

Maybe Claire would do the honors. After all, she had had such fun with both her pregnancy announcement *and* gender reveal party. Maybe she had an extra cake with an unknown color inside of it just hanging out inside that annoying red bag she was always carrying around.

As the newest pregnant sister sat still, wondering if older sister had already texted ahead with the news and trying to convince her legs to start the journey toward more judgment, she very noticeably felt crazy kicks from something inside her abdomen. Knowing now that it was a baby she wondered how she could have missed that before. It was like the show the gang always used to make fun of "I didn't know I was pregnant!" where woman after woman thought they were dying and then ended up delivering a baby on the toilet. Never in a million years did she think that this would be her life. Maybe she really was as dumb as Claire always said she was.

Thinking about an actual person being inside of her physically sickened her. She didn't want to do this. Was there any way to get out of this? Any way at all? Her biggest problem last month was that an old lunch died in her locker and created such a stench that the rest of the row of lockers complained about her to the school office. Now she had to worry about a whole other person? Being a mother? What kind of sick joke was this?

There was so much to worry about already in life. She didn't have the emotional capacity for one more thing.

Every night before bed, she would stand in front of the mirror in her room and try to see what everyone else saw. Was she really beautiful? Or did Daddy just say that because he had to— being her Dad and all. Her forehead was too broad, and her nose had a weird bump in it if she turned to the side. Her skin only looked appropriately creamy if under the Valencia filter on Instagram (why didn't they make "Valencia filter" tinted makeup?) Her green eyes were rather nice, she would tell herself, but if she smiled just so, they would shrink into tiny slits under eyebrows that she plucked to perfection— but still. Her teeth were nice and straight due to getting her braces off just last year, but too much of her gums showed when she smiled. Spending long hours with her favorite TV characters, she would revel in their perfection while worrying about her own flaws. Daddy used to tell her that she was beautiful every day. Mother mentioned it every now and then, but she didn't sound that convinced herself. Elliot once said "You look nice" but that was it. She knew that soon he would tell her more— much more. But what if he didn't think she was beautiful because she just wasn't? She tried it on for size. *Beautiful...Beautiful.* Was she? Her self-critique was usually at night, but honestly this important question very rarely left her mind.

But right now, her finger was poised above the seatbelt release button and she was frozen in her seat, worries about her own beauty fled from her mind. Who cared about the bump in her nose when she was about to have to disguise a huge body bump? Felicity suddenly decided— no need to worry when the jury was definitely in. She was not beautiful. Never had been, never would be. She was just a mistake. A teenage screwup. An awkwardly shaped body about to become a balloon.

"Well." Claire spoke first. "Time to face the music."

CHAPTER SIX
Claire

Claire didn't know if it was possible to be angrier with her sister than she was right at this moment. Pregnant? How stupid was she? She turned fifteen three weeks ago, and she wasn't able to responsibly sustain the life of a plant or animal let alone a baby.

A few years back Felicity begged and begged for a guinea pig. She would just DIE without a guinea pig. She thought they were SO CUTE, and life would not be the same if she didn't get one. Mother tired of the begging and finally bought her a cute little red guinea pig which Felicity promptly named Scipio. Three weeks into life with her new little buddy, she tired of cleaning the cage and complained that her room always smelled like urinated cedar chips. Four weeks in she begged to give him away as he wasn't learning any of the tricks she tried teaching him, but mother told her to give it some more time. When the neighbor's dog "accidentally" ate poor little Scipio one-month in, Felicity shed no tears. How did the guinea pig even come to be hanging out on their driveway unsupervised? Claire had been suspicious of the entire event, but Felicity claimed to be grief stricken and refused to discuss it.

And now the guinea pig murderer was to be a mother. What was wrong with the universe?

Not to mention, this attention-pulling stunt now made something glorious and beautiful in Claire's life now seem tainted and dirty since they were now occurring at parallel intervals. Claire will still be celebrating her new life when BAM, Felicity would steal the show with hers. And oh by the way, Felicity would also need everyone to do her job for her while laughing about her "super baby" which had come to save the world. The title "Grandma" seems a whole lot less glamorous when a fifteen-year-old mother is involved.

Pregnancy was no longer about Claire and this beautiful phase of life that she worked so hard to earn. It was now all about a sad mistake happening in her teenage sister's life.

Felicity wouldn't even admit how serious this was. She had done nothing but crack jokes since they left the hospital. Perhaps not dying was a relief, but still— this had to bring some thoughtful introspection of its own. Right? Rethink the path she was headed down? Dump her loser boyfriend who did this to her? Ask for help to do this right? Be concerned about what kind of life she could offer a baby right now?

But perhaps the part of this that made Claire the angriest was another extremely non-youth pastory thought.

How dare Felicity be better at conceiving a child than she was.

Claire had worked for years and prayed desperately for this to happen for her. Married for six years? Check. Bought a house and dedicated herself to making a lovely home? Check. Endured years of specialty doctor visits, sobbed with devastation at every negative, and begged God for a miracle? Check. Followed every rule ever made in regards to increasing her fertility and then maintaining the perfect pregnancy? Check.

Felicity sidled up to her greasy boyfriend with the shifty eyes— who knows how many times, maybe even just once or twice, and it just happens for her? That easy?

Even as the thought crossed her mind, Claire felt like a fifteen-year-old spoiled girl herself instead of the twenty-seven year old mature professional, but she couldn't help herself; *this wasn't fair.*

They had started trying for a baby only a few months after the honeymoon. Sure it was early in their life together, but they both wanted a big family, and it just made sense to them to start on it sooner rather than later. They both had intense baby fever, and not being able to make one as quickly as they thought they should be able to was frustrating. After a year of no baby, they went to a specialist who swore that everything looked fine— they just needed to keep trying. Three years later and dozens of doctor appointments later, here she finally was— swollen, pregnant, and happy.

And Felicity? Did she have to go through any of that? Did she even appreciate what she had been given? Did she know how many women would kill for a chance to be thirty-three weeks pregnant?

Also— how was she not swollen? Glancing over at Felicity's hands resting gripping the seat belt as if frozen in position, she noticed her hand still easily wearing her favorite thin gold ring with a light green stone — her promise ring from Daddy. How did her ring still fit? Also, a promise ring to keep her virginity intact until marriage? Um, time to take that piece of hypocrisy off, dear sister.

She was relieved to finally be at her mother's house so that Mother could take over the difficult job of impressing the true nature of the situation on Felicity. If anyone could get her to take this seriously, it was Mother. Claire was exhausted, emotional, and seriously starving. She didn't have anything left to give to this situation right now.

If there was anything that her mother excelled at, it was creating a discipline to fit the crime. When Claire was eight and skipped her violin and piano practice, but lied and said she did them anyway, she had to practice double time for the next week with her mother sitting in the room observing her every move. When Claire was eleven and had a screaming meltdown over not winning her violin studio's solo competition, she was made to go hear the winners perform and write an essay on "appreciating the success of others". When Claire was sixteen and snuck out of the house wearing a mini skirt and a cut-off shirt to meet some friends for a movie, her parents grounded her for the next month with reading assignments on modesty and becoming a lady.

Her parents had always been quite strict with her although she noticed years ago that now they tended to be a little softer with Felicity, even before it went from *they* to *she*. Perhaps this had something to do with the age difference— getting tired because they were older the second time around and not worrying as much about the small stuff. They always claimed that she was their miracle baby since the doctors told them that they probably wouldn't be able to have any more children after Claire was born. And, of course, in these last five years, this softness toward the baby of the family had increased at an alarming rate.

Felicity was allowed to wear things Claire wasn't as a teenager. Her curfew was more varied and lax than Claire's ever was. Her boyfriend wasn't under the intense scrutiny that Trevor had to go through to prove himself worthy.

Well guess what, Mother? Miracle babies can do some not-so-miraculous things, too. Guess that mini skirt and exposed belly button isn't looking all that bad right about now, huh?

A smug sort of relief replaced her anger as the two sisters climbed out of the car and silently walked past their mother's colorful flower gardens toward the two story white house. Just the sight of it immediately flooded her with happy memories from her childhood. There was no reason this should have an effect on her.

Her thirty-six weeks of pregnancy was a source of pride for all of them. No need to let her sister's screw up affect her joy. Claire had waited too long time for this happiness to allow Felicity's stupidity to get in the way.

Now it was time for her to drop the bomb, stand back, and watch her sister get caught in the discipline explosion. Claire was nothing except for the messenger. A messenger with a slight "I told you so" chip on her shoulder. A chip that was perfectly square and faultlessly pressed.

CHAPTER SEVEN
Julie

Julie Reagan sat back on her heels and surveyed her work. The mulch rings around her row of apple trees had begun to sprout a spattering of unwelcome weeds, but after some attention, the pristine condition of dark mulch untouched by errant weeds was restored once more. Tugging off one light purple gardening glove and careful to keep them away from her spotless khaki shorts, she wiped dripping beads of sweat off of her forehead under her matching light purple visor and fantasized about a glass of ice cold tea inside the coolness of her air-conditioned house.

It was a hot, North Carolina June day, and perhaps she could have put this chore off for a slightly cooler one, but Julie couldn't ignore her apple trees. *He* planted them for her.

Remembering the day all too well, she froze in that awkward position on her heels and wished she could turn back the seasons of growth on these beautiful trees to the day that they were planted as seedlings. Watching as he cut sod, measured the center of each ring, dug a hole for each tree, and lovingly planted each one as if it was a work of art and he was the master artist, she fell even more in love with him that day. As they talked, laughed, and worked together, she enjoyed learning how to properly plant a tree. It was far more involved than she realized. She remembered watching her husband work up a sweat while she listened to the birds softly whisper a love song to the afternoon.

It had been a fun afternoon. She hadn't realized its significance at the time— it was just another day. Just another pearl dropped onto the beautiful string of pearls that was their life together. Little did she realize at the time, it would be their last one.

Harry, her light gray cat, lay down beside her and whined for water.

"All right, boy. We can go in and get something to drink. What do you think of the weeding job that I just did? Pretty spectacular? Why, I think so too, thank you for saying so."

Patting him gently on the head, she stood, ignoring the way her knees and ankles creaked and refusing to feel silly for her need to talk out loud. She didn't use to carry on conversations with her cat, but if she had learned anything, life has a way of changing you.

Maybe she should cross stitch that onto a pillow.

She could just see it now— *Life changes you. Talk to your cat.* Perhaps yellow stitching on a light gray or cream pillow with a cute cat leaping across the lower half? Felicity would get a kick out of that one. It was the family joke. Every Christmas both of the girls received a small, rectangle, cross-stitched pillow. When she realized that they secretly made fun of their "old lady pillow collection", she started secretly making fun of the tradition, too, while pretending to be as full of motherly wisdom as usual.

Watching Claire unwrap her *"When they clap, you bow. You always, always bow"* pillow stitched in thick layers of blue thread on a white pillow with a tiny brown violin in the lower left corner, Julie had the hardest time keeping a straight face. After an awkward pause, Felicity burst into laughter soon followed by Trevor and Julie, with Claire being the last to chime in. That long ago violin recital where nine-year-old Claire stomped off of the stage, refusing to bow with a glare and a stubbornly raised chin because she ended Polish Dance with a squeaking string instead of a smooth up-bow double stop was officially never leaving their family pages of hilarious stories. Felicity wasn't even there, and yet even she could recite the entire event down to the light pink hemline on Claire's cream dress that day. Claire had a rough time laughing at this herself, even all these years later, claiming that the performance was *almost* perfect. Julie put her words of wisdom on a pillow this last Christmas because if Claire was going to be a mother, she needed to learn to laugh at herself. It was the only way.

Working out the creaks while striding the distance between her garden and her two-story white house, she let herself think back to the day they bought this 3,500 square foot beauty with the open floor plan and newly updated kitchen.

"We can have more kids," he said.

"How many more?"

"As many as you want."

"Ten?" Impish as ever, she flirted with him, the love of her life.

"Why stop there? Let's go for twenty. We need to fill this bad boy right up," he said, gesturing around their house.

"Twenty? Now that sounds exhausting!" She laughed, hooking her arm through his and leaning her head onto his shoulder.

"Exhausting? Nah. But we'd best get started right now." He winked back at her.

But just then five-year-old Claire came into the kitchen requesting a snack. Working on more children had to wait until later.

However, as years of Thanksgivings rolled by without the table filling up like she dreamed, as family game night participant numbers remained stagnant, and as those extra three bedrooms evolved into a guest bedroom, a sewing bedroom, and an office, her dream died a slow death. The tiny bit of hope that the doctors gave her at the possibility of another pregnancy disappeared over the long years of waiting. Until the surprising miracle of Felicity's birth.

Now it was just her, Felicity, and Harry her cat rattling around the house she had worked so hard to make a home. Since half the time Felicity wasn't even talking to her, Harry was her main companion of choice these days. Well, that and her brother Gordon, whenever Julie could convince him to come the whole half hour across town and share a cup of tea with his lonely sister.

Lonely? Maybe that was too strong of a word. After all, she did have a child still at home, a grandchild on the way, an older daughter who worked hard to stay in contact multiple times a week, her Sunday school class ladies, her brother who lived close enough to come help out when the sink started to leak, and her beautiful friend Harry who could be counted on for constant companionship. Lonely definitely wasn't the right word. Best reserve it for a much more extreme case.

Walking into her kitchen with Harry trotting faithfully by her side, she stopped for a brief sip from the sweating glass of ice cold tea on the long counter before going to the oven to check on the progress there.

Satisfied with the level of crispiness, she pulled tonight's casserole out of the oven. Layered egg noodles, cottage cheese, green onions, a tomato beef sauce, topped with bubbling cheddar cheese— she had the Pioneer Woman to thank for posting this delicious recipe. She hoped Felicity would like it. Her mouth was producing embarrassing amounts of drool just smelling the odors wafting from her favorite white casserole dish. Her stomach added in its opinion with a very convincing growl.

Sighing, she leaned down onto the counter over her "To Do" list to make sure she hadn't forgotten anything. It had been a good day— linens washed, refrigerator cleaned out, coffee date with Claire, gardens weeded, and Felicity's room picked up.

Felicity's room, what a chore that was. She had to don a HAZMAT suit to enter and remain unscathed by a possible plague.

When Felicity got home, Julie would have to teach her of the magical thing called a trashcan that should be emptied on a regular basis, along with the many places that are surprisingly enough not a trash can— under the bed, in the closet, or in a bag on the floor of her closet. Yes, a banana will still go bad and attract an ungodly amount of flies, even if you can't see it! Who raised that child?

A frown creased her usually calm brow as she realized how late it had gotten. Speaking of Felicity, where was she? She should have been home a while ago. Why hadn't she texted? Or called? Was something wrong? The emergent condition of the trees' mulch beds had distracted Julie from the late hour, and in spite of the intense heat Julie suddenly felt chilled. She picked up her cell phone from next to her "To Do" list on the counter and called Felicity's number, but her call went straight to voice mail. "Go for Felicity," her daughter's voice grunted through the phone at her. She hung up without leaving a message, since she had learned the hard way that Felicity never listened to her phone messages.

"Where r u?" She texted instead, careful to use the proper text lingo since she had been criticized on this matter before. *"Do you think you're writing a term paper, Mom? It's just a text!"*

No reply.

The rule was strict. She could hang out at Elliot's house with friends, but she needed to be home by 4:45, their agreed upon time so that they could do an early dinner together before Felicity moved onto her next social engagement. The oven clock said 6:00, her cell phone said 6:03, and the wall clock said 6:08. Whichever one was right, it was still clearly much later than Felicity's usual arrival time. Did she get in an accident? Should Julie call the police? Was Felicity kidnapped? Was she lying dead on the side of the road somewhere? Or was she dead in an abandoned section of woods?

Brad used to caution her about immediately assuming worst-case scenario, but in this instance she felt justified letting her imagination swing to wild places— especially after that impossible day five years ago that proved that worst case scenarios sometimes actually happen.

She would never forget that phone call. She had been pacing the kitchen just like this. Dinner was growing cold on the table. She was angry. Angry that he wouldn't care enough to call to tell her why he was so late for dinner. She called and called him, but no answer. And then her phone rang with a blocked number. When she answered it, her breath froze in her throat and she just knew.

"I'm so sorry," the strange voice said. *"Brad Reagan is your husband? I'm sorry to tell you that your husband had a heart attack and he, well, he didn't make it."*

"Make it." It was as if life was an elitist club that he didn't get the bid to. Life changed for her then— one of the biggest changes being her ability to choose hope over anxiety. The worst had happened to her— twice. What was to stop it from happening again?

Tapping her fingers against the swirled brown granite countertop, she felt the anger once again win out over the fear. An hour and fifteen minutes. It had been *an hour and fifteen minutes.* Felicity knew how she would worry. Why would she do this to her mother?

Was it that hard to send a text message? Julie had seen Felicity's thumbs fly across the screen with the dexterity of a spider fleeing from a shoe heel's crush. If there was one thing her second daughter was extremely talented at, it was sending a text message quickly, silently, and expertly. Julie had caught her once texting during prayer at church while using the hymnal to shield the phone. At church!

Casserole forgotten, satisfaction over a perfect weeding job gone, suddenly her mind was on her youngest daughter— the one with the wild red hair and equally wild attitude. If she wasn't dead on the side of the road, where was she? Was she still at Stephanie's house? Perhaps she was with Elliot? Felicity had been dating him for almost a year now, and she had changed so dramatically over the course of the year that Julie barely recognized her little girl anymore. Julie tried to talk to Felicity frequently about this change, but Felicity had become quite belligerent where Elliot was concerned.

Wanting to keep an open mind, she had invited Elliot over for a family dinner, and one thing had been quickly clear to her, he was no Trevor. It's not that she expected that she would find two Trevors, it's just that Elliot fell so far short of the Trevor bar that he was truly in a different league— the kind of league that you warn your daughters about.

Where Trevor was a reserved intellect, it seemed that Elliot quickly and loudly spoke every thought that occurred to him. Where Trevor chose the career path of a youth pastor with a heart to serve others, Elliot proudly announced that he wanted to make as much money as possible either as a lawyer or a doctor, or maybe he would get lucky enough to win the lotto. Trevor kept his hair short and neatly combed. Elliot let his blonde hair grow to his shoulders, and from all appearances, he often forgot to wash it.

Of course, if she was being honest, Felicity was no Claire. The entire basket full of odd socks that she found today in the corner of Felicity's room was enough evidence to stand up in any court of law. *An entire basket full of odd socks?* Why? Just why? Was it so hard to match them up? Her first thought? She had failed. Failed as a mother to teach Felicity to properly clean her room and organize her clothes. She still had a little time left before Felicity would be moving out— was it too late? Could she still save her daughter?

Heart heavy, she stared forward and saw the two adorable baby pictures hanging side-by-side on the only magnetized side of the stainless steel fridge. One baby was laughing into the camera, fat rolls decorating each limb. The other baby was serious, a ball of curly brown hair framing dark brown eyes.

Julie remembered baby Claire who refused to sleep for the first two years of her life, hit all milestones in a slightly delayed

47

fashion, and who clung to Julie desperately, screaming if anyone else dared to hold her. Julie never thought there would be a day when Claire would not only be such a strong woman, but would also be grown up and living all the way across town. Felicity had slept a full night from day one after birth, hit all milestones ahead of schedule, and asserted extreme independence from hour two when she pushed her tiny head up away from Julie as if to say "Hey lady, don't get too close!" Even from the beginning the two sisters had been very different, but Julie hadn't minded. She took the good and the bad of both babies, and did her very best to raise them into godly young women. It had been easier back then. In the physical exhaustion of those early years Julie had convinced herself that it would get easier once the kids were sleeping through the night, potty trained, and able to dress themselves. Surprise surprise, it did not. The physical exhaustion exchanged itself with a rare kind of emotional exhaustion; for example emotional exhaustion from when they don't come home and you aren't sure where they are.

Julie paused at the counter, brushing her shoulder length brown hair with too many streaks of silver to count behind her ear. Her brown eyes were surrounded by laugh lines— "happy crow's feet" she jokingly called them, but tonight she wasn't laughing. Something was wrong. Something was horribly wrong with her baby. She could sense it. The explicit romance novel she found under Felicity's bed was a clue. The recent threats about a hair dye job were another clue. Purple highlights? Really? Purple dyed over red? *What was she thinking?* Her attitude and moodiness swinging fast enough for family whiplash were yet another indication of trouble. How could Julie fix this? But first, what was it specifically that she needed to fix? Biting her lip, she worked to turn her worry into prayer.

"Be anxious for nothing, but in everything by prayer and supplication, with thanksgiving, let your requests be made known to God; and the peace of God, which surpasses all understanding, will guard your hearts and minds through Christ Jesus."

Her gaze fell on the verse that she had cross-stitched long ago, framed, and hung in the empty wall space between her kitchen counter and the row of white cabinets. Philippians 4:6-7. She found that she needed this reminder far more frequently than she cared to admit.

Julie prayed daily for both her daughters, and sadly, her prayers for Felicity these days were marked with more tears than joy. And as soon as the prayers stopped? Guilt. Surely she was doing something wrong as a parent. She wasn't getting through to her daughter. At all. If only Brad were still here, he would know what to do.

Washing a few stray dishes while she waited, she glanced up into the kitchen window and was surprised to see both of her daughters headed up the walkway together. Claire's mouth was drawn into a tight line, and Felicity looked nervous. This couldn't be good. Those two didn't hang out unless it was a matter of national security. Was this about Claire's text earlier? Something was wrong. *She knew it.*

Her joy at seeing that Felicity was still in one piece and not being held captive in a sewer hole somewhere was replaced with a new concern.

Scooping up Harry who was now purring at her ankles, she hurried to open the front door, ready to ream out a certain Felicity Sarah Reagan about her late arrival tonight and the extra twenty gray streaks she was responsible for today.

CHAPTER EIGHT
Felicity

Tiptoeing into the familiar house while holding close some unfamiliar news, Felicity was struck with the rich smells of deliciousness wafting out of the kitchen. Her stomach churned with a weird mix of hunger and fear, but she was forced to ignore it. No time for eating when you have to tell your mother you have an entire being stuffed up inside of you.

Claire led with a grim "Well, mother, it looks like you're going to have two grandchildren" and then stepped back as if to get out of the range of fire.

Mother excitedly mouthed the word "Twins?" before catching the mood and seeing the evil tilt of Claire's eyebrows. Curse those brows. Felicity would swear the majority of her sister's talent lies there alone. Hand those brows a violin, and Felicity's money would bet on them out-fiddling Claire's arms from the start.

Mother turned an unreadable face toward Felicity. When mother gets angry, she gets quiet. Too quiet. The quiet of a pond with no waves or ripples because a horrible monster lives below the surface. The quiet of the entire world of cross-stitching descending into a moment of silence. Time to lighten the mood. Clearly.

"Yup. Well, the more the merrier, right *Grandma*?"

Mother wordlessly walked into the living room and then sank onto the couch as if her legs could no longer hold her up. She appeared to be having a stroke. Felicity looked closer. Was her eye *twitching*? Weird.

Mother swallowed hard and whispered "When— how— why—" She trailed off and then said so softly Felicity had to lean in to hear, "I have failed."

Claire rushed to her mother's side with enough panic to suggest the house might be on fire. *Drama queen.*

Draping an arm around their mother's slumped shoulders, Claire jumped in with details because of course she would want to pound in the nails while the wall was already falling.

"The doctor did an ultrasound and measured the baby at thirty-three weeks, but I haven't been able to get any details from Felicity beyond that." Claire looked eager to share. Too eager.

"Thirty-three weeks!" Their mother turned ghastly pale and stumbled over the simple words— still at only a whisper.

With mother doubled over, Claire sinking so low into the couch she would probably need all of them to pull her back up, and Felicity standing in the middle of the room as though she were auditioning for *The Voice*— Felicity took a moment to smirk as the entire picture most likely looked quite comical. What's the big deal, people? It's just a baby! People have them all the time!

"Who would have thought? Your second daughter is a Fertile Myrtle!" She punctuated this remark with two thumbs pointing at her belly and an attempt at a Claire raised eyebrow look. She didn't know how much she looked like Claire at the moment, but the look on her mother's face let her know that she got the message across.

Silence. Silence filled with an awkward combination of emotions that Felicity couldn't put her finger on. Pity? Were they feeling sorry for her— again? They were looking at her like she was a stranger. What's the matter with them? This wasn't her fault! She didn't ask to get pregnant! Why were they staring at her like that? Stop it! Were they focused on that pimple on her nose? Rude! Have they no manners at all? Her back started to ache and her legs began to tingle. *The Voice* audition ended with two rejections from the sanctimonious judges.

"Soooo, yeah. You all know. And I know. And better yet, your eyebrows all know. So I'm going to head up to bed because well....I'm pooped."

Silence. Still? She had never before seen her mother speechless, without her usual witty quip in response to whatever fun nonsense Felicity threw at her. It was confusing— making her feel even more tired. She expected hysterics. Maybe some yelling. Or fainting. Silence? Really? It's like going to a Fourth of July fireworks show and instead of exploding brilliance being offered only a dark black sky sheathed in, well, darkness. Rolling her eyes and awkwardly shuffling out of the room while trying to knead her lower back with her fists, Felicity headed for the stairs. Passing the large clock in the hallway, she noticed it was only 6:20. Eh, that last Red Bull must have just worn off. Time for bed. Who cared that she now had the bedtime of an eighty year old. Thirty-three weeks meant that this wouldn't go on for too much longer, right? After all, how long did pregnancies last? Felicity realized she had no idea. Guess that's what she got for blocking out all of Claire's annoying, look-at-me-I'm-so-special-because-I'm-pregnant chatter.

"No." A strong voice stated clearly. "No. Felicity Sarah Reagan, come back in here right now." The steel in her mother's voice could have built a skyscraper.

A full namer, eh? Felicity silently debated just ignoring her and continuing on to her gloriously beautiful bed. After all, what was Mother going to do to her if she disobeyed? Pretty sure the disobedient line was already maxed out. Once you reach "pregnant," there aren't many ways left that you can disappoint your parents at fourteen…oh right— fifteen. Her birthday was already over this year? Really?

Deciding not to push that button tonight, she dragged her feet back into the living room. Felicity kept her head down to allow privacy to that poor nose— to the pimple that seemed to capture their attention so dramatically. Bet it was growing a bump now too. Standing in the doorway, she kicked an invisible spot in the carpet with her bare toe.

"Have you— have you been having sex with *that boy*?"

Huh? Was mother choking on something over there?

"If by *that boy* you mean Elliot, then apparently so." Dig deeper into the carpet. Very important not to look up.

"Why— *why* would you do that after everything we've talked about?"

"Because he loves me. He accepts me for who I am. He loves me for exactly me."

"*I* love you for exactly you. *I* accept you for who you are. And we have been over and over the importance of abstinence at this point in your life."

"Um, no. You're always trying to get me to study more, watch less TV, eat better."

"That's *because* I love you. I want you to have a future that you will be proud of. I want to see you find some goals and work toward them. I want your life to reach beyond a couch, a TV show, and a bag of salty chips."

Felicity whipped up her head and finally made eye contact with the piercingly dark eyes of her mother. Mothers are so clueless sometimes.

"But those are the things I love! Don't you get it, Mom? Don't you see?"

"I see a pregnant teenager who has made some epically bad choices. I see—"

"You see what, a daughter who is NOT Claire? Wake up, Mom. You have two very different daughters. I AM NOT CLAIRE, and I never will be."

"That's not what this is about at all."

"Isn't it?"

"No. I don't expect you to be Claire. I just expect you to care about being Felicity. Right now it's like you don't care. You make the choice to jump off a cliff and then look surprised when there's nothing to catch you at the bottom."

"What you don't realize is that I'm attached to a bungee cord and am having the time of my life. Why do you always assume you know best? What do you know? You spend your days making stupid pillows and talking on the phone with Uncle Gordon. What gives you the right to think you know what choices are right and wrong for me? I am sick of this whole family acting so superior."

"Felicity— you are one of the smartest people I know, and you're just throwing it all away. If you were to just apply yourself, you could do anything you want! Stop making excuses and really look at where your life is heading."

"Oh please, that's straight from the book on Cliché Teenage Parenting."

"Sweetie, it's true. You are so smart. I am in awe of you."

"That's what all parents say. They teach you that in orientation."

"There is no such thing as parenting orientation." Mother said.

"If there was, they'd never have let *you* through." Claire mumbled into a couch cushion while jerking her head towards Felicity.

"Claire." Mother said sternly.

Felicity rolled her eyes.

"Oh yes, of course— I forgot. *Claire* is the only one good enough to get through anything." Felicity said.

"Girls."

"No, it's not about being good enough. It's about being ready for it," Claire snapped back.

"Ready Smeady," Felicity said.

"Girls, please—"

"Please? Please what? Ever since Daddy died you haven't been the Mother that I've needed. You've been lost in your own little world of who knows what. So if I'm not ready, then guess whose fault that is? Not mine, that's for sure."

Mother winced. Felicity felt almost bad. It was Claire's turn to roll her eyes before looking awkwardly down at her own invisible spot on the couch. Mother dropped her face into her hands with her elbows on her knees. Felicity stood tentatively as though she might drop any second. Someone's cell phone rang inside someone's bag, but no one moved to answer it.

"Now if you will excuse me. I am going to bed. Or is sleep another horrible rotten choice that your *bad* daughter is making? Huh?"

No answer as Felicity turned and once again made her way up to her bedroom. Ahhh having the last word— how Felicity did love it. But for some reason, tonight it left a bitter taste in her mouth. If she didn't know better, she would think that it tasted very similar to regret.

CHAPTER NINE
Julie

Julie leaned back on the couch; feeling like her body was about to snap in two. Never before in her life had she felt so completely betrayed.

Claire left quickly after Felicity went upstairs. She mumbled to Julie something about food, practice time, and a missed call from Trevor. Felicity must have fallen asleep right away because after Julie said goodbye to Claire, she went upstairs and knocked on her door, hoping to talk this through now that the initial shock had worn off. No answer. When Julie opened the door quietly, Felicity was passed out on her bed snoring. At least she was sleeping on her side and not on her stomach like she usually did.

Staring at the limp body of the sleeping girl turned woman overnight, Julie felt disconnected from her daughter.

A few years back, an unmarried adult in the church stood up to confess that she was pregnant. She begged for the church's forgiveness, saying that God had forgiven her, she had forgiven herself, and it was time to move on and be the best mother she could be. Felicity sat beside Julie during the announcement, and afterwards, Julie gave Felicity a hug.

"Please don't ever make that mistake. Even though I'm sure she will make a fantastic mother, things will be harder for her because she won't have the help of a husband. I don't want that for you." She said.

"Of course not, mommy! I would never do that!" Felicity said.

"Promise?"

"Pinky swear promise." And then they both laughed as their pinkies tangled together.

The teenager getting ready to begin high school in the fall that was sleeping in front of her no longer did pinky swears. Or called her Mommy.

Felicity was wearing braids and playing with dolls two years ago. Who was this pregnant, belligerent teenager and what did she do with her little girl?

Sure she knew there were problems— but *pregnant*? How did this happen? Julie really had suspected more of a "I cheated on a test and I feel so guilty" or maybe a "I watched an R rated move. I'm so sorry!" or maybe a "My body is changing and it makes me feel uncomfortable and awkward". Because of course Julie noticed when Felicity started wearing mostly hoodies and needed bigger jeans. But Julie just thought it was a too-many-calories phase. Felicity was a comfort eater. Since dating Elliot she seemed to be missing her Dad even more than usual, asking to look at picture albums and hear the story of how her mom and dad met one more time. This was always followed up for a request for a specific food item— raspberry pie, fudge ice cream sundaes, homemade French fries.

A sadness settled over Julie. It was a deep sort of sadness that settled between every bone and covered each organ with a film so thin and sticky that the removal process would cause more pain than relief. Why would Felicity do this to her? She was having sex?

When? Where? There were specific rules, curfews, boundaries. Were they not enough? Placing a strict system in place, Julie only allowed Felicity to be in certain places at certain times when certain adults were present. And then she would grill Felicity about each day— where she was, who she talked to, what she watched, when each event happened. Had Felicity been lying to her all this time? What was she really doing when she told her she was going to Stephanie's house with her mom there to supervise? Was she being dishonest this whole time? Talk about misplaced trust.

And where were they doing it? Upstairs in the room that Julie just cleaned? She thought she kept a close eye on them when they were here. The door was always supposed to be kept open when they were in there alone. How did she miss this?

The sadness settled even more firmly. Her sweet, innocent girl was experiencing something meant for adults. A time to celebrate a new life— yet she was still such a little girl herself. Felicity wasn't ready for this. She couldn't appreciate the magnitude of what was happening inside of her. No matter how snarky Claire had been when she said it, she had been right. Felicity just wasn't ready.

And what was she planning next? If she was having sex with Elliot, was she planning on running away with him too? Had Julie lost her baby girl forever? Why hadn't Felicity talked to her about any of this before she announced an almost fully cooked baby? They used to discuss everything. Now she was having sex, and Julie had to hear about it in the worst way possible. Scratch that— the worst way possible would have been actually IN the delivery room. How considerate of Felicity to give her a few weeks of prep time.

Still, Julie had to wonder, why didn't Felicity come to her as soon as she started feeling strange? Because of course if she was thirty-three weeks pregnant, she had to be feeling it for a good long while now. And did it make Julie the worst mom of all time that she didn't even notice that such a life-changing event was happening to her one child left at home? Was she too wrapped up in her own loss and loneliness to be there for her daughter? Was Felicity right?

The fear and sadness was quickly replaced by embarrassment. She was the mother of the pregnant teenager. What would people say? Julie was sure the gossipers would go crazy with this one. "Did you hear? Julie Reagan can't keep her daughter under control! Can you BELIEVE she's pregnant! And at fifteen...such a shame. Tsk tsk tsk."

What would her friends say? Her family? The responsibility of this sort of news always fell back on the parents. This was all Julie's fault. Somehow, her daughter not keeping her legs together would fall back on Julie's own personal failures. Not protecting enough. Not teaching enough. Not impressing the seriousness of this enough. Julie sighed. She had been teaching abstinence. Should she have been teaching birth control instead? Did this pregnancy happen because Felicity lost her father at such a vulnerable age? Was she not enough for her daughter?

Each thought tumbled into another one, sending her confusion and anger on an endless loop.

What would Brad say if he were here? It was comforting to know that he had been spared from having to see his daughter make this mistake, but at the same time, Julie could have really used the backup right about now. She missed the security of knowing that he would always take care of her and guide her through difficult situations when she just didn't know what to do next. He had been her rock.

Her stomach lurched. She was going to throw up. Her daughter was having a baby. At barely fifteen.

Running to the sink in the kitchen, she dry heaved for a few minutes before wiping her mouth and sinking down onto cold tile floor, which was spotlessly clean.

Did it matter? Did it matter that her floors were the cleanest floors in the neighborhood? Her daughter was pregnant at fifteen.

She had failed. How she had failed— where it had happened— she had no idea. But clearly she had.

Placing her flushed cheek against the cold tile, she rested her tense body onto the floor, trying to calm her churning stomach. It was then that the thought hit her.

How dare she.

How DARE Felicity get pregnant. How dare she have sex even after all she had been taught. How dare she continue seeing Elliot after Julie had expressed explicit disapproval of him. How dare she make such a huge life decision before she was ready. How dare she not even care. How dare she put Julie through this after everything that she had already been through. This took "selfish daughter" to a whole new level. The fly-breeding banana found in her closet this morning now seemed like an act of kindness compared to this blow.

Was this a bad dream? Was God judging her? Punishing her? Forgetting her? Why was this happening to her?

The coldness from the tile seeped through her skin and blended seamlessly with the sadness that had overtaken her.

CHAPTER TEN
Claire

Claire sat in the light green glider chair set in the far left corner of her little bub's nursery rubbing her belly, gliding slowly, and thinking back on the weird evening: Felicity storming upstairs with a parting jab, her mother's shocked silence, a tasty looking casserole in the kitchen calling her attention, and her mother saying go ahead because she wasn't hungry anyway.

After Felicity went to bed, Mother pressed her for information— juicy tidbits— anything, but really Claire knew nothing. They both knew that it had to be Elliot's baby, but other than that the entire pregnancy remained a mystery. Felicity had been moodier than usual the past few months, but given the fact that "moody" was one of her main descriptors on a normal day, no one thought too much of it.

It was nauseating to think of her sister having sex, let alone to discuss the details of this with her mother. The tension was so thick in her childhood home that Claire could have mixed it into some creamy pudding. *Mmmmmm pudding.* It had been too long since she had some thick, delicious chocolate pudding. Claire snuck away as soon as possible, taking the rest of the casserole at her mother's urging. Good thing. If hunger was the best sauce, then being pregnant and starving made a simple meal taste like life-saving manna. The subtle green onion flavor with the simple ingredients of the noodles was amazing— and was this cottage cheese? Genius. She needed to get this recipe.

When she finally arrived home at 8 p.m. (why was traffic so horrible tonight?), she finally reconnected with Trevor who said that he was on his way home from the youth group activity. She had forgotten all about him during these past few hours. Not that he would have had his phone on him to read her texts while he was with the youth group, but if she had been texting as this situation unfolded, that conversation would have been a doozy. He claimed to be full from the pizza that had been ordered for the activity, so she ate his share of casserole before retiring to the baby's room. Those noodles slipped down easier than ice water during the heat of the day.

Ditching the bath idea because she was out of the energy required to get it ready, she rested in the nursery, her favorite place to be these last few weeks of waiting. She should get up and practice. She needed to stand, go get her violin out, and practice. Practice was needed by her. Practice— now. She rehearsed the right lines over and over in her mind, but for some reason her body didn't obey. She continued to sit.

Rubbing circles on the top of her belly, she beamed when she got a kick in response. There were times that she was just completely overwhelmed with how much she loved her little guy. Little bub. Samuel Lewis Bailey. *Her baby.*

So much prayer was poured into this pregnancy. The first trimester hit her hard, the second knocked her down, and the third trimester kicked her while she was down. But it would be worth it. Very soon. Anxious to meet her bub, she loved to spend time in his room; the room that would soon be home to *her baby*. Soft green walls with dark brown furniture, it had become her baby haven. Filling it with personalized touches such as the monogramed painted canvases and the wooden letters spelling SAMUEL that hung over his crib— she just knew that he was going to love his room. A few weeks back the church had thrown her a baby shower, and between the piles of brightly colored cloth diapers and adorable tiny clothes, her label maker was busy for days finding places for all of his new stuff.

She looked around the room contentedly— a wall painted light gray and white chevron, a crib fitted with matching sheets, a soft bear rug, a closet full of clothes organized by size, a reading corner with a wall full of books begging to be read, a silver edged mirror over the changing table ready to show the eyes of an exhausted new mother, and of course this glider, all set to be an ideal nursing station with a monogramed quilt carefully placed over the back of it. The room smelled new and fresh, ready to welcome its newest occupant. She had worked on this room for months, conceptualizing it long before she even became pregnant. And now it was perfect. And ready.

The memory of staring at the pregnancy test and wondering *why* at yet another negative was just that now— a memory. Clutching her very flat stomach and feeling helpless at her inability to force pregnancy to happen for them was just a thing to look back on as not her best moment. Claire was willing to work as hard as it took to achieve the things that she wanted in life. It just seemed so unfair that this one thing, the thing that she wanted more than anything, had nothing to do with how hard she worked or how faithfully she prayed. But now it was happening. Now she was back in control— well, as much as she could be. She knew now that she was not the one ultimately in control of her life. But the little things? She could micromanage those to her heart's content. Trevor often said that her attention to detail was her biggest strength and her biggest weakness all at once.

"Thank you, Lord." She silently prayed. "Thank you for sending me my baby."

It was time, and everything was now perfect. The only thing that would make this more perfect was if her Dad were still around to meet her baby. He would have been an awesome Grandpa. One for the books. With his good-natured laugh and unlimited patience, he would have made all other Grandpas look like slackers in comparison. Feeling the sadness creep over her, she let herself think of him for just a moment. The world lost a bright, shining soul when he left it.

She missed him. Whenever she started to think about the pain of losing him, she was always reminded of how thankful she was to have him in her life for as long as she did. For twenty-one years she was the luckiest daughter ever. She would treasure her memories and the childhood that he gave her with all the intensity that was within her. What a gift he had given her.

Staring at the wall, she saw her "To Do List To Finish Nursery" lightly taped onto the changing table mirror.

Smiling, she remembered how Daddy used to tease her about her obsessive need for lists. When she was ten, he claimed that there had never been a more organized lemonade stand in the history of their neighborhood. When she was thirteen, he pointed out that she perhaps didn't need to alphabetize her locker contents. When she went off to college, he both praised her and laughed at the labeled boxes/containers that looked like a professional organizer had packed her things. And when she got married and her day went flawlessly with twenty different check sheets checked off to perfection, he told her how proud he was of her for using her gifts and abilities in such wonderful ways. She wondered what he would say of this beautiful nursery that she designed.

What would he say about her having baby lists which had now all been triple checked? Freezer meals, bags for hospital, cleaning and organizing to be done before baby, people to be immediately texted and called, people she owed thank you notes for the shower— everything had been checked and checked again except for perhaps a few more freezer meals that she found on Pinterest last night that she would definitely make as soon as possible. Confident about what was ahead, she had her binder full of lists to thank for the level of preparedness she had reached. Now she could just sit back and enjoy the experience of becoming a mother.

A few more rubs on her belly. There was a foot! No a hand! No that was his head— or spine? No matter. Her long fingers tapped gently as if playing the fast sixteenth notes from the third movement of the Wieniawski violin concerto. This earned her more kicks. She smiled. Was it possible to love anyone as much as she loved this little person she hadn't even met yet?

Interrupting her musing, Trevor wandered in. "There you are. I knew you would be in here." He knelt down next to the glider and placed a soft kiss on her belly. "Hey, bub! Are you just about done cooking in there? We can't wait to meet you." He turned to Claire and added, "And you, Mommy? Did you finish your bath and practice?"

Mommy. She could really get used to being called that.

"That was the plan, but today has gone wrong in so many ways."

"What is it? Is something wrong with the baby?" She loved him for the panic that he infused into these questions.

"No, no, nothing like that. I just found out some rather disturbing news today." She stared once again across the room at the perfectly organized changing station she set up last week. And Felicity? Where would she change her baby's diapers?

He waited for her to continue, looking concerned with a small wrinkle on his handsome brow that showed how he deeply cared. In spite of the news, she smiled before continuing.

"It's Felicity."

"Yeah what's up with her? She didn't come to the scavenger hunt tonight at church. We even got the pizza from Dominos— I know it's her favorite. Is she sick?"

"Not exactly. She's— well— she's pregnant."

His mouth dropped open, and she could see him calculating the damage of announcing that the youth pastor's teenage sister-in-law was with child.

"She came to my office at school and told me that she thought she was dying. I've never seen her so subdued. She perked back up on the ride to the ER, but then when we got the news— wow. My mind was seriously blown. Felicity—having a baby? The craziest thing is, she is only a few weeks behind me in the pregnancy. She could have this baby in a month or two."

Trevor sighed. "I had a bad feeling about Elliot from the start. Felicity is a good girl, but even good girls get led astray in matters of the heart. What did your mom say?"

"My mother? Not much to Felicity. After she went to bed, she had a lot of questions for me. Apparently she had no idea that Felicity was having sex— or at least had it at one time. I've never seen Mother so confused and, well, sad."

"I can imagine. None of us could have predicted this."

"I am honestly afraid for that baby. If you could have seen her putting back that Red Bull on the way to the ER, you would understand. No concern for how she's treating her body or taking the necessary vitamins to grow a healthy baby. And remember when I told you before, I'm pretty sure I've caught her drinking several times these past few months as well. Pregnancy is like practicing for a concert. You put in the good work, you get good results. Simple as that. *Drinking* while pregnant? Seriously? This will end badly— mark my words."

"But what about God in this equation? Don't you think that perhaps he has a bigger plan than the work that we put into it? Don't you think he could protect her baby anyway?"

"Well, sure. God has a plan too. But he honors those who honor him. He blesses the good," Claire said.

"But God lets it rain and the sun to shine on both the evil *and* the good," Trevor responded.

"What are you saying, that God's going to bless Felicity through her disobedience and carelessness?"

"No. I'm just saying that it's not our place to call out the end of the story here. We know that God is good, but the truth of the matter is, life isn't always fair."

Claire thought about her fertility struggles and bit her lip, looking away from her husband's piercing blue eyes.

"Why do you always have to be in your youth pastor mode? Why can't you ever just be a husband who will complain with me about my sister?"

"Do you honestly think that this is just about me being a pastor? This is who I am. This is what I believe. I can't separate parts of myself away from that."

Claire nodded. They ended up in this discussion often. There were many times when Claire felt out of her league to be married to a man of God. Maybe she wasn't spiritual enough or perfect enough, but goodness knows she tried.

"Still, you have to admit that Felicity having a baby right now is all kinds of insane."

It was Trevor's turn to nod.

"Yeah. Hard to picture her in a maternal role. Last time she saw me she said that Lancaster Pennsylvania just called, and they want their Amish Boy's hair back."

"Well, you have been parting it kind of weird lately." His short blonde hair was normally brushed forward or spiked, but it had been put into a middle part the last few weeks. Claire hadn't said anything before, but now that he brought it up...

He feigned shock. "Not you too! Can't a guy just try a new hair style without being mocked around here?"

"You're the one who brought it up." She giggled at the look on his face.

"Well then I guess I'll keep my hair AND my massaging fingers to myself."

"No!!! NO! You promised!" The tired pregnant lady who missed her relaxing warm bath was almost shouting in response.

"Well, all right. I will give you your nightly neck massage AFTER I hear you say three nice things about my hair." The glint in his eye was just evil.

"Three? It's going to take me a while to come up with that many," she teased.

"Then while I wait…massaging fingers just turned into tickle fingers!" He reached for her.

"No! Stop! I might pee on the new glider! My bladder control is shot these days and you know it!" Jumping up, she ran from him laughing and giggling. She didn't get very far.

Wrapping strong arms around her, holding her close, and breathing warm air onto her neck, he whispered into her ear "I love you."

Breathless from her attempt at an escape, she smiled before echoing an "I love you too."

His hand reached up, stroked her hair, and then went to her jaw. Turning her face towards his, he claimed her lips with a long kiss.

Felicity long forgotten, all Claire could think of in this moment was intense gratitude. If she was going to go through all of this for parenthood, there's no one else she would rather do it with.

Ending the kiss, Trevor's expression became pained.

"Sweet, there is one bit of bad news that you need to know."

"What?"

"Well, as you know, our principal, Dr. Brown, has been having some heart issues."

"Yes. What does this have to do with us?"

"Today he told me that he needs to have a pretty major surgery to correct some blockage in his arteries. This surgery is scheduled in a week, and it comes with a long recovery period which means—"

"Summer school," Claire finished for him. Her heart sank as she realized where this was going.

"Yes. As I am vice principal, he needs me to step up and cover the last three weeks of summer school administration duties."

"But your paternity leave! They promised you!"

"I know, and I'm so sorry. But I can't get out of this. It will mostly be half days, and you'll have your mom to help you— "

"Will I? With a second new grandchild in her house, you really think she's still going to be able to help me?"

"Well, summer school ends August 1st, and you're due July 6th. If you are late at all- that means that it's practically only a week or two before I'm home full time for almost the entire month of August. And when did you say Felicity was due?"

"Best as they can tell, July 27th."

"Then perfect. Your mom can help you during those first couple of weeks, and then when Felicity's baby is born, I'll be back at your beck and call 24/7."

"I don't like this. It isn't what we planned." She turned her face away from him to hide her hurt and not-very-adult pouting.

"I know. I'm so sorry."

He cupped her chin once more and brought it back toward his.

"I love you. We will make this work."

She was silent as he kissed her again. Way to destroy her carefully charted plan and then cover it up with a kiss. It was easy for him to be calm about this; he wasn't the one about to pop. "Make it work?"

If Felicity wasn't on the books for a delivery now as well, she would be confident in her mother's help and not worry about this as much. But now?

Now she would probably have her baby on the living room floor because no one would be here to drive her to the hospital. She would deliver in a thunderstorm, no a tornado. Immediately following the birth she would be on her own for all-things-baby after a quick check from the paramedic sent by the 911 operator. That's when the tornado would upgrade to a hurricane. Probably the house and the town would both be destroyed while she was trying to cope with new motherhood— completely alone.

Her Week-Of-Go-Time List clearly said that Trevor would be here for her. She had checked it off already. You don't mess with the list!

Make it work. Sure.

CHAPTER ELEVEN
Julie

Julie picked herself up off the floor, made herself a steaming cup cf chamomile tea in her favorite navy blue mug with textured edging, and sat quite still in a tall white fabric chair at the pristinely polished dining room table.

It was late, but Julie couldn't calm her wildly thrashing mind enough to actually sleep.

Time to make a plan. She didn't want to make a plan. This was grossly unfair that after twenty-seven years of parenting and at forty-nine years old she had to start all over again with a "plan." But here she was.

The worst part of all of this was the memories it invoked. Decades-old memories. They always called Felicity their "miracle baby", but they never truly explained to the girls why. She couldn't believe that she was on this side of things this time. Pushing back against the rush of emotions, Julie focused. This was about the plan, not her history. She had reminisced enough for one day already.

Should Felicity put her baby up for adoption? If she kept the baby what would that look like? Would they live here? If no, where would they go? Was she going to want to marry Elliot? What kind of life would that baby have with a mother who couldn't keep up with her own hygiene or show up at the expected time?

It was no secret that Julie wanted more kids— so many more kids. She wanted to fill up their spacious home with as many kids as it could hold, but her body had other ideas. She was twenty-two when Claire was born, thirty-three when Felicity was born, and now she was forty-nine— too old for another miracle not to mention the other half of her baby-making team was no longer with her. But she didn't feel too old to hold another fresh life, rock big eyes to sleep, kiss soft cheeks, stroke a small head, and grasp fingers that were a fraction of the size of hers. She was counting on the healing powers of Claire's new baby infusing their lives which still felt raw from the loss of her husband.

Claire's baby was supposed to fill the void, a baby in a different location to which she would travel Grandma-style and offer assistance. After a few sleepless nights, she could then come home to her own home of quiet bliss and catch up on some ZZs, a perk of not having another newborn herself.

A baby in her own house wasn't entirely awful, but the thought of Felicity giving birth in the near future and being a mother herself while still under their roof? It sounded complicated, confusing, and just plain wrong. Obviously Julie would have to take care of the baby, but whose baby would it be? Would Julie be the mother? Or Felicity? What does Felicity want this to look like? Or was she planning on adoption? Was she even old enough to make a decision this big? Should she decide for her? Would Felicity let her? Should Felicity even get to decide if she would let her?

Standing slowly and walking to the counter where she last saw her cell phone, Julie picked it up and went back to the table. Hitting speed dial number 2, she waited for the comforting voice on the other end to assure her that she wasn't as alone as she felt right now.

But of course, voicemail. "Hi this is Gordon. Sorry I can't get to the phone right now. Leave a message and I'll call you back." *Beep.*

"Hey, it's me. Call me as soon as you get this. There's been a development with Felicity, and I need to talk to someone. Nothing's wrong. Well, yes something is wrong, but no one is in the hospital. Yet, anyway. Just call me. It doesn't matter how late it is."

Hanging up, she placed the phone back on the table. If she didn't talk to someone soon her mind was going to explode.

The dynamic between her daughters tonight had been even more tense than usual, and Julie was pretty sure she knew why. Claire had struggled her entire life to do well. Good grades were a challenge, but one great trait that Claire had was dedication— the ability to stick to a task until it was conquered. Learning the violin at an early age had been a lifesaving measure for her. Struggling grades righted themselves into flashy A's with her music practice a part of her daily routine. Giving her brain a way to organize itself had been the secret to success for her. Well, that and her determination to do well no matter how many hours of sleep she lost to study and practice. Felicity, on the other hand, never struggled. Naturally bright, knowledge came easily to her. Skills and studies were not a challenge. As a result, Felicity never cared enough to truly try at anything. Her report card was equally split between A's and B's. Felicity bragged often that she never studied for a single thing. Watching her girls navigate their gifts, Julie realized more than once that there was a gift in the struggle. Struggling transformed Claire into the fantastic musician that she was today. Felicity would do well to have some struggle in her life. How could Julie convince Felicity that it was worth it to truly work at life? To apply herself? But now here they were again, Claire struggled to get pregnant. Felicity did not. It was a lifelong pattern repeating itself in the girls. And she could tell that this bothered Claire, as it often did when they were younger and took startlingly different amounts of time to study or work. This created a tension that Julie wasn't sure how to help diffuse. It wasn't Felicity's fault that she didn't struggle. And yet, it wasn't Claire's fault that she did. It just was one of those things that simply was.

Just then she heard footsteps padding slowly towards the kitchen. Even if they weren't the only two in the house tonight, she could tell by the sound who they belonged to.

Felicity rounded the corner into the kitchen, rubbing sleepy eyes and in her pink pajamas looking like a ten-year-old girl searching for her lost doll.

"Mommy?"

She hadn't called Julie that in years.

"Yes?"

"Is there anything to eat? I woke up, and I was just so hungry."

"Light green Tupperware— second shelf on the far left. Claire took dinner, but I had her leave some for you in there."

"Ok thanks."

Julie's stillness elevated itself to statue level. Felicity moved sluggishly to the refrigerator, obviously still asleep just a little bit. Julie usually loved half-asleep Felicity. The edge was gone. There was a sweetness in the unguardedness. Half-asleep Felicity reverted back a year or two before the Elliot/extreme sarcasm phase.

The silence lasted a minute. A whole sixty seconds in which Julie searched for words to capture what she really wanted to say without setting Felicity off and making conversation impossible. The grandfather clock in the hall struck midnight with loud bell thunks that sounded a lot like the thumping in Julie's chest. It was a sound that Julie was so accustomed to she usually ignored it, but tonight it captured her whole attention for a whole ten seconds because it was safest place to rest her thoughts.

"Sweetie?"

"Yeah?" Felicity found the container and popped it into the microwave with a slightly cracked lid.

"Do you want to talk about it?" Julie's fingers gripped the mug so tightly she was afraid of shattering it. But her voice stayed calm.

Felicity was leaning against the counter with a simple t-shirt on with elastic banded pants pulled down quite low on her hips. Her belly was obvious for the first time. Yeah, there was a baby in there. How did she not see it before?

"Not really."

"Tomorrow?"

"Maybe."

The microwave beeped. Felicity took out her food, grabbed a fork, and headed back towards her room.

"Felicity?"

She paused in the doorway of the kitchen, turning slowly back towards Julie.

"I just want you to know that I love you. We will get through this. Together."

"Okay." Felicity mumbled before quickly whipping back around to leave.

But not before Julie saw it. One lone tear escaped from the corner of her daughter's eye and dripped down her cheek. She wanted to run to her. To wrap her in her arms and ask her the one thousand questions on her mind. She wanted to sob into the shiny red hair she used to brush on her gorgeous toddler. She wanted to hold her close and beg her for answers. Why did this happen? Was this Julie's fault? Why would Felicity do this to her?

But Julie forced herself to stay still and calm as she watched her daughter in the princess pajamas disappear up the stairs. Once she was gone, Julie's head dropped into her arms on the table. The plan could wait. They had seven weeks— right?

CHAPTER TWELVE
(five weeks later)
Claire

Labor. Claire was convinced that if pregnancy was the joke, then labor was the offensive punch line that nobody got.

After their final birthing class a few weeks ago, she typed and laminated a very specific birth plan. Trevor laughed at the laminating part, but she was getting some music laminated for the bulletin board in her office and figured why not do it at the same time? Everyone appreciated the efficiency of a laminated document. Why should this be any different?

Of course her plan depended on a crucial element. Such a tiny thing really. Miniscule, but apparently important. Claire always assumed that her body would go into labor on its own. When the baby was ready, the magic would begin! Her biggest worry was having her water break while in the grocery store, or feeling contractions that made her cry out during the quiet moment of reflection at church. How embarrassing that would be!

Who knew that her body would grow to the size of a blimp and then just keep right on going past week forty with no end in sight? As the weeks clicked by, it got increasingly difficult to maneuver and breathe, giving her anxiety attacks about getting the fun started before her lungs were completely squashed.

Her birth plan indicated natural labor as her birthing method of choice. She had completely strategized the upcoming experience after her diligent research from birthing class and after reading no fewer than a dozen books on birthing in love.

Her body would start softly in the privacy of her own home. Perhaps she would get in a warm soothing bath and relax to music until the contractions got closer. Trevor would then rush to get her to the hospital, concern etched on his face as he assured her over and over of his love and appreciation for all she was doing to bring his son into the world. Maybe he would run a red light to get her there faster. She would smile wisely and look glowingly beautiful even in the midst of the contractions while placing one hand softly on her swollen belly. Eyes shut, mouth drawn in a line of concentration, chest rising and falling with deep breaths as she found strength from within. Upon arriving at the hospital, she would be whisked to a private room overlooking the city. Her hair would be perfectly moussed and gently resting on her shoulders to be ready for the many "after" pictures. They would set up the CD player with soft Baroque music floating through the room, but they would barely make it through the first 4 songs because her Samuel, eager to meet her, would come bursting into the world in that first hour, a self-motivated starter from the very beginning. Pain would seem minimal because she would be so overcome with love, nothing else would matter. Plus, her pain endurance level was scary high. It always had been. This, combined with her fierce ability to concentrate, would get her through. The entire experience would be beautiful. A memory she would treasure for years. A story to say "it wasn't that bad" to other expectant mothers who were fretful about the approaching experience.

Of course she knew that she needed to be flexible and all, so she was okay if they didn't get the CD player set up before Samuel was born. She was a reasonable woman. She *would* accept music from her iPhone. And if by some horror she did start labor softly in the grocery store— that was okay too, just as long as her water didn't break in the produce section and she could be back home in her warm, birthing bath within the hour.

But it turns out, it doesn't matter how carefully laminated the typed birth plan is. A beautifully scripted sheet of lies is still a sheet of lies.

Her body didn't kick it into high gear by itself so she had to be induced at 41 weeks. The baby was getting too big, the doctor said. Time for him to come. Picturing a ten-pound bowling ball trying to work its way out of her private parts, white faced and worried, she quickly agreed to the induction.

Waking up at 6am the morning of the date she was given, she waited for the call that said she had a room at the hospital. Sitting next to the door with her bag packed, staring at a cell phone, and willing it to ring for hours and hours does not a fun morning make, she learned. The call finally came at 10am— sort of.

Ring ring.

Claire jumped with glee, grabbed the phone, and said "Hello?" with breathless "The Waiting Is Finally Over" joy.

"Hi, is this Claire Bailey?"

"Yes."

"This is Grace Hospital. We are calling about your induction."

"My room is ready?"

"Yes, you can come on in— oh wait a minute."

There was a pause with indecipherable whispers in the background.

"Sorry." He said. "I just got another call with a more emergent case. Someone needs to be rushed into a C-section and they will now take the empty room. We'll call you the minute something else opens up."

Click.

Now Claire considered herself to be a lady, but the names she wanted to call that "more emergent case" woman who just stole her room were not even remotely close to names a lady should use.

It was official. She would be pregnant forever, and it was all *that* lady's fault.

The call finally came for real at 2:10 pm. By this point Claire had convinced Trevor to load up the car with the overnight bag and infant car seat. When her cell phone rang again, they were circling around the hospital in their car.

"This is ridiculous. They haven't even called you yet." He said.

"But when they call again, I don't want someone else to snatch that room right out from under me— again! We need to get there quickly or else we might not get in today at all."

"So? Is it really the worst thing if we go in tomorrow instead of today?"

"Oh, you're right. I forgot that you're the one who can't breathe, sleep, or hold pee for longer than twenty minutes. Let's go with your thing. Do you want to live with this version of me for another day?"

"You're right. We should get going *right now*. Why don't we just wait in the lobby? Why wait from so far away? I mean— do you realize how long it will take us to PARK?" He said with mock seriousness while nodding to that last point.

"Wait, have you been hanging out with Felicity again? What's with the sarcasm?" she whimpered.

After a very un-like Trevor eye roll—which she ignored— they loaded up, went to lunch at her favorite café right next to the hospital, and then drove circles around the hospital.

But it paid off. That call came in, and she was strapped up to the fetal heart monitor on the open hospital bed ten minutes later with the entire floor of nurses gaping at her in wonder at the excellent time she made.

The only problem? She was exhausted from being on edge for the past eight hours, waiting for and willing that call.

She tried not to think about the fact that she didn't get to do any laboring at home— in spite of her fervent pleas to God and squats and consumption of five pineapples plus the spiciest Chinese food on the takeout menu and every "how to induce labor" suggestion on her BabyCenter group discussion post.

After they were done commenting on the speed with which she got there, the nurses put her in the smallest delivery room possible. No windows. They said that they would move her as another became available, but still. She had to start her journey of motherhood on a hard bed where she could reach out and touch both walls while wearing a scratchy, cold gown that showed her entire backside. They stabbed her arm full of needles dripping fun stuff like Pitocin and an IV drip after suggesting she trade her tight fitting black underwear for horrible white mesh underwear and ginormous pads. This. This is where sexy goes to die.

Trevor forgot the Baroque CDs at home in their rush to get out the door, and since they didn't know how long they would be there, they decided to save the battery on their phones because they also forgot their chargers. The chargers were also on Trevor's list. He had two things he was supposed to remember: the CDs and the chargers. *Two things.*

Her natural labor ideal was ditched after six hours of no progress on the Pitocin. The baby did not come quickly. The baby didn't even come sort of quickly. Hour after hour ticked by with little to no progress and a lot of extremely painful contractions that were determined to make her lose her sanctification. Um, was this supposed to feel like this? This felt like it was killing her— not bringing her through a beautiful birth. Hello? Is everything okay here? How was she supposed to keep this up for an unspecified period of time? How could she concentrate on the finish line when she didn't know where the finish line would be? *Epidural* escalated very fast from a dirty, bad, horrible word to the most magnificent word she had ever heard.

Before breaking her resolve and asking for the epidural, she took several long, hot showers to help manage the pain. Her perfectly made up hair soon became a wet, stringy mess guaranteed to look like a rat's nest caught in a rainstorm for all of the "after" pictures.

Ten hours into labor when Trevor ate a sandwich with onions and a strong southwestern sauce during his quick trip down to the cafeteria, he reeked so badly she wanted to scratch his face off. Starving wife in labor, and he chose the foods most likely to make her vomit. Good going, hubby. If he wanted to get close to whisper his adoration of her now, someone would have to provide a gas mask for her first.

As her laminated plan was ignored check by check, it sat sadly neglected on the wheeled bedside table under a plastic cup full of ice and apple juice. After a few hours, it got over its sadness and began viciously mocking her. It began as a subtle "hahahahaha" that quickly led to an elegantly composed song of mocking in A flat minor. Stupid key with flats. Who wants to play you anyway?

How did other women do this? How did they survive the pain? Only one thought put a smile on her worn out, tear-stained face. How would the little sister who whined for days after getting a flu shot make it through this torture?

The image of Felicity sitting on one of these beds in a scratchy gown of her own, being told she had to put on this mesh underwear and trade in every last bit of her dignity for her coming baby made Claire actually laugh. Hysterically. And then she cried. Hysterically. Just because it seemed like the most logical progression of emotions.

This was never going to end.

CHAPTER THIRTEEN
Felicity

In her room listening to music, Felicity did not appreciate her mother waltzing into the room like she owned the place.

Tearing out her ear buds, she snapped, "It's called *knocking.*"

"I did knock. Did you not hear me?"

Felicity looked at the volume at which her music had been and didn't answer. It wasn't her fault if she needed to drown out the world for a little bit.

"Anyway, I just wanted to let you know that Claire's induction is well under way. They started her late yesterday at the hospital."

"And I care, why?" she snapped back before lying back on her bed, putting her ear buds back in, and clicking the music up another notch.

Her mother looked like she wanted to say something, but instead turned around and quietly left.

"Shut the door!" Felicity shouted over her music.

The door clicked shut and her infuriating mother was gone. She should really put a lock on that door. The pest problem was positively unmanageable around here.

Why would she care what Claire was doing? A rocky relationship at best had turned into a non-relationship even faster than usual these past weeks due to their dual pregnancies.

Claire tried to "help" Felicity by bringing her prenatal vitamins, inviting her to her childbirth class, and buying a little yellow onesie that said *World's Best Aunt.* Felicity knew her sister better than anyone, and she knew perfectly well that these gestures were Trevor's suggestions, not Claire's. She saw the look on Claire's face when the pregnancy announcement was made in the ER five weeks ago. Just once, she wished Claire would say what she really meant instead of channeling this passive aggressive super sister who never had a negative thought. Because of this, each of these sisterly olive branches were met with:

"Why? Trying to spread the guilt around?" and "My kid told me that it's going to just walk out." and "Oh really? Teaching our kids to lie on a onesie. Classic."

She didn't care that Claire was in labor. She didn't want to think about having to do that herself. Her plan was to wing it, much like that English final she took a few weeks ago. That one turned out awesome. An A-. No prep. And she didn't do any of the required reading. Not too shabby. She didn't like English and didn't want to spend any extra time on it than absolutely necessary. Winging it and cramming were inventions of the brilliant to save the time of the bored. So she blocked out all of the thoughts about labor by blaring Katy Perry's latest single until her ears buzzed. If she didn't think about it, it didn't exist.

Also high on her list of things she didn't want to think about— the ten million conversations with her mother that all started the same.

"Sweetie, do you want to talk about it?"

"Have you decided what you're going to do about the baby?"

"Can we talk about what's going to happen in a few weeks?"

Silence. Felicity was good at this game. After unsuccessful attempts to talk it out, her mother always fell back on a safe topic. Food.

"Does anything sound good for dinner?"

Felicity wanted to bite out "How about a giant platter of LEAVE ME ALONE." But she always went with the no-fail response— silence. When you're freezing out a parent, you can never have too much silence.

Closing her eyes, she thought about her Daddy. She had never needed to freeze him out. Calling her his pumpkin, teasing her about her creative need for a mess, laughing with her over the silliest of jokes, walking with her through their quiet neighborhood on warm and chilly days alike— Daddy never let her down. He tempered Mother when she became anxious and unreasonable. He lectured Claire on being nicer to Felicity. He stuck up for Felicity when she started to berate herself. She was just entering the awkward age of ten when he died. One day she felt all grown up and ready for junior high— the next, constantly reminded how she was still yet a child. And it was when she came home after being teased at school for being "that Wendy's girl with the red hair" with "hey, burger girl!" or "can you bring a frosty over here?" or "sing us the pretzel bun song!" She walked in the front door desperately needing his bear hug. Or perhaps to hear him say softly "you are my pumpkin" in his endearingly low voice that it made her feel so special. But he wasn't there. And Mother said he would never be there again. Feeling rejected and alone for the first time in her life, she often wondered if she would ever recover.

A tear slid down her cheek and dangled on her chin. Wiping it furiously away with a hand sporting a chipped dark purple manicure, Felicity wouldn't let herself think about him right now.

What he would say to see her like this. What he would do to Elliot. She wouldn't even let herself dwell on her usual favorite memory— their long chess games where he often told her that it was a rare gift to be able to process the game as well as she could. She hadn't played chess since, and thought that he might take back his compliment since her real life game was going so badly.

Pushing her mind away from the shore of hurt, she pulled up the Facebook app on her phone and clicked to see the activity of her classmates out of habit more than anything else.

Lydia: Awesome pool party today! Loving my new red two-piece.

It would be a while before Felicity would be caught dead in a two-piece again. Although, a pool party sounded way more fun than her current status— "sitting on bed."

Samantha: The Fault in Our Stars is such a great movie. I bawled the whole way through it! #thefaultinourstars

Not allowed to go to any movies right now as part of her grounding. Her mother hated her. Clearly.

Ashlee updated her location as *the Caribbean.* Her family must have left on their cruise.

If Felicity had a family that went to the Caribbean every summer, no doubt she would not be pregnant right now.

Facebook was even more depressing than usual.

Jake posted the results of the quiz: *Which month of the year are you?*

Loser. Who cares if he's a December? What does that even mean?

Julie Reagan: Claire is progressing nicely- 7 cm dilated. Grandbaby will be here soon!

Gross. Who let parents on Facebook? And more importantly, why does she have to see this stuff in her feed? Isn't it enough that she has to share a house with her? One quick *unfriend* button took care of that problem nicely.

She was feeling crummier than usual today, even with the new bar set for her definition of "crummy". Felicity tried to switch positions as another annoying cramp hit her side. If she hadn't been told five weeks ago that she was pregnant, she certainly would have figured it out by now. Her stomach hadn't ballooned out like Claire's, but her mother's OBGYN, Dr. Greenwood, had told her that it was because of the baby's positioning and something about the shape of her uterus. This was why she seemed to be widening more than changing into a round pregnant ball. This super fun fact didn't make her any less uncomfortable now though.

Her energy had been fading even more, cramps would come and go, the headaches that she had been getting intensified, and random kicks caught her by surprise. All of it? Extremely annoying and quite unappreciated. She had become a stranger in her own body. Not sure what to expect next, she wouldn't be surprised if her alien body kicked her out soon and her spirit was left to roam the earth and look for a new body to inhibit. Hey— that would make a great movie! Although, if she were writing it, she would be sure that the lady with blindingly red hair searched for a second body with soft blonde hair. With no body bumps.

Why couldn't she just be dying? Dying would have been much more fun and dramatic, and the sympathy she would have gotten would have been made up of more parts sympathy and less parts judgment with whispers following her everywhere she went.

She would have preferred "Poor girl. Cut off in her prime. Such potential! She's so smart and pretty." Instead of "What a slut! Can you believe she was having sex? Surely God will judge her for her disobedience and carelessness!"

She wasn't a slut. She was a girl trying to make a go of it with a guy that she loved. Out of all the teenagers having sex, it was quite unfair that it was Felicity that got pregnant. Stephanie often bragged of her sexual prowess. Elliot also had been with two other girls before her. TWO. Gloria at school apparently had been having sex for two years. Was she pregnant? Was anyone else at her school pregnant? Nope. Just her. So much for fitting in.

When she told Elliot about the baby, he had been decidedly cool towards her. Apparently she managed to hit a "first" for him— earning him the title "Daddy" for his sixteenth birthday.

"Are you sure it's mine?"

She gave him her best imitation of Claire's glare of death, and he muttered a half-apology. How could he even think that? He knew that it had been her first time. Did he think she was getting something on the side while dating him? She said, "I love you!" What else did she need to do to prove her faithfulness to him? For the last few weeks he had been busier and busier, picking up more hours at McDonalds and playing extra gigs with his band. He said it wasn't her; it was him. But she knew better. He didn't want her to have his baby. Like she had a choice.

This baby was ruining her life already. Annoying. And completely unfair.

Before her ultrasound last week, she had asked Elliot if he wanted to come see a blurry black and white squirrel version of their baby, but not only did he not laugh at her awesomely clever joke, but he declined, saying that he didn't feel comfortable coming. Comfortable? Want to talk about not being comfortable? How about her body attacking her from the inside out? Did he think that this was comfortable? When she tried to bring up her aching boobs and sore hips and back pain, he held his hands over his ears and said, "La la la la la la – you are ruining the romance here" while backing away and grabbing his Xbox remote. Romance? Did he mean sex, or did he mean their relationship beyond sex or are those two things the same? Pregnancy was really making her rethink what they had, and what they did. It seemed innocent before. Now, she wasn't sure. If this is how sex made you feel, Felicity wasn't sure that she was on board with this anymore.

Felicity wanted to talk to Mother about all of this— Elliot, the sex, and what was going on now with her body, but the gulf between them was too wide. It was like the Grand Canyon was between them and talking through things would require one of them to successfully jump across it first. Sometimes Felicity wanted to rewind back to when she could tell her Mother anything, before the canyon separated them. It was lonely over here.

Mother had been extra bizarre these past few weeks. At first Felicity just thought she was being weird, but then after a few too many awkward conversations Felicity had to upgrade her description to bizarre. Felicity didn't like talking about her private parts on a normal day, so why should pregnancy make that any different? The stuff going on down there was no one's business but her own! Mother's persistence at trying to discuss these things was maddening.

Not to mention, Mother seemed quite embarrassed when she had to tell her friends about the second grandchild. Nothing like the gushing that Mother went through to announce Claire's pregnancy. Humph, always the favorite, that Claire. And then there were the questions mother kept asking about adoption. Give the baby up for adoption? What a crazy question! How was she supposed to know? How about, let's talk about how to go back nine months and not have sex without a condom! Got a time machine in that casserole of yours? Nope? Then not interested.

Kids from church and school had been avoiding her like the plague as if finally listening to their parents when advised not to hang out with that super bad influence girl— Felicity Reagan— the girl dumb enough to get pregnant in the eighth grade. "Pregnancy isn't contagious, you jerks!" She wanted to shout more than once, but instead she found a safe corner and kept to herself. The old crew all of a sudden became super "busy" and when she texted Stephanie to see where the gang was hanging out, Stephanie acted surprised and then asked, "Gang? What gang?" before making up some lame story about her parents not letting her hang at all this summer. Felicity knew she was lying. Stephanie's daily Facebook posts were all about "the gang" and their daily adventures with basement hopping. Plus, when had Stephanie actually ever followed her parents' rules?

As someone who loved hanging out with other people and who thrived on conversation and company, this new no-friends isolation was hard. It made her feel somehow as if she were not a whole person. But at least isolation was better than the alternative at this point: judgment. Lots, and lots of judgment— with the cherry of "you really should have known better" on top.

Never before had she been happier to see the start of summer vacation. Being 38 weeks pregnant was excuse enough to stay in her room and refuse to participate in life. It was summer break. Nothing was expected of her. That's why she was able to do nothing but position a pillow in the small of her back, lean her head against her padded headboard, and turn into a gassy, pregnant statue. Her back pillow of choice today was the crocheted pillow "You is strong, you is kind, you is important", gifted to her the year Mother read *The Help*. She was betting Mother would take back some of those words right about now. Or maybe just revise it to "You is snarky, you is mean, you is a disappointment." Or maybe "You is fat, you is gassy, you is rude."

Mother tried to get Felicity to go shopping at the mall with her, or go out to lunch, or go visit one of her Sunday School ladies in the hospital who just had surgery. But after a painful pedicure appointment (which really was just a trap for Mother to deliver a detailed lecture to Felicity on taking care of herself now that she was pregnant), Felicity refused all of her mother's socialization attempts. She was tired of dealing with the stares, the gossip, and especially the mandatory counseling sessions at school. People annoyed her even more than usual right now. Yes, she knew that premarital sex was frowned upon. Yes, she knew she wasn't supposed to get pregnant at 15. Yes, she knew that she was a giant disappointment to her family, friends, and teachers. Yes, she knew that her potential wasn't being met.

If this was chess, she would make her next move so surprisingly clever that they would all gasp at her brilliance in delivering a checkmate even when all seemed lost.

She adjusted her ever-broadening body and realized she must have dozed off mid-rant to herself. Must have been more tired than she realized. She felt like she could sleep another week. What woke her up? *That.* Another ridiculously strong cramp hit her, and all of a sudden she realized that she had wet her bed. What? When did that happen? Oh gosh, embarrassing! She jumped up and a cramp stronger than anything she had ever felt before pulsed through her body. Felicity fell to the floor with a cry.

CHAPTER FOURTEEN
Claire

Claire was still only eight centimeters dilated, and yet the clock on her labor had officially hit twenty-six hours. The offensive punch line to pregnancy hit level ridiculous ten hours ago.

Thankful that her epidural definitely helped make the waiting easier, she napped on and off as her body let her, but the epidural came with high levels of guilt. Her friends had warned her about mommy guilt. She just didn't realize that it would start this early. She hadn't even met her baby yet! Was the epidural hurting her baby? The articles on Facebook conflicted on this point. Was this projecting what kind of a mother she would be? Because she couldn't do this the way she wanted, was the rest of her motherhood journey going to go horribly wrong as well? Had she set a precedent for failure? Was giving up on her ideals giving up on the only right way?

Trevor helped as much as he could with the guilt that came pouring out of her mouth like lava from the motherhood volcano. At first he was supportive with endless amounts of patience.

91

"There's no reason for you to be a hero," and "There's no shame in accepting help when you need it," and "What do you mean you're a failure? I've never been so proud of you as I have been these last nine months. You're doing awesome!" and "If it wasn't safe, they wouldn't offer it to you. Think about how many babies have been born successfully with an epidural before this!"

But when encouragement morphed into a lecture on how motherhood requires flexibility, and she might as well start getting used to that now, she told him to go take a walk. "Go, just GO." Anywhere except to the cafeteria if he was going to get more mind-numbingly bad smelling sandwiches that would make her question the seriousness of his marital vows to her— she very sweetly said, not yelling at all.

He had only just left when she already missed him, feeling the silence of the room start to suffocate her. Grabbing for her phone on the side table, she wanted to text him to tell him to come back right now! But instead of grabbing the phone, her fingers pushed it off the table onto the floor, and in her numbed state she couldn't get up herself to retrieve it. It was like a slap from epidural guilt karma.

It was a full thirty minutes before he returned, but before she could start in on how inconsiderate and selfish he was to abandon her like that, she noticed a strange look on his face.

"What. What is it? Where did you go? I dropped my phone and ran out of juice! I am doing this for YOUR child! Why would you leave me?" Hysterics blended nicely into an ending sob. Labor wasn't doing much for her dignity on any level.

"Sweetie you told me to leave you alone for a few minutes, remember? And I meant to come back sooner, but, hon?"

"What?"

"I have some news that you might not want to hear."

"What. Felicity had her baby?" She smiled at her own joke. She had been working hard at this and last she heard, Felicity was locked in her room with only her bad attitude for company.

"Yes." He looked pained, knowing how she would receive this.

"Are you kidding? That's not funny."

"Not kidding. Six pounds three ounces. She gave birth ten minutes after Mom Reagan got her here. Apparently it all happened so quickly, they still look in shock."

"How would you know what they look like?" Claire shot out. Ticked, tired, and feeling a little bit murderous at this bit of news.

"She's—" awkward pause "She's actually in the room next door. I ran into your mom in the hallway.

Stony faced, she was silent as she let this sink in. "Boy or girl?"

"Boy. Healthy. Good set of lungs. He's actually really cute. He has Felicity's red hair." He smiled, but then forced a straight face when he saw her reaction to this.

"So let me get this straight. Our child is no longer the first grandchild, my sister did the natural birth I wanted, she was only in pain for an hour max, and her extremely careless pregnancy care *didn't* result in a baby who was born with two heads?"

"Why are you glaring at me?" Trevor asked. "I've been here helping you!"

"Except for when you abandoned me," She pouted.

"But aren't you happy for her? Maybe she can find a nice family to adopt her son and can move on with getting her life back on track."

"Does he have a name?" Her glare seemed to intensify with a thought.

"No, no name yet."

"Well then we better pop this kid out before she steals the name 'Samuel'. I could see her doing that just to spite me."

"Come on— she wouldn't do that."

"Wouldn't she though?"

Claire lay back on her bed, feeling numb from more than just the epidural.

CHAPTER FIFTEEN
Felicity

The room reeked of motherhood. From posters on the wall showing bare chested women with fat babies attached to them to the stack of tiny diapers towering next to her bed, all of it was just too much pressure.

Lying on a layer of bricks that was disguised as a hospital bed covered in itchy white sheets, Felicity wished that she could be somewhere else— anywhere else right now. Pain ripped through her body in weird places that she didn't want to think about, and she was tired— so very, very tired. Feeling too fragile even make a joke, Felicity wondered when this would all finally end.

There had been a few moments when she thought that she was going to die— that her body would explode into ten million pieces— that her punishment for spreading her legs was this most brutal and agonizing physical torture in the same spot that once brought Elliot such pleasure. But now it was all over, blessedly so, and she wasn't sure what was next.

Before rushing off with the baby, Mother leaned over and kissed Felicity's sweaty forehead and whispered. "I'm so proud of you, baby. Good work. Your baby is as beautiful as you are."

Proud? Mother was proud of her? She did something right? Also— beautiful? Really? Felicity didn't want to admit how badly she needed to hear that, so she turned her face away all the while tucking away the memory to pull out and replay often in her mind.

She was tired of the last few months constantly feeling two blinks away from a nap. She was tired of everyone hounding her with questions about how this baby came to be. She was tired of being asked what she was going to do with this baby. She was tired of the not-so-subtle guilt manipulations. She was tired of Elliot's mind games, and she was tired of feeling so incredibly alone.

Turning her head over to her left she saw a small glass bed with raised sides. Inside was the tiniest person she had ever seen. Two arms, two legs, ten fingers, ten toes, button nose, little lips, slight chin dimple, eyes that looked right through her— yep it was a baby all right. It was hard to believe that just hours before he was still a part of her. She couldn't wrap her mind around the fact that she grew him inside of her. Her body. Her son? *That* came out of her? Weird. And decidedly— gross.

During one of the conversations with her mother that was one-sided and completely uncalled for, mother had insisted that the minute Felicity met her baby, she would feel differently. She would care. An invisible thread would string from the baby's heart to hers, connecting them in a way she had never been connected before. A thrill greater than a caffeine high combined with a sugar rush would fill her veins and create an euphoric moment of love. She was supposed to bawl with joy while wrapping him up close to her and doing what? Talk to him? He seemed a little young to go over and over how much he had disappointed her, which was the stripe of parenting that she was accustomed to these days.

For a second, Felicity *almost* felt something. Something inside of her *almost* felt concern for this tiny person. But then she handed the warm bundle back to the nurse and the almost feeling disappeared. In its place landed a strong sense of disconnection.

Now, a few hours later, as Felicity stared at this tiny glass bed with an even tinier occupant, she felt nothing. Her heart didn't pitter-patter, the music didn't crescendo for a dramatic moment, and the only rush she felt was from liquids that were still pooling out of her. Disgusting. Why would anyone actually want this to happen to them?

Slowly rolling onto her right side and purposefully putting her back to the foreign baby who everyone claimed was hers, Felicity closed her eyes and gave into the exhaustion weighing on her. Maybe when she woke up, this nightmare would be over.

CHAPTER SIXTEEN
Claire

This was it.

This was the moment that Claire dreamed about for the last five years; the point in the future where she had focused on as her someday reward and joy. *It was her someday.* The journey had been long and difficult. The path was strewn with debris and was windy and dimly lit. The experience had been lacking in the magical moments that she dreamed should be there. But she made it. She was here now— the long awaited arrival into motherhood. None of the hardships from the journey mattered anymore because she was about to become a mother. Samuel Lewis Bailey— he was almost here.

She was finally in one of the big birthing suites with umpteen hours of labor behind her, and people were shouting "PUSH!"

Completely ignoring the repulsive things that her body was doing and yet focusing keenly on the moment, Claire was relieved to have made it this far. Several false starts whetted her appetite all the more to complete this journey successfully. And here she was. This was it.

She was so blessed. Trevor was right. It was ridiculous to focus on Felicity during such a time. This wasn't about Felicity, Felicity's baby, or the ridiculous sibling competition that had always been between them. This was about their son. Their long awaited, perfectly made son that God had sent to them as their own little miracle.

Wanting to remember this moment forever and yet to get it over with as soon as possible, Claire emotionally dangled with painful indecision between rushing through and pausing to enjoy. She wanted to bathe her emotions in this experience and yet she was dying to be done with it so that she could get up and take a long, steamy shower before snuggling down to cuddle her new bundle and to get to the next part. Birthing her child had stretched her further than she thought possible, and she wasn't even referring to her stomach now webbed with stretch lines. She knew that she would laugh with Trevor later about the laminated birth plan. Motherhood was already turning her into a better version of herself. Didn't go according to her carefully charted plan? She was okay with that. See that? Growth!

He was almost here, and that's all that mattered. Waiting four-and-a-half years to unwrap this present, she was finally untying the bow to reveal the gift below. It was hers now.

Closing her eyes she leaned into it, putting her entire body into bringing life to her little bub. The rest of the world blacked out for a minute and then she peeked open her eyes and stared, riveted at the scene in front of her. Trevor's eyes lit up. A tiny person was lifted from the end of her bed. The nurse reached for some weird looking scissors. Her husband grabbed the scissors and helped cut the cord that tied her to her baby. The doctor and nurse wrapped her little bub in a white blanket with light blue and pink stripes on the edge. She couldn't see his face yet, but he was here. *She did it.* She had a baby.

She swept her gaze across the room as they carried her baby across it, and she noticed that the still-lingering summer sun was flooding the room with a bright light. The hospital that had held her prisoner for the past thirty hours seemed less like a prison and more like a place of celebration. A heavy weight fell off of her shoulders— *finally.* Finally this part was over. The empty baby warmer that had been sitting in the corner of the room now had an occupant and was surrounded by people cleaning the occupant up so that she could meet him for the first time.

Her baby.

Her heart flooded with happiness and tears of joy sprung into her eyes.

Thank you, Jesus. Thank you for my baby. She silently prayed.

Would he smile when they locked eyes for the first time? Would he grab her finger? Would he know her instantly and coo at her breast? Would breastfeeding go easily for them? What color were his eyes? His hair? How big was he? Was he cute? Of course he was cute, how could he not be!

"Good job, mama" Trevor beamed to her and gave her a quick kiss on the cheek before hurrying back to the warmer. "We have a son!"

She wanted to celebrate, scream, do a dance, yell to the world, "I JUST HAD A BABY!" But first, she wanted more than anything to hold him. *Her baby.* He was here! She was almost regretting her insistence that he be cleaned up before their first moment, but really she didn't think it would be as magical as it should be if he was covered in— well, her. She needed to shower his head with kisses, hold him close, whisper how much she loved him into his ear, beam with pride for their first picture together, and caress his cheek to help him remember her touch from all those months inside of her. All of this would be more enjoyable if he was clean. She could already feel his warm form imprinted into her arms. She was ready.

The doctor, nurse, and Trevor were all over by the bed warmer with him. She was jealous that they already knew what his face looked like. What did his eyes say? Were his lips pooching out for her? Did he have hair? On a scale of ugly to handsome, how far did he leave the other babies in the dust? Did he look like her or Trevor? The suspense was killing her!

Heads bent over her little guy, the doctor and nurse were working furiously on— what? What exactly were they doing? Why was it taking so long to clean him up?

"Trevor?" she called. "Is he okay?" Was he supposed to be crying? The room that spent those glorious thirty seconds celebrating flooded with a tense silence just as a cloud shadowed the sunlight filling the room. Was the silence a bad sign? Elation leaned into alarm.

She tried to lean up on her elbow to see better, but the epidural still hadn't worn off, and she was too physically exhausted to fight against it not to mention she was beginning to feel a bit light headed. Falling back onto her pillow, she waited.

"He just needs a little puff of oxygen. Labor was hard on him too!" Her husband called back, not leaving his son's side. Even though his words were assuring and exactly what she needed to hear, his tone was etched with concern. She could read him and always knew instantly if he was lying just by looking into his eyes, but now his back was to her. She couldn't see his eyes. Why was he hiding his eyes from her? What was he afraid she would see?

What happened next happened so quickly that for a minute Claire thought she might be dreaming or hallucinating or both. More people started running into the room— doctors, nurses, and young people wearing official looking white coats but who looked like they should still be in high school. A new infant bed was wheeled in with a lot more wires attached. The new people were all whispering. Trevor got blocked out of the circle around the baby and stepped back nervously looking over white-coated shoulders. The baby was still silent. Too silent. Why was her baby so quiet?

101

Did he need more than one quick puff of oxygen? Claire couldn't see what was happening to her baby or what they were doing to him.

The room suddenly became freezing. Her arms, which should have been holding her baby right now, started shaking. And then her legs followed suit. Before she realized it her entire body was shaking involuntarily on the birthing bed. Coldness or fear— she wasn't sure.

She wanted to jump up out of bed, push the white coated people aside and scoop up her baby— giving him his first kiss from her and making everything all better, but she couldn't move. A nurse draped a heated blanket over her and the shaking slowed down from quarter note equals 150 to 120.

"Why…why isn't he crying?" She managed to whisper through clenched, chattering teeth. The room was silent. Everything was moving quickly over in the corner, but no one was explaining anything to her. Trevor stood by the baby.

"Is he okay? Please tell me he's okay!" A hoarse whisper was all she could manage.

One of the new people came over and knelt down next to her bed. "We need to take your baby to the NICU for some observation. He isn't keeping color on his own, and we're not sure why."

"*Samuel.* His name is Samuel."

"Ok. We're taking Samuel to the NICU. We'll come back and update you when we can figure out what's going on with your little guy."

"The NICU? But the NICU is for babies who are premature! Samuel isn't early at all! I was forty-one weeks with him yesterday! I carried him full term!"

The new person with kind eyes patted her hand. "Did you have any concerning ultrasounds or markers during your pregnancy? Did you have any testing done on his heart?"

His heart? No, why should she? She had the perfect pregnancy. Every day was flawlessly performed. She meticulously followed everything on her pregnancy "Dos and Don't Dos" list, practically guaranteeing health to her unborn child. The nurse's question brought a million questions to her mind, but Claire just said, "no."

Another hand pat. "Mostly likely it's nothing. I'm not trying to alarm you. I just had to ask."

And then she was gone.

The bed with her baby wheeled away. Trevor waved to her to let her know that he was going with the baby. The doctors left with the bed holding her most prized possession. The other nurses left. The residents left.

It was like the scurrying exit of the orchestra at the end of a long concert. One by one they all fled the stage like the building was on fire. Except for some strange reason she remained, frozen to her seat and unable to move.

Claire looked around the large room that minutes before had seemed tiny because of the crowd. She drowned in the sudden aloneness. Her arms still hadn't held her baby. Her deflated stomach no longer held a life. He was gone and yet she hadn't met him yet. Where was her baby? Being flexible with a laminated birth plan was one thing, but this was just cruel. Why was this happening? She had just had a baby. Didn't she?

Squeezing her eyes shut, she felt an overwhelming desire to cry but for some reason she couldn't. She had been a mother only a few minutes, and already she was a failure.

CHAPTER SEVENTEEN
Julie

Julie hated hospitals. No matter how many years passed from the worst day of her life, every time she walked into the hospital the events of that day came flashing back as though they had happened yesterday. Each time she lost her breath for a moment as the emotional pain assaulted her yet again. This never got easier.

And yet here she was, camped out in the waiting room, simultaneously taking a break from the moody teenager high on hormones while waiting to hear a "He's here!" from Trevor.

These past few hours had been such a blur. Going up to Felicity's room to bring her a snack. Seeing her writhing on her floor moaning in pain. Trying to get her to the car. Calling 911 when it was clear Felicity couldn't walk by herself. Holding her hand in the ambulance. Telling her it was going to be okay; that she was doing great; that Julie loved her. Watching the pain in her baby's face. Wishing she could take it all way. Arriving at the hospital. Running next to the stretcher holding her girl's hand. Arriving on the Labor and Delivery floor. Seeing the commotion as someone yelled, "She's pushing!" Standing at the foot of the bed and watching her first grandson come bursting into the world. Hearing him wail. Feeling her heart pound in a way it hadn't pounded in a long time. Going to her daughter's side, pushing back her sweaty hair, and whispering, "You did a good job, sweetie." Holding him. Feeling that tiny body melt into her arms. Looking into his face framed by a glorious headful of red hair and realizing— from the beautiful red hair to the fairy kissed dimpled chin, Felicity's little baby looked just like the little baby that haunted her dreams. And like Brad. This moment was gloriously dangerous. Julie wanted to scream and cry and yet looking into this tiny face was like having all her dreams come true. He was here.

It was only a few hours later that she realized that she had forgotten her cell phone at home in all the commotion. About one day a week, she tucked her phone away and disconnected herself from the phone's many distractions, simply enjoying the stillness of real life around her. Today was the day that her phone was turned off and stored at the bottom of her jewelry box. Trevor had been calling the house phone with labor updates, and there really wasn't anything else pressing enough to require a cell. She went most of her life without a cell phone and valued the ability to cut herself off from the world when she needed to refocus, but she hadn't realized how dependent she had come to be on it. Right now she needed to call her brother to go make sure that Harry got some dinner and to text Trevor to see where they were at, both in the hospital and in the labor progress. Thankfully Trevor ran into her in the hallway a while back, so at least she knew that the waiting wasn't yet over for her other grandson.

Claire requested that only Trevor be in the delivery room, and Julie was determined to give Claire the space she wanted until she was ready for visitors. So Julie waited in suspense to hear the good news.

Poor Claire had been at this for over a day now. Julie almost warned her about the entirely unmagical thing called getting induced as she had experienced it with Felicity's birth, but she didn't want to cloud her eldest daughter's excitement with the harsh reality of what was probably to come.

"But don't worry— no matter how horrendous the birth is, once you hold your little baby for the first time, it will all seem like nothing because it gave you your baby," she had told Claire, trying to prep her for the bad by giving her a glimpse into the good.

Claire's face beamed in response, truly glowing with love. She was going to be so good at this. Emotionally prepared for the new journey, physically having put in her time to make every day count— Claire was going to be an amazing mother.

"Thank you, Lord for making this happen for my sweet girl," she silently prayed. "And help us— help us figure out how best to help my other sweet girl."

The black cloud on the blue, sunny skies of her grandmotherly happiness would have to be Felicity. If she had been difficult before they knew that she was pregnant, these last few weeks she had been extra troublesome in her surly attitude. Barely agreeing to see a counselor at school, she had refused to talk in her sessions and had pushed Julie away every time she tried to discuss the heavy issue at hand.

Certainly she was not the first teenager to ever be in this mess, and certainly there were options to keep Felicity's potential intact as well as to provide a good life for the baby. But it was difficult to settle on an option when Felicity rebuffed their attempts to discuss it with her.

Julie smirked as she remembered Felicity's face when Julie had asked a few days ago if she had lost her mucus plug yet. The horror in her eyes; the scream of "GROSS! MOTHER! STOP!"; the plugging of her ears; the backing quickly away— she had just earned herself a Christmas pillow reading, "Don't knock the mucus plug." Definitely a yellow pillow. With green thread.

The whole situation was awkward because it was an adult situation with adult consequences while Felicity was still very much a child.

This reminded Julie of when Felicity was still a toddler. If she tripped while running and skinned her knee, she did not want help. She did *not* want comforting hugs or mommy kisses on the boo boo. She did *not* want a band-aid. She did *not* want a visit to the doctor. She didn't care if these things would help make her feel better. Fiercely independent, she would go somewhere to be alone, cry to herself, and self-soothe— welcoming absolutely no parental comfort or intervention.

When she was a toddler, Julie used to laugh at the cuteness of her stubborn independence. Now it was just extremely scary. A new life was involved, what was Julie to do?

Julie sat up long nights deliberating the best intervention choice. Should she set up an adoption for Felicity's baby? Should she take the baby home for a few weeks until Felicity was ready to make a decision for herself? Should she help her raise the baby? Should she wait for Felicity to ask for help?

After feeling like her head would explode, she would call up her brother Gordon to discuss the impossible confusion.

"You know I would love another baby. I've always wanted a big family."

"But just think about how adoption has helped our family in the past. Felicity could give someone else that gift."

"But what if she regrets it in ten years?" Julie asked.

"What if you raise the boy as your own and *then* she regrets it in ten years? Does she just get to take him then? *Away from you?*" Gordon gently added his concerns.

Julie wished in the worst way she had her phone so that she could call Gordon now. She wanted to tell him that little baby boy looks just like Brad and like— well, him. It made her heart stop for an instant when she looked into those blue green eyes which were so familiar to her. Something in her heart immediately attached itself to his. He was a part of her. Even if Felicity wanted to give the baby up for adoption, could Julie even give him up at this point?

Julie twisted her hands in her lap, remembering their many conversations heavy on questions, light on answers. Gordon was so wise, having raised five kids with his wonderful wife Sally, but even he didn't have a magic ball that gave all the answers in such a gray situation. There wasn't a one-size-fits-all answer for teenage moms. Through the years she had seen many teen moms step up and do a amazing jobs as mothers. The question was— would Felicity be one of those?

Just then, she saw him.

Running down the hallway to keep up with a tiny bed on wheels surrounded by people in white coats— he didn't look well. His blonde hair was mussed, his normally cheerful blue eyes were tired, and his mouth was drawn into a tight line.

"Trevor!" She stood and shouted. Did he see her? "Trevor!"

He turned, waved, and then pointed to the entourage in front of him. "I'm going with the baby!" he yelled back over his shoulder as he continued to move, not offering any further explanation.

The baby? He was here? She had two grandchildren? Yay! Wait— why were they running and where were they taking the baby?

A sinking feeling settled in her gut as her sunny blue sky was suddenly flooded with black clouds. Memories came exploding back. That day so long ago when she was the mom in the Emergency Room holding back tears. That day when her baby was the one rushed away from her. That day when all her dreams were ripped away with a cart full of lifesaving devices hurrying, hurrying before it was too late.

Was her grandbaby okay? Was Claire going to have to face the unthinkable too?

"Oh Lord please no." Dejectedly sinking back into her chair, she lowered her head to pray.

CHAPTER EIGHTEEN
Felicity

Felicity was hoping he would visit, but she refused to get her hopes up. He had made it pretty clear that he wasn't interested in having any part of this the last time they spoke. Too proud to beg, she looked away so he couldn't see the hurt in her eyes after he once again weaseled out of spending time with her when she stopped by McDonalds to catch him after he was finished with his shift.

Perusing the ridiculously healthy hospital menu in hopes of ordering some food, she was wondering where the donuts were or perhaps some delectably greasy fries when a timid knock sounded at the door. Immediately bristling, she prepared herself for yet another friend from church with a parent who said that they were "praying for her". Right. *Gossiping about her and just wanted to come get the latest scoop was more like it.* She wanted to say to these people, "Congratulations— you are BETTER THAN ME because you have never EVER made a mistake in your life! He who is without sin— cast the first stone. Ready for that stone anytime now. Did you want a cookie for your good aim? Awesome. Okay now leave. NOW."

Pressing her lips together and holding completely still, she used her now super power of silence in hopes of discouraging the wrong person from visiting, but the door slowly creaked open anyway. About to feign sleep, she caught a glimpse of him and her irritated glare turned into a dazzlingly bright smile.

Hesitating in the open door, he looked as though he wasn't sure if he were welcome. His long hair was combed, his cloudy gray eyes looked nervous, and those extremely kissable lips were slightly parted as if he wasn't sure what to say.

"Hey." Her smile widened as she stared at him. *He came.*

"Hey." His voice was low and comforting. Like honey in warm tea on a scratchy throat.

"Is this the baby?" He gestured to the still-sleeping baby. Felicity thought back to an hour ago when the baby was screaming and definitely not asleep. Thank goodness the baby had the good sense to time his nurse-needed tantrum to not be at the same time as this visit. Felicity seriously needed some Elliot time. She wanted to joke, "Nah, this one's a rental." But she resisted her usual sarcastic response.

"Yeah. A boy." She watched as one bushy eyebrow was raised and a glimmer of a smile appeared on his lean face.

"Cool." He sat down on the edge of her bed, careful not to bump her or the baby's bed in the crowded room. She suddenly wondered if she smelled funny at the way his nose wrinkled.

"And you? You doing alright?"

She nodded, not willing to share the sordid details of the past hours with him.

"It wasn't that bad." Shrugging her shoulders to sell her point, she barely refrained from wincing at the pain.

"Good." He reached for her hand and stroked it softly. "You look good."

"Good" was a close cousin to "beautiful". Right? She blushed, half hating herself for needing to hear his compliments so badly and half just giving in to the feelings that she had for this boy.

110

They had a baby together. That meant something in a relationship, right? The mistake was made. Time to own up to it together, right? The slow strokes on the top of her hand sent tingles straight to her spine.

"So have you decided what you're going to do?" He asked after an awkward pause in which he cleared his throat three times.

"Do?"

"With the baby. Are you… are you going to— you know— keep it?"

"Dunno. Haven't really thought it through." Averting his gaze, she reached over and grabbed a tissue from the nightstand to pretend-blow her nose while really wiping away the two tears that suddenly appeared out of nowhere. Tears? What was wrong with her?

"What do you think I should do?" It was her turn to clear her throat before responding.

"Dunno." He let go of her hand and stood up, turning around to intently stare at the breastfeeding photo on the wall across from her.

There was another pause. A silence. A strange sort of silence that sparked with a thousand unsaid words. Were her unsaid words the same as his or was she thinking about the baby while he was wondering what he was going to pick up for dinner on the way home?

"Well, it is *our* baby," he suggested, turning back around with widened eyes after getting a good look at the knockers on that poster.

"Yeah." Was he staring at her boobs through the hospital gown? Self-consciously she reached for her chest to make sure that the fabric was covering them all the way. Why were there slits in the gown there too? How much for a gown without holes?

"Pastor Trevor is always telling me to take responsibility for my actions, and maybe this is what he meant," he said.

"You mean my brother-in-law Trevor? Not only did we have a baby out of wedlock, but we had a baby on the exact same day they had their baby, completely scooping their first grandson deal. In the Claire world of competition, that's reason for at least a year of the silent treatment." She let go of her gown, wanting to roll her eyes as she imagined the indignation and low digs she would receive from Claire as soon as soon as they saw each other again.

"I dunno, he's been pretty cool the last several times we've talked." He turned back to the breastfeeding poster. *Really?*

"When did you talk to Trevor?" She was curious as this was the first she had heard of this. Plus, she wanted him to stop staring at the poster and stare at her. Maybe a holey gown wasn't the worst thing in the world after all.

"Couple of times since you told me about— you know— the baby."

"Like counseling? Therapy? Or congrats on the baby, bro?"

"Ha. The first one. It was his idea. It seemed dumb at first, but I really enjoyed our two talks after that. He's a cool guy."

"Yeah he is. Who knows what he sees in my sister." She mumbled, not wanting to admit that she had always been quite fond of him as well in spite of his annoying preacher ways and that horrible middle hair part that he insisted on keeping.

"So what did he say about our baby?" Felicity's interest was piqued. Did Trevor think she should give the baby away? He was not her mandatory therapy counselor at school because of the family conflict of interest, so she hadn't discussed this with him and that made her sad. Honestly his opinion meant more to her than that of her sister. She wished she could trade Claire for Trevor without ever having to see Claire again.

"He wouldn't tell me what to do. He just said to pray about it and think about what the right thing for the baby would be."

"Well, he is OUR baby." She quoted his earlier statement, feeling a sudden urge to pee.

"Yeah." He replaced his large hand softly on top of hers, and she felt that blessed tingle once again.

His lips curved up into a full smile as his piercing gray eyes held hers for the first time since walking into the room, promising— promising something. Felicity wasn't quite sure what, but there was definitely a promise there. She now knew one thing for sure— this baby wasn't going anywhere. They were a family now.

CHAPTER NINETEEN
Claire

More than anything Claire wanted to march upstairs and see her baby who was still being held captive in the NICU, but unfortunately she found that just shuffling from the bed to the bathroom was the maximum of what she could handle right now. She wasn't exactly sure what was going on, ahem, down there, but even the smallest of movements caused immense amounts of pain, and her body was not interested in obeying the usual commands like "take a step forward". Marching was out.

The fact that her baby was down a long hallway, up two flights of stairs, and down another impossibly long hallway meant that walking it on her own was out of the question. What fool designed the mommy recovery floor so far away from the NICU?

Thankfully, Trevor spent the night on the bed/chair thing next to hers, and after breakfast, he promised to take her up to meet their baby. Fluffy pancakes, real maple syrup, strawberries, yogurt, a banana, coffee— breakfast never tasted better than when it was the first food she ate after a thirty hour birth. EAT ALL THE FOOD.

114

Trevor ran down to the cafeteria and grabbed his own breakfast sandwich, and Claire was tempted to eat part of his breakfast too. *Ravenous* didn't even begin to describe how she felt.

The time finally came for them to journey up to their son. Part of her wanted to hustle up there to meet him. Part of her wanted to delay it as long as possible, giving him all the time in the world to snap out of whatever he was fighting before she got there. Maybe she could bring him back down with her if she waited long enough. All the other moms seemed to have babies in their rooms with them, including Felicity down the hall— who she was still avoiding and would probably avoid for the rest of her life. It hurt that Samuel wasn't in a little bed in her room cooing at her, watching her every move, bonding with her, and lying trustingly in her arms that had been waiting for him for so long. She *needed* him with her.

Reluctantly she left the tray full of empty plates (after her very thorough demolition) behind, only taking with her the paper cup of coffee to finish on the ride up. Trevor often teased her about how long it took her to finish her coffee, frequently having to reheat it several times throughout a morning before she slowly sipped her way to the bottom. In turn, she poked fun at his guzzling technique as if all the water on the earth was disappearing right now, and he had to down as much of it as possible before it was all gone.

Her husband glanced now at the mostly full cup of coffee tightly gripped in her hand and smiled, but he didn't say anything. Their familiarity over such a small thing calmed her, and she smiled back at him. Things would be normal again soon.

As Trevor wheeled her up from the recovery floor to the NICU floor, she tried to find a comfortable spot on the wheelchair lined with large cloth pads underneath her. Not possible. Biting her lip, she settled for "just not in immense pain", balancing on the seat as gracefully as possible. Excited to finally meet and hold her baby, she was also a little nervous.

The nurse checked on her every few hours last night, and each time the nurse woke her up, she reached for the phone to call the NICU to see if there were any updates. Every time she called during her broken night of sleep, she was given evasive answers.

"We're just observing him for now."

"We'll know more after rounds."

"We're running a few tests but haven't gotten any results back yet."

Claire wanted to reach through the phone and shake them. The least they could do was to tell her what the heck was going on with her baby! She spied their evasiveness hidden in their technically correct answers. She was no fool! She needed answers, and she would stay on the phone *forever* if necessary until someone gave them to her. They had her baby! But she found that every time she opened her mouth to demand that this is the least they could do, her throat became suspiciously too scratchy to speak clearly. So she would whisper, "thank you" and then hang up.

Not getting a chance to meet him after she had spent so much effort getting him here was extremely disappointing. It was more than disappointing— it was heartbreaking. Why hadn't she gotten to meet her baby yet? Okay so she might have gotten carried away with her laminated birth plan, but wasn't it enough that she graciously went with the new plan? Was expecting to hold her baby asking too much? Why was so much change from her ideals required of her?

Now her birth story was ruined. It was stolen from her by the Neonatal Intensive Care Unit. When she would tell and retell the story of birthing Samuel, there would be no rainbow and fireworks moment of that first meeting when he was seconds old. There would be this awkward gap in time where he grew hours old without her being a part of the story at all.

Exhausted, emotional, and overwhelmed, these last eight hours after his birth had been healing in many respects. She appreciated the warm blankets that were given to help her stop shivering. She loved the helping hands that got her to the shower so that she could wash the birthing grime off of her. The cool, clean sheets on the hospital bed that could be raised and lowered to help with the impossible tasking of getting comfortable soothed her in a way she never dreamed possible. Bits of sleep seemed like hours of rest. Her body felt emptied and a slow process of restoration had begun. Truly she had never felt anything like this before.

While she was being put back together physically, all she could think about was the tiny part of herself that had been taken away. While her body seemed whole for the first time in months, her heart, sensitive from the recent expansion, felt strange. Loneliness and hurt combined with broken expectations to create a new depth of sadness she had never reached before.

Trevor was silent as he pushed her along. She wanted to ask him what he was thinking right now. She wanted him to hold her close and never let go. She wanted him to say that this wasn't her fault, that it was just a misunderstanding, and that there was absolutely no reason that the NICU had detained their son all night. She needed to assure Trevor that she would argue their son out of there like she was arguing her way out of a speeding ticket. She wanted his face to lose the worry and instead beam with pride like it did when Samuel was first born. Now that it was a full eight hours after his birth with no change, Claire could detect some disappointment on her husband's face. Was he disappointed in her? Afraid of the answer, she remained quiet.

Clutching her now lukewarm coffee, she lifted it to her lips and took a small sip after he pushed her onto the elevator and they were momentarily still. The first cup of caffeine in a year, rushing in tiny swallows down her throat, fueling her empty energy basin, and reminding her of her love for the full octane brew was the lone bright spot on today. Well, that and this nonsense getting cleared up in 3-2-1.

They had to press a buzzer outside the NICU and wait for someone to let them in. Once the heavy door creaked opened, Trevor directed her to a room to the right side of a large room. In the large room there were many isolettes and many babies. In the side

117

room separated from the crowd of sick babies, walled in only by windows? There was only one baby— her baby. He was waiting for her.

Excitement coursed through her, and the nervousness fled. She was about to meet him. *Her son.* This was it.

Crossing the threshold into the small room, Claire's eyes immediately raced to the center of the bed to see him. As she was pushed toward him, she eagerly stretched her neck forward to take it all in as quickly as possible.

A small, limp form lay still. More wires than she could count were attached to him— attacking his body like moss smothering a stone . His tiny, raised bed was surrounded by machines and monitors. She could only see the small bits of his face not covered by a large blue and white tubing contraption, stretching like an angry, upside down cross up both cheeks and traveling from his nose to his forehead and beyond to a machine that Claire had never seen before. Eyes were tightly shut as if holding in the weight of the world. The top of his head wasn't visible under a tight white cap that rested under the elaborate strapping, keeping the blue and white tubing contraption in place. Naked except for one of the tiniest diapers she had ever seen, his miniscule size made the puffy Pampers wrap seem massive. Right above the folded down diaper, his umbilical cord had a tube running out of it held in place by stiff white tape forming a semi-circle around where his belly button would hopefully someday be. The small portions of skin that she could see were covered in red rashes, bloated and puffy, with an overriding yellow tint.

Trevor stopped the wheelchair next to their son's bed, and she could see more clearly. From the way the tubing was taped into his nose, it would seem that this machine breathed life into their son. Another tube that she didn't notice before snaked into his mouth. Dried blood and frothy spit crusted together around this tube, making the awkward placement in the corner of his mouth look cruel and unusual. His lips were chapped and flaky— dry like the desert in a windstorm. The screen next to his bed read sets of numbers that were constantly changing— 98, 92, 94, 88. With the 88, the screen started flashing and the beeps intensified in volume and pitch. A low hissing noise combined with the beeps to create a strange sort of duet. Stickers decorated his chest, with wires attaching them to more wires, which eventually led back to the machine with numbers as if those machines were the mothership that took over where Claire's body left off. One side of his forehead was awkwardly taped up with a port not attached to anything, but there was more dried blood along with a yellowish paste around the base of the port leading nowhere. His neck was thick, decorated with many rolling chins, held high by a blue chin strap connected to the breathing tubes as if to keep the mouth pressed tightly together around the tube there. The smallest feet in the world were bandaged with multiple Band-Aids on the heels. His hands rested palms up on a faded blue blanket with yellow ducks under him. The whole room was bathed in sterile air except for the faint smell of her son. *The smell of birth.*

He was right in front of her, but he seemed so far away. The bouncing baby taking a bath in a kitchen sink while laughing in the commercials seemed like an entirely different species than the strangely swollen body with floppy, weak limbs in front of her.

So this was motherhood. Nothing prepared her for this. The piles of freshly washed diapers, the bins of carefully folded clothes, the bed with a tightly stretched crib sheet, the books on parenting that she devoured, the classes she attended on childbirth and breastfeeding; nothing prepared her for this moment— the beginning of her motherhood.

She reached a trembling hand up to touch his small arm resting closest to her side and whispered "Hi, mister. It's nice to finally meet you, Mr. Samuel Lewis Bailey. Mommy's here now." She barely recognized her voice.

His arm was warm— hot— feverish. A bracelet was taped around his wrist. NBClaire Bailey- it read. *He was hers.* Lightly tracing her finger down his arm, she put a finger into his open palm, waiting for him to grab her finger while popping open his eyes and smiling wide as he recognized the one who worked so hard to give him life.

Nothing. His eyelashless eyes remained tightly closed— his only action being a slight rise and fall of his chest. Beep, beep, beep. Hiss, hiss. Beep.

Claire turned to the nurse and cleared her throat. "Can I hold him now?"

The nurse who had looked so welcoming when they entered turned cold. At least she had the courtesy to look chagrined, averting her eyes before firmly replying. "No. He really can't be moved right now. It's critical that we keep him as still as possible."

Claire desperately needed to hold him. If she could gather his limp form into her arms, she could *will* health into him. If she could kiss his brow, she could transfer healing love stronger than any of these machines. If she could hold him tight and protect him from all of this, perhaps she could help him get better. But they said *no*. Who was this nurse to keep her from her baby? How did they know that holding him wasn't exactly what he needed? He *knew* her. He needed her.

"Please. I really need to hold my baby. Please let me hold him. I haven't gotten to hold him yet." Her voice cracked and broke. Her arms, empty and eager for the touch of her baby, reached out as if to show the nurse how badly they needed to be filled.

"I'm sorry. It's not in his best interest right now. I would let you if I could. I'm so sorry. He can't be moved." The unyielding nurse protectively put her hand onto the side of his bed.

Claire lowered her arms, feeling rejected while grabbing back hold of the coffee cup that she had perched between her legs.

A strong arm wrapped around her, and with a start she realized Trevor was crouched down beside her wheelchair.

"It's okay babe. He knows you're here."

No. It wasn't okay. That was part of her lying there. Part of her heart. Part of her soul. Part of her will to live. *She* grew him. She gave him life. Why was this nurse keeping him from her?

Looking at the sick yellowish hue of his skin, she wouldn't let herself voice the one thought that persistently knocked against her heart— *did she do this?* Was this her fault?

CHAPTER TWENTY
Claire

They huddled in the corner of their son's isolation room clasping hands and praying for their baby while they waited for rounds. According to all of her middle of the night phone calls, magic was accomplished during these rounds. Answers popped out from the walls like rain on a foggy day. Claire had never needed answers more.

Even though her eyes were obediently closed in prayer alongside her husband, she kept peeking them open to steal glances over to the bed that held her baby.

"Lord, please help Samuel right now." Trevor caressed their son's name lovingly with a shaky voice. "We don't know what's wrong with him, but you do. Please give us strength as we are both so tired. And please give Samuel strength as he fights whatever this is. You are a good God, and we praise you for your goodness. But we beseech you now— please heal our son. Please put easy breath into his lungs and life into his body."

Trevor kept going, but Claire wanted to protest his wording, *"We praise you for your goodness."* This wasn't good. A baby that looked like that was not good. Starting life with sickness instead of health was not *good*. When asked if she wanted a boy or girl, she always laughed before replying, "We don't care. As long as the baby is healthy!" Well the baby wasn't. What does that mean now? "Goodness" wasn't the first thing that popped into her mind. Unfair, wrong, mistake. *Maybe*. Good? *No*.

Clearly God was putting them through a trial— judging them perhaps for a past wrong. This wasn't God being good. The triteness of the phrase she had said before herself a hundred times made her feel nauseous now. "Oh your Grandfather died? Well, God is good." "Your house burned down, you lost your job, and you are now bankrupt? Well, God is good!" Why did she ever say that? Why? How was God still good even when bad things were happening? It sounded like a pat phrase you use in horrible situations like offering a Band-Aid to someone who just had their arm torn off as if this meager offering of a phrase would somehow patch it all back together.

This wasn't good. This was a mistake. She had said a million times before that "God doesn't make mistakes" but did she really believe that? This seemed like a pretty blatant mistake to her. Maybe if she found the right words, she could change his mind— alert Him to the wrong here. Maybe if she begged hard enough, He would fix this mistake and heal her son. If she just started saying praying words maybe the scale-tipping prayer would come to her. With just the right formula, maybe her prayer would make God realize what a horrible mistake He was making.

"Dear God, please, please, please—" she silently began, but stopped as she noticed with her one eye peeking open that the crowd of people wearing white coats was joining them in the room.

It was time. Searching their faces, she looked for happy eyes delivering good news. Perhaps there was a medication that they had just discovered to help him get better quickly. Perhaps they had overreacted and he was just extra sleepy these first hours— they were here to free him! Perhaps her son had already proven to them that he was a fighter and had won his battle with— whatever this was.

Suddenly feeling hopeful, Claire wiped the tear off her cheek that she didn't even know had escaped, sat up straight in the hardest wheelchair in the world, let go of Trevor's hand, and nudged his shoulder for him to stop praying and pay attention.

Some of the doctors looked old and seasoned. Some of them looked too young to even be out of med school yet— just like the ones who were in the delivery room. But all eight of them wore the same curiously stern expression as if delivering a lecture to a classroom of rowdy students.

Deciding that she didn't want to be sitting for this, she stood up cautiously, gripping her cup of coffee as if it was lending her strength, and shuffled the few steps back over to stand next to her baby. She placed her free hand on the side of his open bed, careful not to disrupt any of her son's equipment.

Trevor followed beside her and draped one arm once more around her shoulders. She leaned into him.

Once in place, she nodded toward the crowd of doctors. She was ready to hear. No one would look her in the eye.

They led with a lot of medical speak that went right over her head. In that moment she would have traded all her schooling and violin practice for a medical degree so that she could understand what they were saying. They seemed to be talking mostly amongst themselves— assigning tests to be done, labeling his chart with more information about him, and guessing treatment paths.

"Does he have a name?" One smiling doctor finally looked up and addressed Claire and Trevor directly when the team of doctors seemed to be wrapping up their unintelligible agenda.

"Samuel. Samuel Lewis Bailey." Claire responded, eager to assign something to him that was according to The Plan— eager to share even this small part of who he was with the intimidating team of doctors. If they understood what an amazing baby he was, starting with his awesome name that Claire and Trevor labored over for months, maybe they would work harder to help him get better.

The row of doctors was quiet for a brief moment, nodding in a sort of synchronized unison while marking something onto their charts. She took the opportunity to jump in with a question. Finally.

"How much did he weigh?"

"What?"

"You know— when a baby is born, the doctor announces 'Eight pounds, one ounce, twenty-one inches long!' so that the birth announcements can be sent out. But the thing is, no one told me how much he weighed so I can't do that. They took him away so fast that step got skipped, and I just really need to know. Did you weigh him? Do you have a number for me? So I can send out a birth announcement?"

Eight sets of eyes began searching their clipboards before one of the youngest looking doctors gasped out a number as if expecting a cookie for finishing the scavenger hunt first.

"Seven pounds, eight ounces! Um…but no length was recorded. Wait— is it written down somewhere else?"

Claire was silent as they all searched for Samuel's birth length in their stack of paperwork before them, but she couldn't wait any longer for her next question.

"What's—what's wrong with him?"

"I'm sorry, what?" The doctor who seemed to be leading the huddle wearing thickly rimmed glasses and a lot of hair gel leaned toward her with a smile, and she realized that she mumbled her question too softly to be understood.

Trevor's grip around her tightened, and he echoed her question with clearer articulation. "We were wondering— do you know what the root cause of all this is? Is there an underlying reason he's so sick?"

The same smiling doctor volunteered. "Well, we're unsure the exact nature of his breathing issues, but he seems unable to maintain a high enough oxygen count on his own. Hopefully we'll be able to wean him off some oxygen later today and see if his body is able to breath on its own. Right now he requires 100 percent oxygen. We think it might have something to do with extra fluid he's retaining that is pressing down on his lungs. We are also doing a heart Echo as well as few other tests later today."

"No, but *why*? *Why is he sick?*" Claire tried again, this time achieving enough volume to be heard. Barely. Her follow up "Did I do this?" was whispered so quietly that she wasn't even sure that she said it.

The doctors all exchanged glances and smiles disappeared.

"We've sent his blood work to the lab to be tested for genetic abnormalities. The results won't be back for several days."

"Genetic abnormalities? What does that mean? What do you think he has?"

"We don't know for sure— and won't know until the test results return from the lab, but we suspect that your son might have…Down syndrome."

Down syndrome.

She felt it before she saw it. Warm puddles around her thinly slippered feet. Wet warmth splashed up on her bare ankles. A dark stain spread quickly over the floor of the small room like a shroud over happiness. Confused, she looked at her hand— empty. Coffee— she was holding coffee. Where did the coffee go? Staring down, she saw the now empty cup where it had landed at her feet. She connected the wet feelings with the dark brown spots. She realized her hand was numb and suspiciously empty of the cup holding her favorite brew. The coffee— the coffee was on the floor.

Staring at the mess on the floor, her mind was muddled. This wasn't part of The Plan. How was she going to clean this up?

CHAPTER TWENTY-ONE
Felicity

All Felicity wanted was to feel normal again. It wasn't fair that she was physically destroyed while her classmates were off enjoying an awesome, pain-free summer vacation, dressed and clean without worrying about what else was spilling out of them. Would she ever get normal back?

After Elliot left, she took a short snooze and then puttered around the room, prepping her things for a long shower and feeling almost happy in spite of the hospital gross covering every inch of her. Frowning as she pawed through the ridiculously neat bag that Mother packed, she couldn't find anything that she actually wanted. She didn't get a chance to pack for this hospital stay because it happened faster than anyone thought it would, and of course her favorite sweet pea body wash was nowhere to be found in her duffel bag. Mother had put some stuff together while Felicity was sleeping earlier today. Figures she would get it wrong.

She picked up the tank top, underwear, and pajama pants—all clean but absurd choices. (Hello Kitty pajama pants, really?), her biggest concern was what her mother did while in her room. Did she snoop around? Read her stuff? Look through her music on her iPhone before bringing it and her charger to her? Did she discover the box of magazines hidden in her closet? Her mother was a nosey, prison-guard-like room searcher. Was a little privacy too much to expect?

The nurse said that Felicity would feel some pain and discomfort, but after her short nap honestly Felicity felt great. Well, great enough to respond with a sarcastic "Ready to hit the marathon trail" with a sassy thumbs up when the nurse came to probe about her private parts once again.

What does a girl have to do to be left alone around here? Would the blasting-the-music trick work with the nurses? While ten shades of annoying, at least her nurse seemed only too willing to take the baby back to the nursery so she didn't have that little guy staring at her all day. When asked if she would be breastfeeding, she started laughing so hard things started to hurt. Breastfeeding? Um no. Her breasts were hers and were not up for auction here.

Did they have a "Take the baby. Give him formula. Leave me alone." sign she could swap out for the standard "Do Not Disturb" sign on the door?

Turning the water on as hot as it would go, she slipped under it and sighed. Wow that felt good. The only thing that would make this moment better was some sweet pea body wash.

While relaxing under the water, her mind kept churning. Elliot's visit got her thinking. Maybe having a baby wasn't the worst thing to happen to her right now.

Could they be a little family of three? Would it be a mistake if she gave the baby away? Would she regret it in a few years? She couldn't really picture life with a baby, but she couldn't picture life without Elliot either. He was her soul mate. He was the Edward to her Bella. He was the August to her Hazel. The attentive Elliot who dropped by today was an Elliot she hadn't seen in a while. He seemed legitimately willing to give them another shot. Maybe the baby was the glue that their relationship needed to be held together.

How would it look during one of their basement hangouts, though? Would the baby stay in the corner? Would Felicity just need to push him around in a stroller thingy wherever she went? What would her friends say? Well, that is— if they were still her friends. If she showed back up with a tiny person, would she become more popular with those girls who actually loved babies? Or would it ostracize her even more?

Felicity tried to specifically picture one of her favorite activities with a baby tagalong, and yet she couldn't grasp how it would look. Maybe this is just another thing that she should wing. Couldn't be that different from a final exam— right?

Surely her mom would help. It was no secret how much her mom loved babies— and this one had her genes in it. Super Grandma! Surely she would make sure the baby was fed and taken care of, and Felicity could just claim mother rights when Elliot came around and wanted to see his son. Diapers? Ewwww gross. Non-negotiable. Definitely a grandmother chore.

Perhaps they could try this as a trial thing. See how it goes for a few weeks and then decide. If the baby's presence helped Elliot decide to choose her— cool. If not, surely someone else would still want the baby after a few weeks in Grandma's nursery. Do babies come with return receipts?

Felicity grinned to herself, feeling ridiculously happy as she turned off the water and started to towel dry. Ouch, stepping out of the shower wasn't as easy as it used to be. Curse this awful sensitivity. Felicity had never been more physically miserable than she had been this entire hellish experience of creating another human being. What kind of fool would actually sign up for this?

CHAPTER TWENTY-TWO
Claire

Claire's soul felt heavy and misshapen.

Lying on the hospital bed and trying to breathe normally, Claire keenly felt the heaviness pressing down on her chest. As she stretched out on her back for the first time in months, she tried to relax and enjoy the much-missed comfortable position, but her mind wouldn't let her. Just as the twinge in the small of her back recognized the familiar position, her chest couldn't take it anymore, and she started gasping for air. Quickly flipping over onto her side, she could pretend. She was still pregnant. She could still breathe. Her baby wasn't sick. He wasn't being questioned as to whether or not he was normal.

A few months ago she ran into Wal-Mart before work. Her treat basket was empty, and she knew that she wasn't going to get through the eight-year-old group lesson at 1:00 without candy or stickers to offer to the well-behaved. On a strict schedule, focused on the mission, and not in the mood to socialize, she had been most displeased when the greeter at the door stopped her to chat. He seemed off somehow— his speech was slurred; his eyes were slanted funny; he was short; his neck and bare arms were covered with bushy black hair. The look on his face suggested that he wasn't working with a fully stringed instrument. Was that Down syndrome? Her attempts to sneak past him unnoticed were not successful.

"Hello!" He shouted except it really sounded more like "Hewwo!"

She ignored him, refusing to make eye contact. Her goal to power walk by unnoticed was thwarted by two carts in front of her crawling to a stop and blocking off the narrow aisle. Impatiently, she stopped and tapped her foot in its still pre-puffy glory days. She was going to be late.

He moved closer, shrinking the distance between them with a few clumsy steps.

"Hewwo!" He shouted again. "My name Maphew. How you?"

It was then he crossed into her personal space bubble, walking even closer and leaning in for a hug. *A hug.* Curse those carts in front of her blocking off a quick exit! How did she get out of this sweaty, unwelcome moment? She didn't know what to say to him as she squared her shoulders and backed away. She could barely understand what he was saying to her. He was decidedly different from those she might normally hang out with, and he offered no value to her or her mission to get treats for her teaching basket. He made her immensely uncomfortable. Avoiding was her best option. Mumbling about needing to go while ducking out of the hug and running away with an "Excuse me" to the carts in the way, Claire got out of there as quickly as possible. She hated the awkward feeling the entire encounter gave her. The neatness of her square world offered no space for a circle.

Immediately pushing the memory off like a dirty jacket that she couldn't wait to discard, she had pushed that morning out of her mind and forgot about the child masquerading as a hairy man as quickly as possible. And she had successfully forgotten. Until now.

There was a breastfeeding poster across from her bed. She stared at it now, but she didn't really see it. Her hands became instantly clammy, and her chin trembled. Shutting her eyes, the next thought took her breath away.

Would that be her son someday? Would he be a greeter that made everyone uncomfortable? A grocery bagger who couldn't be understood? A seat-filler in life who held little value other than warming a seat?

Would the world go out of their way to avoid her son? Would he be the one making people feel awkward? Would he not have the common sense to not hug the cranky pregnant lady glaring at him?

She blinked ten times and licked her dry lips. Her shoulders all of a sudden seemed tighter than if she had just finished five hours of violin practice. The clamminess on her hands spread to her whole body.

She glanced at her side table and saw where she hastily flung the paperwork on Down syndrome that the NICU doctors had given her. This "list" was on top:

Possible vision problem or crossed eyes

Possible heart defects

Intellectual disability, mental retardation

Extra large, protruding tongue

Short height

Tiny white spots on the colored part of eyes

Excessive flexibility

Poor muscle tone

Upward, slanting eyes

Small, abnormally shaped ears

Short neck

Gap between toes

Small nose

Flattened facial features
Simian crease on palm of hand
Short fingers and small hands

She closed her eyes and felt a sudden urge to vomit. *Mental retardation?*

From the many hours spent with her curly-haired Cabbage Patch baby at age six to the many prenatal appointments this past year; nothing even once suggested that her path of motherhood might veer off in such a direction. Shouldn't there be some kind of warning for this sort of thing? Shouldn't someone stand in the way with a large sign that said, "WARNING! Cliff up ahead. BRACE YOURSELF!"

There had been no signs. Life filled her with dreams to how this would go, and those dreams included no cliffs, no warning signs, and nothing remotely regarding Down syndrome.

Surely this was all a mistake because dreams don't lie, right? Her dreams had been extremely specific about how this was supposed to work.

She would get pregnant, look adorably cute while pregnant, deliver her sweet and beautiful child, and be thrown at long last into the club of motherhood. This club was the one where you complained about how little sleep you were getting all the while convincing the crowd that your child was the cutest, smartest, and most talented. After paying some hefty dues and staying on the waitlist for too long, she was ready for the bragging rights to begin.

Her dreams then skipped ahead to when he was four. Forget teething, crawling, and walking. The big milestone would be at four with his first violin lesson. Maybe it could even happen at three-and-a-half if he was ready for it, which, her dreams promised that most likely he would be advanced enough to start early. Discipline and talent would combine perfectly for her son, creating a masterpiece musician before he had even learned to read. Beginning with Suzuki Book 1 and a tape-made blue pinkie house for the bow, leading all the way to Carnegie Hall or perhaps a highly coveted orchestra seat, her son would have every advantage and ability to achieve.

Little Samuel would attend the best music camps, enter (and no doubt win!) the most competitive solo competitions, and study on scholarship at the most prestigious schools. He would learn from her mistakes and go so much farther than she ever did. When listening to her collection of Isaac Pearlman CDs, her first thought was always— "Someday that will be my son."

Her dream was always fuzzy on certain details, like where to get the money to purchase his million-dollar violin or perhaps how she would win over Trevor's dream to see him in the ministry. But one thing was always clear. He would leave a mark, make some noise, *be great.*

Was that so wrong? Was that a bad desire— wanting him to love music? To be great? For him to feel the rush of adrenaline that came with competing and performing? The sweat on his palms as he raised his violin to his shoulder, the shaking of his arm as he drew his bow, the intense concentration on his brow as he recalled every note of that concerto, the soaring of his heart as the music collided with the moment in the most perfect way possible, and the calculated breathing as he refused to start the tempo too fast in case he got in trouble with the sixteenth note passage on page three— all the while knowing that thousands of people were watching, waiting, literally holding their collective breath to hear his solo. Nothing could compare.

This. This was her dream for her baby. And yet they say that he might have Down syndrome?

Why would God do that to her? He promised to "give us the desires of our hearts." To see her son experience a thrill and love for music was her desire. Intense desire. Why would God set him up for a life in which this was impossible?

One question she couldn't even ask aloud, but she couldn't stop thinking, was— what if he was deaf? Would he not even be able to enjoy the one thing that got her out of bed every morning?

What if he not only couldn't hear and process the glorious strains of music, but he also couldn't hear her soft voice talking to him? What if the reason he wasn't getting better was because he couldn't hear her desperate pleas to him to do so?

She understood that there were people with disabilities in the world. She knew that some families dealt with this on a daily basis. She knew that God was still in the equation for these families. But the thing is, that was fine for them. It was easy to watch this happening in *their* lives— far away from her. God obviously made them extra special people ready to take on this extra special burden. But her? No way this should happen to her. She was the over achiever who went into depression over an A-. The thought that such an awkward, low IQ human being would belong to her? This didn't seem right. Did one plus one all of a sudden equal four? She worked hard and should be rewarded accordingly. What you sow, you reap. Right?

She wasn't a horrible person. Maybe after all of this was over, she could smile and say "hello" to the Wal-Mart greeter. Maybe this was what God was trying to teach her through all of this. She could be kinder. She could be more gracious— accepting. Next time she walked past the greeter with her perfect baby in her cart, she would refrain from cringing. He didn't have to be her best friend, but maybe she jinxed herself by being so rude.

"I promise to never be rude like that again if you will spare my son from having Down syndrome. I promise to try harder at being a youth pastor's wife if you let the test results come back negative for Down syndrome. I promise to be a better person. Just please. Please. Please…" her silent prayer ended with an audible whimper.

Her mother had always said that she was lucky in life. Things naturally fell into a pattern of her favor. The sun smiled kindly down on her. She married the man of her dreams when she was only twenty-one. She won a prestigious orchestra chair. She got pregnant when it looked like it might never happen. This luck had to balance this out now for her. There really wasn't any other option. Well, and prayer too. Of course, God wouldn't let such a huge mistake happen to one of his most loyal followers. God is good— right? *Right?*

The doctor was wrong. He had to be. There was no way her son would grow up to be just like the greeter at Wal-Mart. Her son was going to be a concert violinist! He was meant to achieve great things in life!

She would just wait— oh so patiently— for those tests results to come back negative and then for that doctor's apology for his obnoxious "we think maybe...". God would heal her son from his breathing problems, and he would live a normal life with their normal family with extraordinary talent. It's the only ending to this story that made any sense.

She thought of her favorite verse of *Amazing Grace* that Trevor often sang to her when she began to get anxious:

"The Lord has promised good to me,
His word my hope secures.
He will my shield and portion be,
As long as life endures."

He wouldn't fail her on bringing the "good" when the stakes were so high. He never had before. He promised.

Just then her door popped open. What happened to her "Do Not Disturb" sign?

It was a familiar red-haired person, wheeling a glass baby bed holding a red-haired baby. She looked suspiciously happy.

"Hey, sis." Felicity greeted her cheerfully.

Claire stared at her sister with a baby. A perfect baby. She tried to blink and look away but her eyes wouldn't let her.

"They told me I needed to do some walking, and then they said you were right down the hall. Of course I figured stopping by was the neighborly thing to do and all."

Claire still couldn't come up with any words.

"Hey, where's your baby?" Felicity asked, glancing around the room.

"He's—" Claire stopped to clear her throat. "He's upstairs. Just having some tests run. Hey, do you know where mother is?"

Mother had stopped in briefly to gush how proud she was of Claire, kiss her on the forehead, and promise that she was praying for sweet Samuel. Then she said she had to go home and pack some stuff for Felicity and that she would be back to visit again as soon as she could. But that was hours ago. Did mother forget about her?

"She's at the nurses' station filling out some paperwork. Oh yeah, she said to tell you that she would be by as soon as she was done there blah blah blah— whatever. Did you see what I did?" She gestured toward the baby asleep in the glass bed. "Can you believe that *I* grew *this*? Kinda weird, right?"

"Yeah." Claire whispered.

"I mean, I thought for sure he'd be crazy messed up, because let's face it— he's my kid. But he's actually really cute and super strong. The nurse swears he's the best baby she's gotten all week. She's never seen a baby with such strong neck control from the start. Apparently that's pretty unusual."

"How nice for you." Must not cry. Must not cry.

Suddenly, she had to know.

"Felicity, when you were pregnant, did you do some drinking? It's okay— I won't tell Mother. I just want to know. I need to know."

"Why do you need to know?"

"I just do— okay? Did you?"

"None of your business!"

"Of course not. You're right. But maybe Mother should finally find out that it wasn't Harry that knocked over her entire angel figurine collection from Dad and broke every single piece. In fact, if I remember correctly, YOU were there that day."

"Okay fine! Yes, I did some drinking. Whatever— just a few times. A few dozen times. But it doesn't even matter. He's perfect. They all said so. Why do you care?"

"I don't. I was just curious." Claire's tone was flat.

"Anyways, Mother says she thinks he looks just like dad. How cool is that?"

"Very cool." Claire repeated dutifully, her tone still not reviving beyond a flat line. "Hey, if you don't mind, I think I'm going to take a nap." She lay back on her pillow, pulled up her blankets, and looked at her sister expectantly.

"Oh sure. I think I'll go take another shower. Can you believe how disgusting all of this makes you feel?"

"Yeah, it's the worst." Claire whispered.

"Okay, bye!"

And then Felicity was gone. Along with the perfect baby that she perfectly grew even though she broke almost every rule of pregnancy ever to be written. The last bit of evidence was in. If Felicity took credit for the perfection of her baby, does that mean that Claire had to take credit in the non-perfection of hers? And if so, *what* did she do wrong?

CHAPTER TWENTY-THREE
Claire

No sooner had Felicity disappeared in a cloud of giddy smugness than a light knock sounded at the door. If it were mother, she wouldn't knock. Trevor had gone home to catch a few hours of sleep, and her nurse was under strict instructions to turn all visitors away. Does the *Do Not Disturb* sign mean nothing around here?

Claire rolled over on her bed so she could face the door.

"Come in." She said.

The door was pushed open slowly, and in came the Pediatrician they had met with three months ago while they were still in the blissfully ignorant stage of pregnancy when her belly looked just like all of the other pregnant bellies and there were no signs of deformity or difference lying below. An older gentleman with kind eyes and a face full of wisdom, this doctor came highly recommended by all the other new moms at church.

"Dr. Martin, hi." She hoped that her voice didn't come across as wobbly as it sounded to her own ears. She pushed herself up to a sitting position.

"Hi, Claire. How are you doing?" He held a worn clipboard with hands lined with veins and wrinkles. His kind eyes seemed unusually sad.

"I've been better." Her smile didn't stretch very far.

"I've been catching up with the NICU staff, and it seems that you got quite the surprise when your son was born, huh?" He leaned his elbows down onto the rolling cart at the foot of the bed so that he wasn't towering over her.

"You could say that." Understatement of the year.

"So, Dr. Wilder sent me down to talk to you about some test results."

Test results? Cold puddled in her belly and slowly inched its way up.

"The ones about the— ummm— genetic abnormality?"

"No. That blood test can take up to a week to process. You didn't request the rushed FISH version of it, so I'm sorry I don't have those results for you yet.

Stupid insurance that wouldn't pay for a rush on tests.

"The results that I have for you now are about your son's white blood count. It seems that your son has what is called Transient Abnormal Myelopioesis."

Claire stared at him blankly.

"Basically, he was born with a type of leukemia."

Leukemia? *Oh my God.* Claire had never in her life said this phrase before, but in this moment it hopped into her mind and refused to leave.

"Now I don't want you to panic. This type of leukemia is not uncommon in children with, um, Down syndrome. But almost every case resolves itself within a few days. Some blood cells haven't decided which side they're going to take yet, but almost always they return to normal within 48 hours." He doubled checked something on the chart and then looked back up at her. No wonder his eyes were sad.

"But— we don't know for sure that he has Down syndrome," Claire protested.

He cleared his throat and looked down again as if something of extreme importance was written there. "Right. Of course. This doesn't prove he has anything other than this white blood cell issue." He looked back at her.

"I just wanted you to know that we are watching this carefully. We will be redrawing his blood frequently to stay on top of his progress."

She nodded. Her voice refused to work.

"I put in a request for a visit from a hematologist so that he can discuss your baby's increased risk for leukemia in the future as well as the plan for today. Has he been by to see you yet?"

She shook her head. Seriously, why wouldn't her voice work?

"Well, he should be by later today to discuss this in more detail with you— answer any questions you might have. This is nothing to be worried about. Right now your son has bigger issues he's fighting. That's what we are focusing on."

He was so sick that leukemia was not his biggest problem? Wasn't it enough that he might have Down syndrome? Wasn't it enough that he was upstairs unable to breathe on his own instead of swaddled in her arms right now? Wasn't it enough that every single expectation that she had about motherhood, down to her ability to actually meet her child had been taken from her? Did he have to have leukemia too?

CHAPTER TWENTY-FOUR
Felicity

Today was the day for Felicity to go home. It had been three days, and the nurse visits seemed less urgent and frequent. Guess the danger of her toppling over dead had gone down significantly from forty-eight hours ago. There was no reason why she should stay any longer in this sterile prison where French fries were banned. Physically, Felicity felt great, but was just tired. She could practically hear her soft bed at home beckoning her. Time to take back her summer vacation! She had big plans. Like, um, well, sleeping a lot more within a much more comfortable and private place.

After the nurses did the first few shifts, her mother took over the care of the baby while Felicity continued to rest and avoid visitors at the hospital. There was no reason for this setup to change at home where she could be in her room with her things and no nurses pressing down on her belly until she wanted to scream in agony. Seriously, what was with that particular brand of torture? If she had known whatever government secret those nurses were after, she would have gladly shared it with them. *Note to self: secret agent should be crossed off her potential careers list.*

Last night she had discussed this whole awkward, messy, annoying situation with her Mother and Uncle Gordon. Nothing like putting it off to the last minute. Presenting her idea to keep the wee one, she wasn't surprised to see the skepticism on their faces. But since Felicity felt like she was doing the right thing, she held firm. As firm as her favorite cherry jello on a hot summer day after being frozen overnight and then thawed only partially.

This was her mistake— her baby— she would do the responsible thing and care for it. Plus, this is what Elliot wanted, and it was important that they stand together as a family. She wanted to blush and smile at the thought of Elliot being her family. He had such a cute butt.

"But what about when you're at school? Do you really want your first high school accessory to be a stroller?" her mother asked.

"Can't you take care of him when I go to school?"

"He's not my baby." Mother replied softly.

"But he's your *grandbaby*. Would you really want me to stay out of school to do something that you could so easily help me with? Would you turn away your own flesh and blood? Would you make me give up on my future just because of a silly mistake? I know how lonely you are. This will give you someone to talk to during the day that isn't a cat."

"I don't think 'lonely' is the right word—"Mother started, but faded off with a look from Uncle Gordon.

"Your mom and I think that you don't really grasp the seriousness of all of this—" her uncle said.

"Seriousness? I just pushed a human being out of my body. I don't know how much more serious I can get here."

Mother rallied.

"No. Stop right there," she said firmly. "First of all, this is not a 'silly mistake'." This is a serious error in judgment on your part that has significant repercussions. Second, I don't appreciate your guilt manipulation tactics. Of course I want what is best for you and your son. But *the best* doesn't always mean what you might think at first. What if the best for your baby means giving him to a home where he has a mother and a father dedicated to giving him a life full of promise and opportunity?" Mother looked unusually stern. The wrinkles on her forehead and around her eyes seemed to be deepening by the second.

Felicity idly wondered if now would be a good time to bring up the suggestion of some Botox for Mother's poor face.

"Adoption?" She pondered the concept and wondered what Elliot would think about adoption. Would he want her if she gave his baby away? Would his eyes still hold that lingering promise if she discarded the one unavoidable thing that held them together? The thing that finally got him to pay attention to her again? "I don't really feel comfortable with that," she said decisively.

"But think of a young couple somewhere who would give anything for a baby. You could give them that. The gift of a life to a couple struggling with infertility—" Mother's voice broke. A strange look passed over her face— a look that Felicity had never seen before. She looked like she was going to say something else, but Felicity rushed to speak first.

"Oh cut the drama. I'm sick of hearing about the infertility crap. Why does everything have to be about you? This is about me. And *my* baby. Just because you had a hard time having more kids doesn't mean I have to give up my baby to complete strangers. Can't you guys help me adjust? Can't he be a baby for us to love? You're always saying that I need to grow up. Wouldn't this be a great first step?"

Mother and Uncle Gordon exchanged a glance that she couldn't interpret. It looked almost like laughter. How infuriatingly condescending. This further strengthened Felicity's resolve to win this one.

"Um, honey," her mother interjected, "the fact that you think that having a baby is a great 'first step' to growing up tells us that you aren't ready for this sort of responsibility. How will you pay for all of the things your baby needs? What insurance will you use when your baby needs to go to the doctor? When your friends are at parties or studying together at a friend's house, how is it going to feel when you can't do any of these things— ever again— for the next eighteen years? How will you still go to college? Get a job that covers the price of childcare too? Motherhood takes a lot of responsibility. It requires constant sacrifice of yourself. Are you ready for that?"

"I'll figure it out." Felicity mumbled, refusing to fully process her mother's words. "Elliot told me that he really wants to be there for me and the baby. As soon as he gets his promotion at work, he promised to kick in enough money to help. I think we can all agree that my having this baby was a ginormous mistake. I mean, an even bigger mistake than the size my body has grown to be these past few months. But he's already here. Shouldn't we just make the best of it? Can't you guys just help me until I can do it all myself? Please?"

There was a long pause. Mother and Uncle Gordon stared at each other, seeming to communicate so many things without saying a word. Felicity smiled even in the tense moment— someday that would be her and Elliot making big decisions together like this. The fact that she had his baby pretty much guaranteed that they would be together forever now.

Mother then went the betrayal route with her next argument. "Remember Scipio?" Low blow, Mom. Low blow.

"My guinea pig? This isn't the same as a guinea pig! Babies are way cuter! No way would I forget to feed this guy. And plus— he won't live in a cage that needs to be cleaned. Way easier!"

"You really think that a baby is 'way easier' than a guinea pig?" Her mother laughed humorlessly. "You really have no idea, do you?" She stood up and turned away from Felicity.

Felicity knew this tactic well. Her mother wanted to say no— wanted to punish Felicity and stay strong on what she felt was the right decision, but she wanted the baby more. It was no secret how much her mother loved the tiny ones— always volunteering for nursery and begging to hold the new babies at baby showers. Plus, this one looked just like Dad— everyone said so. How could Mother give up on that? Felicity was sure that her mother was turning away and avoiding eye contact so that Felicity couldn't see her struggle between wanting to parent and wanting to do something she obviously wanted very badly. Felicity had seen this before. This same battle had gone down when Felicity needed to be grounded from the Six Flags fieldtrip that Mother really wanted to chaperone because one of the ladies from her Sunday School class was going.

Felicity wasn't called "the master argument winner" for nothing. There was even a pillow somewhere dedicated to it. Time to take her *Queen* and sneakily slide it up to block her opponent's *King*.

She was hoping not to go here, but Mother really left her no choice. "It's just that— you mentioned that the baby looked like Daddy, right? Ever since you said that, I totally see it too. I just don't know how I could give away a part of Daddy like that." *Bite lip, lower eyes, turn head away*— Felicity had perfected this act.

When her mother grabbed her purse stated flatly, "I need to go buy a car seat and a few things before we can take him home," Felicity knew that she had won.

Checkmate.

Beaming, she said, "Does this mean that we can keep him?" Mother nodded tersely and left the room.

Uncle Gordon, looking even balder usual and wearing his unstylish round glasses, had a weird look on his face. "That was kind of rough of you to bring up your Dad like that."

Felicity shrugged. She had won; that was all that mattered.

"Why do you really want to keep this baby?" Uncle Gordon asked.

"Um… I believe we just covered all of that. Weren't you listening?"

146

"I've raised five teenagers. I know an Oscar worthy act when I see one."

"Whatever." Pick up phone; put in earbuds.

"I'm just saying, please don't hurt your Mom. Don't give her this baby just to yank it away."

Felicity took out one earbud. "Who said I would do that?"

"Just, be careful. That's all I'm saying. There's stuff that you don't know about your mom—."

Felicity cut him short with an obvious yawn. She then tried Claire's line.

"I was just about to take a nap. Do you mind?" Felicity said, nodding toward the door.

Uncle closed his rather fish-like mouth and backed away.

"Promise me." He said

"I promise; I promise!" Just leave already.

He finally left, shutting the door carefully behind him. Felicity stretched out on the bed. Was it just her, or was the bed actually getting softer? Eh, probably just her body going numb from curling up on a sheet of steel for three days.

Turning her music up, she almost wanted to hum along.

Maybe this baby thing would be kind of fun— a babysitting adventure that never had to end with a hot Baby Daddy stopping by even more frequently than usual. Mrs. Elliot Miller. Oh and look— they already had a ring boy.

CHAPTER TWENTY-FIVE
Claire

Another morning spent in the NICU was making her sleepy. Sitting in a chair by his side, Claire wondered why her new life of doing nothing but sitting was so exhausting.

Sitting by his side constantly, she had done little else but pray and pump. Pray— for the doctors to be wrong, for the test to come back with good news, and for her baby to miraculously become healthy. She continued to pump herself like a human cow attached to a plastic milking machine because she had heard the NICU nurses refer to breast milk as "liquid gold" which could be put down her child's feeding tube. Painful, humiliating, and just plain weird— those pointed plastic cups that got to second base made childbirth all of a sudden seem like a romantic moonlit stroll on a summer night. But *liquid gold* sounded promising. Perhaps it would heal him faster? Help get rid of those machines that were standing between her and her baby? Push him faster onto the other side of this leukemia nonsense?

She was supposed to breastfeed her baby. Hold his warm body close to hers. Cup his head in her hand while he latched onto her and took what he needed. Feel his body curl around her. Listen to his sucks and swallows. Feel his hand gently rest on her breast, his cheeks and lips thirstily pulling milk from her. The liquid gold straight from her to him— no machine needed— let alone all those tubes and the plastic cups sucking her dignity from her.

Even after three days, she still had been unable to hold him, but she gently touched his arms, his hands, his forehead, his feet, and his cheeks as frequently as possible. The wires surrounding him had to be respected, so every move— every touch was a bit like handling something broken that had been glued back together and was still drying. She wanted him to know that she was here. That he wasn't alone. His skin was hot to her touch and slightly scratchy where the mystery rash still lingered. Whispering close to his ear, she begged him to get better. Then she paused and begged the Lord for Samuel to be able to hear her.

His numbers on the screen next to his bed would go up slightly for a few hours, and then just as she was getting ready to celebrate the numbers would plummet back into the range where he needed even higher amounts of oxygen– alerted by frantic beeping, more hissing, and the pounding feet of someone in a white coat running in to adjust the machine output. This rollercoaster ride exhausted her, but there was no getting off of it.

Trevor had been in and out these past few days— going home to catch some sleep that wasn't on a hospital chair, keeping up with his summer school duties, and attending those meetings that apparently couldn't be rescheduled. It annoyed her that he wasn't 100% hers these past few days when she needed him so badly, and yet she knew that he couldn't take any time off work right now with Mr. Brown still in bypass recovery. Plus, she did have her own personal nurse for this three-day luxury stay of oversized pads and over-eager residents interrupting her nights.

None of this was right. This is not how it was supposed to happen. A joyous celebration had been dead-ended by— something. They weren't even sure what. Every time Claire thought of the "Welcome Home, Baby Boy!" banner folded up at home, she was pierced through with sadness. And then she was angry. Then she would get worried that her anger would count against her in test results coming back soon, so she would smooth out the lines in her forehead and pray for those good results to come quickly so that they could use that banner.

A few words into the prayer, tears would pop into her eyes. When she would try to wipe them away, they multiplied like ants on a crumb. And then no matter how embarrassed she was when someone popped into the room and she was sobbing over her son's still body, she couldn't stop. The tears would not leave her alone.

Every time a medical professional walked by who looked like he might have test results, her entire body jumped to attention. A weird tingling started from her toes, rushing quickly all the way up to her scalp. And then the tingle faded into numbness each time the medical professional kept walking, or just checked Samuel's numbers and then left with little more than a "hello" and illegible scratches on those clipboards that they always seemed to be carrying around. She knew that they were illegible because once one of those clipboards was left next to Samuel's bed by accident. Claire searched it over to find what secrets they were keeping from her— what they were really writing about her son. But she couldn't understand a single word other than the fact that they spelled his middle name as "Louis." Who does that? She pulled out a red pen from her bag and fixed it. *Lewis.* Samuel LEWIS Bailey. What else were they getting wrong?

She spent long hours dreaming how this whole situation would resolve itself— putting all of her positive energy into her desired outcome as though if she imagined it hard enough it would happen. In this improved scenario, the doctor with the curly hair and wide smile would walk up to her, give her son an apologetic glance, and say, "Mrs. Bailey we couldn't have been more wrong! We thought he showed some markers for Down syndrome, but the test came back completely negative! He has normal genetic makeup—do not fear. Now we just have to wait for his lungs to get stronger, and you can take him home. My guess would be one, two days tops. A baby this cute deserves to be wire free so that you can at least see his face and of COURSE you can hold him!"

The doctor would then shuffle away to give bad test results to the couple at the edge of the room next door. That couple often took smoking breaks and Claire heard it rumored that the baby was in the NICU mostly to "dry off" because the mother had been a drug user throughout her entire pregnancy. They would get the bad news because they had sown the seeds for a harvest of bad news. Claire would get the harvest from her perfectly planted and maintained crops. All would be right in the world once again.

She would dance with happiness and joy and then call Trevor to tell him the good news. He would send an email out to all the people at church praying for them. She would text her Mother, including at least ten emoji smiley faces. Mother would sigh with relief and tell her of course her baby didn't have Down syndrome—it was ridiculous that the doctors even thought he might! Things like that don't happen to lucky Claire!

In a few days she would take him home. He would be healthy, normal, and ready to inhabit his perfectly decorated nursery. Life would resume, and her biggest complaint would be how little sleep she was getting. She would follow that up with a knowing glance and comment that it was all worth it as she watched her precocious son navigate infanthood.

Samuel Lewis Bailey. Someday when they were at his first symphony concert they would look back and laugh at these days. They would laugh at their fear and laugh at the escaped possibilities. They would laugh because it was untrue. He couldn't be more bright, talented, and typically developing. He was her son. Her "mini-me". Her perfect baby.

After daydreaming so intently, she started to dream of this at night too. Vividly. The emotions were so real. The happiness was all-consuming. Then she would wake up and remember that they still had no good news, and she would crash down emotionally once again. During the day while holding vigil by his bedside, she would add in details to the dream, pressing her mind to send an even stronger positive energy to the completion of this story. She looked forward to the day when she would wake up and think, "Oh yeah. That NICU nonsense was all just a bad dream!"

Of course, she prayed too. Claimed promises. Made deals with God. Such as— if you let my son be normal, I'll try so much harder to be a good youth pastor's wife. If you let my son be normal, I'll gossip less and pray more. If you let my son be normal, I'll never snap at Felicity again.

Felicity. Felicity's baby. Thinking about these two and the injustice at play was making Claire physically ill. If she didn't know better, she would think that someone switched their babies. Her baby was the one that slipped out all pink and healthy. Her baby was the one going home today with his mother. Her baby was the one who would be cooed over at his first Sunday at church— only days from birth. Her baby is the one who would grow up normal.

If Felicity and Claire's baby competition started out so unfairly, what would happen when Felicity's baby walked first? Talked first? Got better grades and had more friends? Cured cancer while Claire's boy was still living at home, dependent on her— forever. Felicity would be standing on the sidelines shouting, "Look what I DID!" as her son conquered the world while Claire's son would fail to even be normal. Claire's cheeks reddened at the thought, and a competitive fist rose up and struck her heart with a maddening tension that put her back into the anger category once again.

Claire leaned forward and rested her forehead against the coldness of the metal edge of her baby's impersonal, sterile bed. She couldn't figure it out. If her improved scenario was what God promised, what she prayed for, what she dreamed of, and what logically made sense— then why did she have a strong sense of impending doom?

Since her face was down, she didn't see him enter the room.

"Mrs. Bailey?" A pleasantly strong male voice spoke after clearing his throat.

Claire's head shot up, embarrassed that she had been caught all but snoozing.

"Mrs. Bailey, I'm Dr. Walker, one of the pediatric cardiologists."

Cardiologist? Heart stuff?

Tall and thin, he had black hair that spilled onto his forehead creating an almost boyish look even though his dark eyes claimed to be middle-aged at least.

"Hi, nice to meet you," Claire murmured, trying to clear the gravel out of her voice.

He held out his hand to shake hers. Firm, strong grasp. Claire instantly relaxed when she sensed that she could trust him.

"I wanted to talk to you about your son's Echo results."

"Oh, okay." Her eyes flitted back and forth between her son and the new doctor.

"The Echo on his first day of life revealed that his heart has properly formed. He has four chambers and everything is working correctly."

Wait— good news? About time. She welcomed the oxygen mask of "good" and breathed deeply. Greedily. Good news.

"I just repeated this Echo today, and even though there are no defects in the heart, there are several large, gaping holes that haven't closed on their own as they are supposed to. We believe that this might be one of the major reasons why his oxygen counts are so low. The holes are allowing too much blood to pass through, creating an unnecessary pressure on his lungs. He has what is called pulmonary hypertension."

She knew "good news" was too good to be true.

The doctor continued, "And since his pulmonary hypertension is in the severe range for someone his small size, we want to talk about a possible surgery that will close at least one of these holes and help his pressures lower."

Wait— surgery? *Heart surgery?*

"We will continue to watch him and if he progresses on his own this surgery won't be necessary. But if we don't see the numbers go down on their own, this will be his best shot at achieving normal breathing without oxygen or the current medications that he is on currently to help those pressures go down."

Heart surgery. On her baby. Who she hadn't even held yet.

This was starting to feel like a joke. Was she being punked? Was the NICU staff about to walk in holding the bouncing, giggling, healthy baby boy that really belonged to her and shout "GOTCHA!" while screaming hysterically? This was probably the idea of that nurse who refused to let Claire hold her baby.

"Do you have any questions?"

Claire realized he kept talking even though she had stopped listening.

"No." She shook her head and tried too once again to pray. But words failed her. How could she pray to a God who would do this to her? There was nothing good about this. At all. Even her positive energy vibes didn't feel strong enough to cut through all of this.

Possible Down syndrome, leukemia, and now heart surgery? This was just all too much.

The beautiful thing called motherhood suddenly seemed like a curse. Was this really happening to her? Was it so wrong to want a normal, healthy baby? Wasn't she supposed to be fruitful and multiply? Didn't that suggest having babies that actually would live and thrive and grow up to have babies of their own? Why— how could God be letting this happen to her and her child?

"Hello, God? Anyone up there? Do you not see what's going on here? Um, you can stop this at any time. Whatever point you wanted to make, consider it made. I will appreciate this child like nothing else. He will be my miracle baby— just like Mother got. I will give you all the credit. I promise. Everyone will know of the miracle that you did for me."

Surely this wasn't the end of the story. "All things work together for good to them that love God"— right?

This was not "working together". This was planting flowers and getting thorny weeds. This was putting in an order for a gorgeous new rug and getting a knock-down-your-house tornado delivered. This was loving and serving God and having him smash your hopes and dreams into itty bitty pieces in return.

Seething, Claire thought about Felicity with her perfectly healthy, red-haired, superb-neck-control baby, and her attempt at prayer was replaced by one thought.

"This is not freaking fair. Why me?"

CHAPTER TWENTY-SIX
Julie

Julie had fully prepared herself emotionally to be a Grandmother. She remembered with Gordon's first grandchild, her sister-in-law Sally had cried, "I'm too young to be a Grandma! Say it isn't so!" But Julie didn't care how young or old she was. New baby in the family? Bring it. After all, she had prayed, wept, and held the hand of Claire through her infertility struggles and then during her difficult pregnancy. She rejoiced louder than anyone else at the gender reveal party; she jumped in to help paint the nursery before help was even asked for, and she was the one to buy the first little outfit for the guy— a black tuxedo onesie with striped pants accompanied by a tiny stuffed violin. It was adorable.

From the beginning of Claire's pregnancy, she had prepped her Sunday School class to be ready for frequent Grandma brags and constant picture flashing— starting with the ultrasound pictures and even some of the shots from Claire's maternity photo shoot. Her Facebook page was about to become one big Grandma banner. Let the baby over-sharing commence! But in spite of all her preparation and readiness, she now found herself in an awkward cross between Grandmother and joint-motherhood with a daughter who wasn't ready to be caring for a baby. This wasn't exactly what she had planned her Grandmahood to look like.

Right now she was watching her surprise grandbaby sleep in the hospital newborn nursery as Felicity packed up her things to go home while waiting for a few last discharge papers to sign. Meanwhile, Claire's baby was fighting for his life up a few floors. Belligerent teenage mom, hurting adult daughter— Julie wasn't sure when motherhood had torn her attention so dramatically before. They both needed her right now. Badly.

Normally her plan to help when her children were hurting was to just be there. Be in the moment, no distractions no rushing. Just listen— really listen to what was bothering them because the problem might not be what it first seems. Hugs— she always gave plenty of hugs. She would then jump in to help solve the problem when appropriate, but this truly was a rare thing. Oftentimes the solution to her girls' problems lay within their own grasp. She merely helped direct them to their tightly closed fists to see what was hidden within.

But today's problems were bigger than a bad breakup, an inappropriate crush, or academic failure. These problems were external and life changing. Bigger than their normal problems, how could she help them understand what she had learned when life had treated her badly? Was this just something you have to learn the hard way or could someone who has already gone through it already help you skip some steps?

She would have thought that losing their father would have prepped her children on how to deal with the unexpected. But then she remembered that this dealing with unexpectedness is something she had to relearn every time she got knocked down. It wasn't a one-and-done truth that sticks with you forever. Dealing with "the hard" is a constantly adjusting battlefield. No matter how well you protect yourself, the bullets keep flying in your direction. You get better at dodging the bullets, and you might don a bulletproof vest, but a bullet is still a bullet.

How could she mourn with and encourage Claire, teach and help Felicity, all the while figuring out what to do with the healthy baby while simultaneously praying desperately for the sick one to come home? How could she simply be there for all of them at once when life was tearing her little family in such drastically different directions?

Julie bent her knees when she realized that she had been standing still a while, causing her legs to lock into place. Looking around for a chair in the hospital nursery, she realized that she wasn't willing to give up her spot next to the baby in order to be more comfortable, so she remained standing.

Holding out a finger, she gently brushed the forehead of her grandson, marveling at his soft skin and his delicate breathing. What a miracle this life was. If God had shrunk down her husband of thirty years into six pounds, this is exactly what he would look like. She couldn't believe how much she felt like she was staring at her husband. This was an unexpected gift.

If only Brad were here now, she would have someone with whom she could share the burden of this time. He could go sit with Claire, so that Julie could continue to just be with Felicity. They could split up and conquer together. But he wasn't here, and Gordon had to return home to be with his own daughter who was visiting from out of town. Julie had been by to see Claire twice so far, but she would really prefer to sit much longer with her so that they could really talk all of this out instead of having to rush back to make sure Felicity hadn't tried to break out of "this joint"— as Felicity referred to it more than once.

Julie was all alone in this. Torn between two daughters and two needy grandsons. The weight on her shoulders seemed crushing.

In spite of herself she suddenly smiled at the baby. Well, not completely alone. Seriously, this little guy was a stud.

Yes, she was livid when Felicity announced her pregnancy like she was announcing a take-out dinner option. Yes, she felt betrayed that Felicity had shut her out completely ever since that announcement. Yes, she missed the sweet little girl who used to trust her enough to tell her even the most personal of thoughts.

But looking down at this dewy-eyed boy with a button nose and lips that begged for kisses, she wondered if this could be an answer to her prayers— the baby that she prayed for those many barren years.

Except— this was Felicity's baby. And Felicity seemed intent on claiming her baby as her own. The teenager who had refused to babysit the neighbor kids because she was afraid of changing a diaper was now demanding to keep a baby that only a week ago she shrieked was ruining her life. Did this have something to do with Elliot? As Elliot faded out of Felicity's life (as high school boyfriends were prone to do), would her desire to mother fade as well?

A dimpled chin crinkled deliciously as his lips moved in sleep as if smacking a request for food. If Julie still had a uterus, she swore it would have stood at attention and saluted at the adorableness in front of her.

As Julie pondered the thought of this baby somehow transferring silently from "Felicity's baby" to "Julie's baby", she found herself thrilled by this concept. But even though she knew she would enjoy the cuddles, the feedings, and every second spent with this new life— what would this mean in the long term? Would he always live with her? Would he move out when Felicity eventually moved out of the house? What would this look like for their family? Would it push Felicity or Claire even further away from her or draw them all closer together? Would Felicity let her adopt her baby? Would Felicity's demands stretch beyond what their relationship could handle?

Stroking that silky smooth forehead in front of her once again, Julie decided to trust. There was a sovereign God who set all of this in motion. He let her teenager daughter get pregnant. He brought this baby to their family for a reason. She sincerely hoped the reason was to bring Julie the baby she had prayed for, but she trusted Him enough to let Him reveal His purpose in His timing.

Taking hold of her anxiety, she handed it over to someone much bigger than herself, and relaxed in the moment. Rejoiced in the moment. It was time to take this guy home.

She had purchased a car seat, a pack 'n play, some formula, a pack of diapers, and three sleepers at Toys'R'Us during one of Felicity's naps. Lydia and Susie from Sunday school had stopped by with a box full of little boy clothes and Gordon even had showed up with some burp clothes and receiving blankets that his wife sewed for the new guy.

In spite of the situation, Julie felt a smile appear on her face and grow until it was practically high fiving her ears. She had a baby so new he still was wearing tags and smelling like first baths.

A thought wiped the smile off her face as quickly as it had appeared. *Claire.*

Was there any new news? Would Claire and Julie soon be hanging out with infants together, commiserating on the difficulty yet awesomeness of this quickly fleeting infant stage? The details that had been passed along to her so far had been few and fuzzy. Because of the responsibility of Felicity and the redheaded grandson, she hadn't been there for Claire like she always promised she would be. This made her feel guilty.

"Dear Lord, please be with Claire right now. Comfort her hurting heart, and heal her hurting son. Help me to settle in quickly with this one so that I can be there for Claire during this time."

Maybe now was a good chance to go by for another visit with Claire? The baby would be fine in the nursery, and maybe Julie could finally talk to her eldest daughter to see how she was really doing beyond her forced "I'm fine, Mom. Thanks." Julie's intentions were good, but just then the grandson in front of her began to wake up and fuss. No time to leave him now. A certain little bundle required Grandma's loving care. He needed her. Bonding in these first few days was crucial. She picked up his delicate body and felt a thrill run through her at his warm touch. Gently placing him up against her shoulder with one hand, she supported his head with her other hand. That red hair was amazing. Thick and luscious, it rested softly against the palm of her hand. Breathing in his delicious baby smell, she felt happiness erase all other emotions for just a minute. Focusing on the elation of that tiny, warm head up against her neck, she didn't even let herself wonder if Felicity was in her room or perhaps running free from the hospital parking lot right about now. This moment was only about the baby in her arms.

CHAPTER TWENTY-SEVEN
Claire

Packing up her room on the Mom recovery floor for her own discharge during a short break from sitting with Samuel in the NICU, Claire sighed with bliss at the solitude of her room. She didn't think she would be able to handle the face of one more person feeling sorry for her while asking her a hundred questions she didn't know the answer to. If pity were a Halloween mask, no doubt it would be one made of nightmares.

Although these last three days had been silent and lonely, the time alone was really just what Claire needed to reflect and pray. Always an introvert, Claire enjoyed the company of other people, but when she was hurting, sad, or just overwhelmed, she needed to be alone to process everything and recharge. That's why the church email that Trevor sent out asked for everyone to please give them space and not visit yet. No one could see the baby anyway, and her soul needed the silence to sort all of this out.

This is why yet another knock on her door equally surprised and terrified her. 90% of all drop-ins so far had been to tell her about yet another health issue with her son. What was she going to learn this time— his heart surgery just got upgraded to a transplant? His head exploded into three heads? His limbs were falling off? What? What could possibly be next?

"Come in," she weakly said, not meaning it at all.

A tall blonde stepped in tentatively, shutting the door softly behind her.

"Hey Claire, how are you?"

Susanna from church— she was the friend who went beyond casual acquaintance and well into "sharing every single detail of pregnancy" status. She was the friend who supported her and laughed with her through the uncomfortable doctor visits and fear of what was to come. The friend whose parallel pregnancy allowed them a bonding experience like no other. The friend who had the darling baby girl a couple of months ago, the baby Claire admired profusely every time she saw the adorable bundle of baby cuteness. Now that baby was a close kin of the baby body wash commercial with the laughing, chubby baby splashing in the kitchen sink.

"Oh hey," Claire said, sinking down onto the nearest chair right next to the bed, relieved to see a friend and yet not sure what to say to her. Claire felt like an entirely different person than the one who had laughed and joked with her friend about labor horror stories at church last week. She didn't deliver her baby on the side of the road, in a toilet, or in the middle of her living room. Guess she avoided the entire list of birthing fears.

"Is it okay that I stopped by? I just really wanted to make sure that you were doing all right. And I brought you some flowers." Claire noticed for the first time the light green vase holding a plethora of colored daisies. Pretty.

Susanna sat gingerly on the corner of the bed where Claire lived the past three days. She balanced the flowers on the edge of the bedside table.

"Yes, it's fine. Those flowers are beautiful. Thanks." Manners always came first. Maybe a friend's perspective was just what she needed to get a better grip on what was going on with her baby. Even when Claire had a lot she wanted to say, she remembered her mother's advice about conversing with friends "Your friend will have a good time hanging out with you if you ask her about herself. Let her do the talking. You listen. Ask her questions about herself. Let her share. She will leave feeling valued and loved." Claire searched her mind for something to ask and was opening her mouth to lead with a question about sweet Emily when Susanna spoke first.

"I'm so sorry," Susanna said.

"Sorry?" For what? Her loss?

"Yeah. I'm sorry that your baby might have— you know— Down syndrome. Poor you! That's so horrible!"

When Claire pictured the moment that friends would meet her new baby, "sorry" was the last word on her mind. Congratulations for sure. Perhaps some envy. Some oohing and ahhing. Sitting in front of her and saying sorry like her child was already dead— it felt like there was a knife in that vase of flowers that had just stabbed into her heart. Sorry? For her baby's existence in the world?

"How are you doing? I mean really. *How are you?* We have all been praying so much for you and your baby. What an awful thing to happen." Blue eyes darkened in intensity as Susanna leaned forward as if to grab Claire's hand.

Claire shrunk back a little, but said politely, "I'm doing fine. Just tired."

"Oh goodness, Emily is already four months old, but I totally remember that after-birth tired. At least you can sleep all night and not have to get up for those constant feedings! That was the worst! Small NICU perk, huh? You can catch up on your sleep in time to take him home."

Did she really just say the words "NICU" and "perk" in the same sentence? Did she even think for a minute that Claire wouldn't trade this entire experience for sleepless nights with her baby who just couldn't get enough snuggle/eating time? Did she really think that it was a perk to not be with her baby in order to take care of herself? Should Claire mention how she still got up every three hours to pump with the hospital grade breast pump to create a milk supply without ever having her baby's help? Or that she would beg her night nurse to wheel her up that impossibly long distance to her baby so that she could sit at her baby's side and watch him sleep because she just couldn't stand to be apart from him?

All of these thoughts sounded too exhausting to express. No doubt speaking any one of these out loud would make Susanna feel bad which would then make Claire feel guilty. And she didn't have the energy for that. Not to mention, sharing these facts would no doubt further intensity the look of pity in Susanna's eyes as she stared at Claire.

"Yeah. Sleep is always good." Claire said instead.

"How is baby Samuel doing today?"

"About the same." Claire turned her head away so that her friend couldn't see the tears beading up in her eyes at just the mention of her son's name.

"We've been praying for him to get better fast."

"Thanks. It's tough to see him so sick."

"I've been praying for you through all of this. I know how that feels. I remember when Emily was born— she had awful jaundice and had to wear a little suit and be under lights for most of a day. It was so horrible to not be able to just cuddle her in bed and do our skin-to-skin bonding time. I hated seeing her like that! So hard!"

Wait. Did she really just compare her child having jaundice to her son upstairs who was kept alive by machines and might possibly have a life altering chromosomal problem? Did she really?

But Claire only said, "Yeah, I remember you talking about it."

"But then after a day she was all better and we could take her home. Then none of it mattered. You'll get that too— your happy ending. This will turn around soon."

"I hope so." *From your lips to God's ears*, Claire thought. But then again, it seemed like Susanna's story was about someone changing a popped string on a violin. Claire's story would need someone to piece back together a violin that had been crushed under the wheels of a semi-truck.

"So you're going home today?" No doubt Susanna was clued in by the neatly packed bag next to the large plastic hospital bag full of random stuff like a lifetime supply of gigantic pads and a plastic squirty thing to clean out your baby's nose even though she didn't have a baby's nose in her care. Who knew that her friend was such a good detective? Claire almost expected Susanna to pat her own back silently for her brilliant detecting skills. At the same time, Claire chided herself for being so snarky. She knew that Susanna meant well.

"Yeah. It's time," Claire said quietly, looking anywhere but at her friend.

Susanna stood and looked around the room. "Is there anything that I can do to help you?"

"I have it mostly done, but thanks."

"Well, I have to go get Emily from Grandma care, so I'll get out of your hair, but I just wanted to say that I am here for you. If you need anything at all— please don't hesitate to ask."

"Thanks, I will." Her mouth obediently said, but the rest of her knew that she would never ask for help.

The friends hugged and the happy blonde left, leaving only the curly brunette behind to stew over the unexpected changes that had been brought to her friendship. Before Samuel's birth, Susanna had always been the one who always "got" her, always made her laugh, always kept her going. Now Susanna couldn't seem to truly relate to anything that Claire was going through. This was an unexpected side effect to having a sick child. The buffer of loneliness that she had been choosing up to this point suddenly seemed like the only option from here on out.

Claire knew that it wasn't Susanna's fault that she didn't understand. Her insensitive comments weren't meant to hurt, but they did. And Claire didn't know what to do with the additional hurt. She was already overflowing with hurt aplenty and had nowhere to put the extra. Could they even still be friends?

CHAPTER TWENTY-EIGHT
Claire

The day began just like the ones before it. Wake up, drag her battered self through the motions of getting ready, grab some coffee, pump milk for the baby, and go to the hospital.

It had been an intense five days since Samuel had been born. Five days of no answers, constant NICU observance, and a battle of thoughts that she was afraid to speak out loud— even to Trevor.

She smiled at all the hospital personnel. She always answered *"Fine!"* and *"Holding in there!"* and *"Of course God has a plan!"* in her emails and texts to concerned friends and family. And whenever her mother called to check on her, Claire insisted that all was *"Fine! Don't worry about me!"* But things weren't fine. There was a storm brewing inside her so dark, she didn't know how to even say it out loud. So she stamped a "Fine!" on the swirling masses of horrible emotions and fear and tried to ignore its existence.

This morning she struggled to find clothes that fit for these NICU visits. It didn't seem appropriate to go to the hospital wearing the elastic banded pajama bottoms she planned to wear during her maternity leave here at home, but her hips had weirdly changed shape and none of her regular pants would pull up over them. Her only option was to return to maternity pants, even though this seemed all kinds of wrong, but she found herself going that direction so she didn't have an awkwardly pinched muffin top while sitting all day in the NICU chair.

Today she chose her favorite pair of dark maternity jeans. Combined with a teal ruffled tank top that wasn't maternity but managed to hide a lot of evil, she felt almost like herself again. Almost.

While getting dressed she thought about how her life was hopefully like a piece in Baroque music. Composers in that era would often write a piece entirely in minor key, often sounding sad and melancholy. But then the very last chord of the piece would be surprisingly Major. Happy, upbeat, ending on a good note— literally. The only difference in the chord would be the third. Raise it a half step, and the structure of the chord was changed entirely, causing the minor tone to end with a Major victory. It was called a Picardy third.

Brushing her teeth, she promised herself that it was her time. This minor episode was about to unexpectedly employ a Major chord. While dressing for the day, she couldn't help but think that her life was about to get the Picardy third that it deserved. She just knew it. This was the only thing that could soothe the storm inside of her.

While driving the now-familiar distance to the hospital, she realized that she had forgotten her to go coffee mug on the counter in the kitchen, so she stopped and got some Dunkin Donuts coffee. Steaming hot, creamy coffee in a paper cup. Much better. She required caffeine to clear her morning brain fog. However did she make it nine months without coffee? Why did she cut it out again?

169

Oh yeah— for the health of her baby. Clearly that was a successful mission.

A light rain staccatoed onto her windshield; it was the perfect rain— almost enough to break up the heat of the past week but not enough to make the ride into the hospital unpleasant.

Settling back in the driver's seat with her hot brew and comfy pants, Claire had a good feeling about today. Today she would get good news. Today the winding tunnel would come out into the sunshine. Today her son would make the progress he needed in order to come home. All of this was just the tiniest of bumps in the awesome road that was her son's life.

She smiled the whole drive to the hospital even when she got stuck in traffic and feared she might miss rounds. She smiled the whole agonizing walk as she shuffled up to the NICU, avoiding her usual very Christian cursing she did about the NICU being so far away from the parking garage. She smiled as she settled into the seat next to her baby and noticed the new baby blanket lovingly placed underneath him by his night NICU nurse. She was so thankful for the awesome people in the NICU who were giving him around-the-clock care. She had since become good friends with the nurse who wouldn't let her hold her baby. She was really a sweet nurse, protecting the baby in her charge at all costs, and this nurse was one more reason why Claire was thankful today. Because of her excellent care, Samuel was going to get better; Claire just knew it. And the fresh blanket today was no doubt her thoughtful work from last night's shift. Blue with white stripes, this new addition to his bed looked like the type of blanket that a healthy baby would use for perhaps tummy time or to grasp with strong fingers while riding in the car. She smiled as she stared at her son, looking for a sign— some hope— some change— something to hold onto.

Nothing. Other than the clean baby blanket replacing the one from yesterday that had started getting a little crusty from a drippy feeding— nothing. Her smile faded, and she felt a familiar sense of dread wash over her.

She felt his presence before she saw him. The doctor with the big teeth and surprisingly hairy wrists was standing behind her with his clipboard clasped to his chest. She couldn't remember his name because there were dozens of doctors, each taking different shifts, and their faces all blended together in a clipboard-writing, monitor-checking, quickly-moving haze. She had taken to identifying them in her own way. There was the hair gel doctor, high school doctor, nice hands doctor, super tall doctor, nervous doctor, the annoying doctor that looked like the arrogant trombone player who she had once dated, and big teeth doctor. Her favorite was nice hands doctor. Her least favorite? This guy who constantly smiled with those annoyingly bright white skyscraper teeth.

In addition to wearing his usual white jacket, he had also donned a decidedly smug, sad expression on his overly-tan face. Claire had never before put the words "smug" and "sad" together before, but the look on his face could only be described that way. A sort of triumphant grief.

She regretted turning around to face him the moment that she did, because before he even opened his mouth she knew what he was going to say.

"Oh good, you're here. I'm afraid I have some bad news." His mouth said the words, but his cheeks seemed to be stuck in a smiling position. What was wrong with this guy?

"Your son's blood work came back positive for Trisomy 21."

Positive. Why did they use the word "positive" when it was negative news? Why was she still drinking this cup of coffee? It had reached stone cold a solid twenty minutes ago. *Keeping holding cup. Do not drop. Do not drop the cup.* Why was he still standing there? Did she just dream those words? He was still smiling. Maybe she had misheard what he said? Maybe he did say negative because it was positive news. Maybe she had just switched that in her mind because she was so jittery from her return to fully caffeinated coffee.

The beeping from twenty different machines combined to create a piercing buzz in her ears.

"Ms. Bailey?" Big teeth doctor leaned closer.

"Yes." Startled she realized a long minute had passed without her responding in the slightest. Looking up, she saw something unwelcome in his eyes. It was masked by politeness— but it was there. Pity. The Halloween mask of her nightmare had just donned extra big teeth.

"I'm very sorry, but the blood work revealed that he does indeed have the extra chromosome that denotes Down syndrome."

What was she supposed to say? Thank you? Yell and curse? Pretend like she didn't care? Her mind had gone completely blank, but he was still standing there, staring at her like she was a hurt puppy that he had accidentally kicked. *STOP STARING AT ME.*

"Do you want to talk to someone about this? Is your husband with you today? I can have our genetics counselor come discuss this with you."

"No. No. I'm fine," she mumbled, eyes dropping to the floor because she was unable to meet his weirdly intense gaze any longer.

She wanted to throw up, pass out, punch his stupid white teeth out, and scream all at once. This couldn't be right. The test had to be wrong. This was a mistake. A giant, awful, terrible mistake. However Claire looked down at her boy and saw it— the slanted eyes, the tiny hands, the short arms and legs, and the extra big belly. She finally stopped ignoring something in her baby that would never go away— *difference.* He was different. He would always be different.

Not knowing what to do or say, one thought gut-punched her with the finality of it all. He would never be a virtuoso violinist. He would probably never be able to even play the violin.

Standing perfectly still, staring at the doctor who was still babbling on about who knows what, Claire felt something inside of her break. Not knowing how to describe this alien sensation, she could only guess that it was her heart, breaking into a thousand tiny, jagged pieces.

CHAPTER TWENTY-NINE
Julie

Rocking her grandson in the wooden rocker inside her living room, Julie felt his warm body leaning into her, trusting her explicitly, silently begging to be loved and nurtured. She smiled. He was home in her arms, and Felicity hadn't given her any grief about the assumption that this is the way it was going to be. His perfect little nose wiggled slightly as his chest rose and fell against her in the sweetness of complete trust. She couldn't help but remember when Felicity was the adorable newborn in her arms. She would have to pull out all of the pictures— this new little one looked so much like Felicity did as a baby. Idly she wondered if that was the last time that Felicity had had that same sweet complete trust for her mommy.

Speaking of her teenager, Julie knew that she should have tried to force Felicity into the full reality of what she had done— to take responsibility for the life that she had created. In good motherland, Julie would have been putting the bulk of baby care on Felicity, making her step up to her new life as a mother. She would

174

have been waking Felicity up with every night feeding, insisting she make each bottle, giving the baby to Felicity each time his sweet lips puckered into a cry, and insisting that Felicity's lily white hands finally be deflowered in the diaper changing world. Julie knew this was how it should be done.

And yet, she didn't— *couldn't*. So Julie let Felicity sleep all day, every day, because she knew that if she forced Felicity to do this the right way, she would fold. Felicity just wasn't ready to be a mom, and clearly she didn't want to try to become ready. And if Felicity folded, Julie was terrified that she would lose this baby too.

Julie couldn't stand the thought. Exhausted though she was from the night feedings and constant care required of her, she was connected to this baby in a way she never would have dreamed a few months ago. Wrapping her arms possessively around him she whispered a promise of love.

So she ignored Felicity in all of this. For now. It was too hard to tear herself away from her new man with his chin dimple and dazzling smile— gas smile though it was. There would be time to sort out titles later. This little guy wasn't going anywhere.

This was all about the moment. About the warm bundle in her arms. About the tickling of the blanket swaddling him against her bare arm. He sighed softly, his body sinking further down into her arms. A few months ago she was filling her days with cross-stitching snark and organizing schedules. This life change certainly wasn't one that she would complain about any time soon. Releasing an appreciative sigh, she watched his lips bend into a smile in his sleep. It was official. He had her heart tightly gripped in ten teeny fingers decorated with perfect fingernails.

Having done this before, Julie was painfully aware of how quickly each stage slips away. This newborn stage especially was like steam rising from a hot cup of tea or a freshly baked pie. She was determined to enjoy every moment to its fullest. The big stuff like sleep depravation and schedule adjusting wasn't worth any negative energy because if she blinked this stage would be over.

175

The time goes so fast. He would soon be talking back and running away from her on chubby two-year-old legs before she even knew it. Looking at the wall across the room lined with two childhood's worth of pictures, newborn to kindergarten to third grade to junior high to high school— Julie added *too fast* to that thought. *The time goes too fast.* She felt as though she had blinked and her other two children grew up. Well, one of them was grown up at least.

Felicity was asleep upstairs— not a surprise as sleeping had been her primary activity since they had arrived home from the hospital two days ago. When they first arrived home, Felicity had walked through the front door and headed directly upstairs to her room. Within five minutes it was silent up there, and Julie checked to confirm. One snoring teenage daughter was collapsed on top of her bed.

Admittedly, it was concerning that Felicity didn't glance around for the baby while shuffling through the house. She didn't ask if the baby would be okay while she went to take a nap. She didn't inquire as to whether baby needed to be fed, changed, or needed mommy. She simply tended to the one that had always been on her mind— herself. And that hadn't changed at all, even as these last couple of days unfolded in a newborn haze.

Julie's sigh of appreciation for the baby was now a sigh of exasperation for her daughter. She just didn't get it. Putting yourself completely behind the needs of a tiny person— that was motherhood. Wanting to take a nap but staying awake because your baby needed you— that was motherhood. Motherhood was at least inquiring to make sure someone was going to take care of your child before collapsing into sleep. Motherhood meant loving someone else more than yourself and caring about his needs more than you care about your own.

Motherhood is messy and exhausting. It requires you to be vulnerable and strong. Fragile and yet in charge. Joyful and yet empathetic. It's sticky and messy and disgusting and awesome.

She remembered when she had a stomach bug but struggled through it to take care of Claire's chicken pox. She remembered long nights of exhaustion when her babies needed her to stay awake but all she wanted to do was close her eyes and sleep for a week straight. She remembered the potty training years when her gross tolerance was stretched to include constant messes. She remembered rainy field trips when she wanted to stay home. She remembered early school mornings doing the work of ten people to get everyone out the door on time— not getting breakfast herself until they were all gone. She had twenty-seven years of memories where she had put herself dead last. Self-sacrifice had become her motherhood uniform- worn every day with the accessories tired and happy. Even Mother's Day breakfasts left her with a huge mess to clean up in the kitchen. Motherhood is full of reward, but one reward that it doesn't hold is the ability to live life with yourself as the primary person of importance. Even that one vacation for their twenty-year anniversary when they left their kids with Gordon and Sally and went on an Alaskan cruise, Julie had been worried about her kids and missed them intensely almost the entire time. It was hard to even relax because she was so worried about them staying safe without her watching eye.

Felicity had been a mother for five days, and already she seemed to have reverted back to the pre-motherhood version of herself: sleeping long hours, waking up only to jump on her computer, tuning the world out while hashtagging her fame on Twitter— or something like that. Julie didn't get hashtags. If you want to say something— just say it! What's with runningallthewordstogetheruntilnoonecanreadthem? Why was this a thing? Maybe she should hashtag #newmotherhoodincludescaringaboutthebabytoo on facebook and see if Felicity would notice. Felicity had stopped commenting "dislike" on Julie's statuses so maybe they were making progress there.

Was Felicity going through a learning curve or was she exhibiting signs that she just wasn't ready for this level of responsibility? Julie thought she had delivered this concept to Felicity through a very convincing speech right before they had left the hospital. Felicity had looked half interested and even nodded in all the right spots. But they had been at home two days, and she had yet to do anything other than tend to number one— herself. Someday, *someday* she would make a fantastic mother. But today? It wasn't looking promising.

"Sorry, little guy," she whispered down to the forgotten baby, promising silently to make up for Felicity's lack of attention. She had lots of practice at this "being last" game, and she planned to use it well. Exhausted, she hadn't slept more than an hour and a half at a stretch since they had gotten home, but she didn't even care. She knew all too well that there were much worse fates in motherhood than lost sleep.

So while a part of her wanted to force Felicity to face her new reality, the other, much more vocal part of her was anxious for Felicity to let Julie handle the new one. To let Julie mother. To let Julie put the baby's needs first. To let the baby seamlessly fit into their family as Felicity's brother, not her child.

Really all Julie really wanted to do was sit in this wooden rocking chair with her arms full, rocking, humming, and bonding with this new little boy. These early days of peaceful cuddling needed to be soaked up like water on a dry sponge. There was no time or energy for fighting let alone tackling a teenager's spirit in order to mold it into a selfless mold. Julie loved this about babies. They force you to stop the constant turn of busy and just be still. Just cuddle. Just tend to the essentials. This gave her plenty of time to meditate on her favorite verse "Be still, and know that I am God."

What an amazing God she had. Looking at the warm form cuddled up to her, she was amazed by the goodness and protection of her God to send her this baby.

She stopped her meditating. "This baby." She was tired of calling him "this baby".

Felicity hadn't even given a name yet. At least Julie hoped that Felicity was kidding when she had suggested "Thor" and "Super" and "Better-Than-Claire's-Baby." Super Reagan. Really? What would his middle name be? Mistake? His bed at the hospital read simply "Baby Boy Reagan." Julie disregarded all of this and had secretly been calling him Michael, the boy name she had picked out years ago for her next child. That child had never come, so the name Michael sat unused in her heart until now. *Michael.* Michael Bradford Reagan— Bradford of course for her husband. This whole situation had her missing him even more fiercely than usual. Oh how she could use his wisdom and strength of leadership right now.

She could practically see the look he would have in his eye— the look that meant he had an opinion to share, but she couldn't figure out exactly what that opinion might be. Perhaps he would confess to her that he thought that her keeping her daughter's surprise baby was a dreadful idea, and yet he would know more than anyone how much her heart was singing right now to have a baby to love and nurture. He knew better than anyone that she couldn't care less about the lack of sleep and the other sacrifices that lay ahead— she had a baby.

It had been five years since Brad was called home to be with the Lord, but there were times when the grief and pain from his loss sucker punched her anew. Staring down at the flaming red hair of the littlest babe collapsed so sweetly against her, she felt a tear drip from her eye as she missed her other half so fiercely she couldn't stand it. He had been an amazing husband and a wonderful dad. Oh sure, they had their tiffs just like anyone else. But his whole life was dedicated, it seemed, to serving others. He cared for those that he loved more than he cared for himself. After decades of leading men's breakfast at church, taking long walks with the girls and listening attentively to their latest girl drama, daily putting his agenda second to making Julie feel like the most loved woman on the earth, Brad Reagan left a huge hole in his absence. That first year after his death it was hard to get up every morning to face each day completely devoid of all color. The second year it continued to hit hard as she struggled to adjust to the empty feeling left inside of her, going through the motions of living while feeling as thought her spirit would never revive. The third year she learned to cross-stitch and to laugh— really laugh again. Laughing was something that Brad had loved to do while he was alive and cross-stitching gave her the time to be still and think about him. Maybe was why she often combined the two.

Remembering her struggle over these past five years to adjust to life without the other half of her soul, Julie wondered if Felicity was right— had she had slacked off on the parenting because she was too busy trying to take care of her own pain? Julie tried to recall specific incidents within the past few years in which she lovingly put her foot down all the while putting herself behind the care of her daughter. The years blended foggishly together until she couldn't differentiate between them at all, let alone pick out specific moments. Julie had been thinking that Felicity's big slide started when she started dating Elliot. But did it start much sooner? Did she break her own parenting advice of putting her child before her own needs? Was all of this happening because Julie had been a bad mom?

She bowed her head over her new little Michael and silently poured her heart out for her youngest daughter. She prayed for wisdom, for peace, for patience, for love, for something to wake up inside of Felicity, something that would help her return to the sweet and loving child that she was before losing her Daddy and having her world completely fall apart. Julie prayed to be able to undo the parenting mistakes of the past five years. Then she prayed for this confusion— for her desire to mother this baby herself and yet her desire for her daughter to learn responsibility. Julie had learned in her life that she didn't need to have all of the answers. She just needed to be able to humbly ask for wisdom from someone who did.

Finishing up her prayer with more tears and a crick in her neck from the bowed position, she finally said amen. Listening intently, she tried to hear if Felicity was up again upstairs and Julie wondered if she should insist that her daughter give the baby a cuddle as well. Silence. Never before had her daughter's negligence made her happier. Never before had she been so confused by happiness.

CHAPTER THIRTY
Claire

Crumpled on a very questionable bathroom floor, Claire wondered if this would ever stop hurting. Locking herself into the one-stall-wonder across the hall from the NICU, she lost all track of time as her mind spun around and around, desperately trying to make sense of all of this, trying to find some possible shred of good to be found left in her life. Her baby who was supposed to be perfect and whole wasn't. And this wasn't even about his health anymore. This was about something much deeper, much sadder, much more life changing. His very genetic makeup was flawed. He would never be normal or extraordinary. He could never be healed out of this no matter how many promises she claimed from God or how passionately she prayed. She couldn't change him. She couldn't will this away. He just *was.*

Down syndrome.

The NICU doctor didn't just smash her dreams; he took her everything, boxed it into a glass box, and then dropped it from the highest cliff in the world down into a valley of jagged rocks below.

If her everything was a diligent ant on the sidewalk that was working hard to carry a large crumb, then the smug doctor was a large shoe, deliberately lifted and brought down onto the unsuspecting ant until nothing was left but a smudged wet black spot on the sidewalk.

She would have to tell people. She would have to admit out loud that their family was forever changed. That their family was *special.* That once you took the innocent tubes off of her son's face, something unchangeable and wrong was hiding underneath. But if she said it out loud, would it make it real? Would this bad feeling then become her entire existence? Couldn't she still dream that hiding under his equipment was the pink-faced, normal baby that she thought should be hers?

The words that popped into her mind which she really wanted to say were words that Felicity might say, not Claire. The painfully honest thought process screaming inside her head right now was not a thought process that she could sweetly relay in Sunday School while others wrapped up the news of her son's Down syndrome with "Bless his heart" and "God is so good". Was she allowed to say out loud what she really thought? Or was it required of her to wear her youth pastor's wife hat with a smile, loudly proclaiming how blessed they were to be chosen for such a special mission?

But really, how would she even make it through that act? She didn't want to do this. Didn't want to be *that* family with the slow, awkwardly different kid. Didn't want to have to deal with a lifetime of heartbreak that would come from a non-achieving son. Didn't want to be the mother of a child who would be so utterly and completely wrong for society— for her.

For some reason the picturesque calendar hanging in her kitchen popped into her mind. Bold letters over a never-ending field of colorful wildflowers under the bluest of blue skies read, "Sometimes hope is a summer field in bloom. Sometimes hope is those first few blades of spring green that dare show among the winter brown. Sometimes hope is buried so deeply under snow that it lies dormant for far too long." She had always loved this page in the calendar, but now she wanted to add "And sometimes hope is dug up by large machines and taken to the trash heap to be burned." She had never comprehended hope being so far gone that it would be burned to ashes. Well, not before this moment right now. There was no coming back from this.

She had been clinging to the faint hope of spring green, trusting that it would blossom into a full summer field soon if she just had strong enough faith. Now? Now hope was a thing of the past. What did she have to hope in now? What did her faith get her? What was the use of her memorized scripture that promised her a great life in return for her obedience?

She didn't want to raise a Wal-Mart greeter. She had worked too hard, poured too much of herself into motherhood, prayed so desperately for a baby. She would be an amazing mother! Why were her efforts to be wasted on someone who would always be a half-citizen? A drain on their family? Why? Why would God make this mistake? "God will never lead you where His grace can't keep you." Clearly whoever said that didn't have a handicapped child because wasn't God supposed to be fair in his leading? If we follow His will, doesn't He reward us? If we give ourselves to Him, don't we get blessings in return?

She prayed for this baby. She claimed promises. She obeyed. She trusted and left it up to him. *This* is what God sent her in return?

Reaching for another wad of toilet paper to unceremoniously wipe her dripping nose, Felicity's baby popped into her mind— healthy, already at home, no abnormal chromosome count. Felicity didn't even want a baby. She couldn't take care of one, couldn't pay for the things the baby needs, and couldn't even summon the emotional maturity to take responsibility for her pregnancy. Claire saw her continue to drink high amounts of highly caffeinated Red Bull even after she found out she was pregnant not to mention the drinking of alcohol that Felicity admitted to while pregnant. Alcohol!!! "Are you kidding me?" She hissed into the empty bathroom. Felicity didn't care about anyone but herself. She only mocked the vitamins that Claire brought her. Wait, back up a few months, she wasn't even supposed to be having sex with her loser boyfriend. She had practically alienated their entire family with her sour attitude. Claire was pretty sure the only reason her mother was still speaking to Felicity was because she had to, being her mother and all.

So to sum up: Claire, the good sister, gets the broken baby. Felicity, the bad sister, gets the whole baby. The farmer who watered his crops— they all died and he starved that winter. The farmer who ignored his growing crops and went out and partied all summer? Had a bountiful harvest.

She wished the doctor with the big teeth was still nearby. She badly needed to punch something, and she couldn't believe she hadn't taken the opportunity when he was obnoxiously smiling right in front of her.

This wasn't fair. Why was God doing this? *Why?*

She couldn't think, couldn't breathe. She wanted to fight this! To change it! To push her boy toward a better future! Never in her life had she felt so completely out of control. This wasn't on any of her lists. Her life plan seemed to be just as much a sheet of lies as her birth plan had been. Suddenly feeling oxygen deprived, she gulped for a breath and wondered if it was possible for hopelessness to smother someone.

She didn't know how to make this right again. Nothing would ever be right again. Nothing would ever be normal. Nothing would ever make her happy again.

Joy died today.

Closing her eyes and pressing her fingers against the painful throb in her temple, she knew what she had to do next. She had put this off as along as possible. It was time to tell her husband. Picking her cell phone back up off the floor, she finally punched out the text to Trevor.

911 please meet in hospital cafeteria ASAP
Message sent.

Should she call and tell him instead of using the dramatic 911 text they had promised to save for emergencies? Perhaps. But she couldn't get her voice to work, and she didn't want to have to explain this over the phone. He would know the minute he heard her faltering "hello" that something was terribly wrong.

She just couldn't do this over the phone. She craved his warm hands clasping hers, blue eyes welling up in tears with hers, a strong shoulder to lean her weary head on, a freshly washed handkerchief lent to her for her tears, and a conversation from the love of her life that would somehow convince her that all of this was going to be okay.

Her phone buzzed almost immediately. It was Trevor.
Twenty minutes. Love you.

Pulling herself off the floor, she brushed invisible crumbs off of her and idly wondered if she had just contracted a horrible disease from lying on the floor of a public restroom. Not that it mattered. Nothing did anymore.

She took her time getting down to the cafeteria, walking slowly and wishing that Trevor were already here to push her down in a wheelchair. All her strength was focused on holding it together, having to put each foot in front of the other seemed like an unnecessarily cruel demand. Without even thinking she grabbed a bag of cheesy chips as she walked through the cafeteria, her old default comfort food that she hadn't had in over two years. This day called for cheesy chips. Paying for them quickly, she refused to meet the cashier's gaze and hurried over to a corner table.

Sitting down quickly, she wiped away some more tears, thankful that the cafeteria was relatively empty. No one was staring, pointing, or pitying her right now. She was still able to hide in her news. The rest of the world still thought that she was a new mom of a rock star baby who was just fighting a simple disease like pneumonia or something. A normal, curable disease that ended with a beautiful baby living a beautiful life.

Opening the bag of chips, she picked up a cheesy chip from the bag and wondered how she was going to get her throat to actually swallow something so dry. Just then she saw him walking towards her with his quick, confident stride. He always walked as if he was walking toward the most important mission of his life. That was one of the first things she fell in love with— the way he walked. Now her heart hurt in a new way as she thought of him feeling this hurt too. Would his walk falter when he learned that he was the father of a child who was medically considered retarded?

She set down the chip and rubbed her fingers together to get the cheese residue off. It didn't go away completely, and she immediately felt sticky.

The love of her life looked panicked. His handsome face was lined with worry. He was sweaty and disheveled, and Claire realized that he probably ran in from the parking garage. Literally ran.

"Samuel— is he okay?" He burst out frantically, closing the distance between them with that confident gait.

She didn't answer, but stood, wrapped her arms around him, smelled the comfort of his usual cologne (sweet but deeply so), and found herself crying yet again on his strong shoulder. Where were all of these tears coming from?

"Claire. Sweetie. What's wrong? Is our baby okay? Did he take a turn for the worse? Is he— is he still alive?"

She sat deliberately back down at the table, waited until he sat next to her, grabbed his hand, and looked deep into his eyes.

"Trevor, our son— he— he has—"

He squeezed her hand, waiting for her to finish.

All of time stopped as she gathered the courage to tell her husband. A hum of noise floated around her and she looked around, surprised. The cafeteria was busy again. She hadn't noticed when the lunch crowd started to fill the room.

"Down syndrome. Our son has *Down syndrome*." The words burned her throat. Unwelcome words. Poisonous words. "For sure. The test came back."

Trevor's face softened. "But he's still alive?" Why did he sound hopeful? Did he not hear what she just said?

She nodded, looking back down at the chips that her clenching insides were rejecting even before she had made the mistake of consumption.

"Why?" She whispered. "Why is God doing this to us?"

A tear slid out of the corner of his eye. "Because He loves us, and He wants us to have the best."

The best? Was he kidding? Did he spend his entire morning smoking something that he had confiscated from the teens?

"Sometimes we don't understand why it is the best. Sometimes it might seem downright wrong. But God is good. He loves us. And this is clearly his plan for us. Therefore, it is the best. I love our little guy. He was made perfectly for us."

He continued.

"I know this is hard for you, sweet. *I know.* I see the pain in your eyes. I wish I could take that away for you. I hate to see you hurting like this. And I would be lying if I didn't admit to some disappointment myself. Is this what we thought parenthood would look like for us? No. And it's going to take some adjusting. But the truth is, I believe in someone bigger who designed this long before our little family was a family. This is exactly how it is supposed to be. Plus, did you see the look in Samuel's eyes? He needs us. He *desperately* needs us. Do I understand all of what that involves? No. But God for some reason trusted us with him. This is His best for us. For our family. For our little boy. And I truly think that we can rejoice in God's best."

Claire, looking back down at her hand holding his, couldn't respond. Her source of comfort was going straight into preaching mode. She desperately needed things too. She needed him to yell and scream at God with her. She needed him to question this mistake that God had made. She needed a husband who would scream alongside that this was grossly unfair. That God was doing this all wrong. That His "best" wasn't good enough for them— try again! They didn't deserve this. Claire desperately needed him to grieve with her— to question God's goodness. She needed him to acknowledge that Claire delivered an A+ pregnancy and didn't deserve the F she had been given.

Instead, he had skipped grieving and gone right to grateful acceptance. Why didn't he understand?

Something about his response made her angry. Her husband who she loved more than anything, who she always could open her heart to just didn't get it. He didn't understand. Freeing her hand from his, she pulled her arm back onto her lap.

After hearing his initial response to the news, she couldn't possibly tell him the things she was thinking— the things that she was fearing— the things that were making her physically ill. She just couldn't. He was ready to scoop up their baby and declare love and thankfulness and perhaps look at her like she was the intruder on their family instead of Down syndrome being the bad guy. What she really wanted to do was to turn her back, walk away, and never come back. How could she say that out loud now? How could she confess how she really felt? He would never look at her the same again. What if she told him she didn't think she could love a baby with Down syndrome? Would those blue eyes that stole her heart stare at her like she was a stranger?

What if she said it aloud— that she wished that Samuel would just die so they could put all of this behind them? That it would be easier to bury a baby than it would be to live the rest of their lives with a handicapped one? What would Trevor say if he knew that she was now happy about Samuel's long list of health ailments because his chances of passing away and her chances of

189

being the dutiful, grieving mother were perhaps higher this way? What would Trevor say to that?

She imagined the wrinkling of his forehead and intense disappointment clouding his eyes as he realized that she wasn't the woman he thought she was. That he made a mistake marrying her. That she wasn't strong enough to live with something that he viewed as a blessing.

Should she just walk away? If she couldn't accept and love Samuel for who he was— would they both be better off without her?

CHAPTER THIRTY-ONE
Felicity

Felicity sat on the edge of her bed, resting her bare feet on carpet that was surprisingly clean for her room and wanting to cry but not really sure why. She stared at the navy blue pack 'n play that her mother had bought and set up next to her bed sometime while Felicity was sleeping. Did this mean that the baby was going to sleep in here? Wouldn't it be hard for her to sleep if the baby did that horrible crying thing during the night? Was this truly necessary? Was there a way to suggest that Claire's old room be made into a nursery so that she didn't have to stare at him all day? She already saw him a ton at the hospital, and she was really needing a bit of a break to get some space and clear her head.

She had never in her fifteen years felt more confused. She felt different, and yet couldn't explain why or how. It was unsettling. Sluggish physically and in an emotional hole of white noise, she didn't feel equipped to handle this right now. Did the baby count as hers if she didn't love it? If she had absolutely no desire to even hold it? But why did she feel so weird? Was this love? Or just a weird kind of depression? Was that a thing? Baby depression?

Speaking of which, where was the baby? The pack 'n play was empty.

She couldn't care less where the baby was right now, but she decided to put the question out there so that she wouldn't be the worst mother in the world. *Mother*— she was a *mother*. The weird feelings intensified at the mention of that word. Her mind refused to accept it as describing her.

These weird feelings weren't going to go away if she had to stare at a pack 'n play all day— not to mention the floor space in her room that it was stealing. What if she needed to put clothes right there? That was her favorite piling corner!

Truly all she wanted to do was put on her favorite faded purple tank top and jeans with slightly tattered knees but always made her feel like the best version of herself, go to Elliot's house, grab a bag of Doritos, curl up on the couch next to her man, and start a Pretty Little Liars marathon. She could then spend the afternoon laughing at his insistence that watching this show was a violation of his mancard all the while seeing him get into it even more than she did. That would help her feel normal again. Maybe she would even take him a picture of the baby on her phone for him before she left to remind Elliot that he has a family now.

A few more tears dripped down her cheek. Why? And where was this coming from? She wasn't sad. And yet, she felt slightly melancholy and strange with a niggling sense of something she couldn't quite put her finger on. What was wrong with her?

Coming home from the hospital, her mother had buckled the baby into his car seat for the first time. Her mother had been the one to lift him out of the car and carry him into the house for the first time, whispering, "welcome home" into his little ear. Her mother had bustled about putting away the gifts that people brought and the free diapers that the hospital had given them. It was her mother that settled down in the rocker with him, holding him close and looking like she felt that one thing that Felicity wasn't sure she would ever feel— love. Her mother obviously had this mothering thing down. Did it mean something was wrong with Felicity if she didn't want to do any of those things?

She missed the days when her biggest worry was her lack of popularity, an upcoming chemistry test, or a giant zit growing on her nose to the size of a second nose— or even a fight with her stupid sister.

Her sister. Her mother had done nothing but chatter about Claire the entire hospital stay. "Oh yay! Claire's going to have her baby soon!" "Why haven't we heard anything yet?" "Is Claire's baby okay?" "Claire's baby is sick OH NO!" "Is Claire okay?" "Why haven't we heard more about Claire and her baby?" Claire, *Claire*, CLAIRE— an innocent name seemed more like a curse word to Felicity these days.

It was maddening. Felicity didn't know why her mother didn't just take her cross stitching project to camp out over in Claire's room and see for herself, leaving Felicity in blessed peace and quiet to focus on her own issues— most importantly— why was this TV remote not doing its thing? So Claire had a sick baby. Who cares! It's Claire. He will get better and start pooping alphabetical sprinkles soon. All the Claire drama was infuriating. Why does everything always have to be about Claire?

The only redeeming part of this annoyance was the attention and questions it kept off of Felicity as she tried to figure out the fastest way back to normalcy as simply a high school girlfriend whose life goals included junk food, TV, and Elliot— not necessarily in that order. How did she get back to normal, and most importantly, how did she stop crying?

She had been home two days. Two very long days that blended together into one long nightmare of too much baby all around her. The freaking thing kept popping up everywhere. Not only had she not been able to find the courage to venture over to Elliot's house, but the baby was starting to encroach on the last of her sanity. Exhibit A: this blue and white cage-like thing sitting next to her bed that looked responsible for parental neglect everywhere. What, do you throw the kid in here and toss him snacks every once in a while? Do they have water feeders that you can attach to the side like her guinea pig's cage used to have?

This baby could not stay in here— it would interfere with her agenda. Her days home so far had been spent napping, Twitter perusing, eating, a Twilight movie marathon, listening to music, and more eating. (It was pretty awesome that people from church were bringing them such yummy meals.) She supposed eventually she would have to emerge from her room for more than requests for food. But then would she have to face the baby even more? Would she have to take over taking care of the baby? She wasn't ready for that.

Was she making a mistake? Should she say yes to adoption? Should she give the little guy up to an already made family? Would it be easier to repair things with Elliot without this extra baggage? What was going to happen to her if she kept the baby? Would it mean good things for their little family? Or would she end up just missing all the fun for the rest of her life like her mother threatened would happen?

Also— why did this happen to *her*? Elliot helped make the baby. Why does she have to choose what happened to the baby? This was all so much pressure. Pressure that she never asked for, and definitely didn't want. It was unfair that a perfectly good summer was going to be spoiled like this. She only had four weeks left before school started back again, and she had yet to do anything fun. What a drag this baby thing was.

She pulled her feet back up onto her bed and sank her head onto her pillow once again. Another nap? Why not? She was tired of thinking— tired of the pressure cooker of life. Pulling up her light sheet back up over her, she rolled onto her stomach and snuggled back into the warm place from which she had just risen. Clean pink polka dot pillowcase, sheets that smelled like fabric softener, crisp comforter— it was sure nice to have a Mother taking care of her right now. Not that she'd ever be caught dead saying that out loud.

She sighed into her favorite pink polka dot pillowcase and decided that maybe she would start trying to help with the baby. After just one more nap. Or two. Or five.

CHAPTER THIRY-TWO
Claire

Claire would never forget breaking up with her one true I-will-die-without-you, high school love. Mark Speck had jet-black hair over a perfect forehead, serious dark brown eyes, and a mouth that was made for kissing. She felt qualified to say so because she had fantasied about this often as a teenager. When he asked her out after months of her obsessing over him and hoping/wishing/praying he would notice her— she felt like she had finally arrived in life. Those few weeks of dating had been pure bliss. *Mark Speck wanted to date her*. But then when he informed her during their usual Saturday night date that he thought they should take some time apart "it's not you, it's me" style, she had been devastated.

She had already started planning their wedding— their life together. He was a piano player who could play anything and everything better than anyone else. They would graduate high school, go to undergrad together— perhaps even grad school, and then settle down into joint careers somewhere in a highly competitive music location, maybe New York City or Chicago. Not to mention he was gorgeous, scrumptiously gorgeous.

Driving home after that date cut short by rejection while weeping bitter tears of high school heartbreak, she thought that her entire world was over. Nothing would ever be the same again. The man she was meant to marry no longer wanted to call her his girlfriend. Life was over. All of her friends at school would know that she had been dumped and would not only feel sorry for her, but would jump into action themselves. All of the other girls who had been so jealous of Mark loving her would now be fighting for his affections. She would have to watch him move onto the all the other prettier, more put-together girls in her class. Granted, she did know that he tended to float from girl to girl before she started dating him, but she thought that she would be the one to change his mind, the one to get him to settle, the one to convince him that she was his one and only. But no. Never in her sixteen years had she faced something so humiliating and awful.

When she had arrived home, her mom took one look at her red-rimmed eyes and asked if her everything was okay. Claire remembered whispering "No" and then sinking onto the dark red couch covered in an off-white knitted afghan before launching into a frantic version of the evening's events. He gave her no warning, no concerns— it was just over. Did she do something wrong? Was she a bad girlfriend? Was she too ugly? Too fat? Did she talk too much?

Claire would always remember her mom coming over to the couch, sitting down next to her, and wrapping her arms wordlessly around her. She let Claire sob on her shoulder for as long as she needed.

No "I told you so" or "He was a jerk anyway" or "You're only sixteen, how could you think he was the one?" Her all-knowing mother just offered silent sympathy, a warm shoulder, and a giant slice of her favorite chocolate cake that had been baked earlier that day. A cake never tasted so amazing. Those delicately moist layers of chocolate sandwiched with fudge-like frosting was enough to keep Claire shoveling large forkfuls into her mouth even though she had sworn off all extra calories that year. As much as she looked back with a smile at this now, she had sworn at the time that it was a healing cake. A cake that dulled the pain from the ending of Claire's one-month relationship.

Now she would give anything to be that sixteen year old again— to be able to eat the cake that broke her healthy diet without feeling guilty. She would love to be able to sit and talk so openly with her mom without Felicity jumping in with snarky comments or worse— showing off her baby. If only she were able to have her worst problem be an ended relationship that was doomed from the start anyway.

To hear "You are beautiful and strong. You will find someone who will love you for exactly who you are. This relationship might be over, but you have so much ahead yet still to enjoy. Forget about Mark. You are so smart. Focus on your studies and stretch yourself to your greatest potential. When the time is right you'll meet the right guy. These feelings for Mark will soon go away."

Her current problem? It would never go away. She couldn't break up with it.

Samuel wouldn't grow out of this. No amount of prayer would cure him. She was stuck.

And yet all she could think about was going to her mother, eating chocolate cake, and crying until everything seemed somehow not as bad. Until the tears were healing tears instead of painful tears that kept squeezing themselves out.

Suddenly her mouth started salivating. She needed cake. This was not a want. This was a need. Her whole foods diet had taken a massive hit this week, but honestly, so had her life so another hit to her diet seemed about right.

Getting up from the cafeteria table at last, she started to walk to the parking garage. It had been one hour since Trevor had gone back to work, leaving her alone in the cafeteria to think. She didn't want to think. She didn't want to go back up to the NICU even though she told Trevor that that was what she was going to do. She wanted to be comforted. She wanted someone to grieve with her. She wanted someone to understand her pain and assure her that it was all going to be okay.

She wanted cake.

Locating her car in the parking garage and climbing wearily into it, her mind was made up. She was going to go see her mommy.

Pulling out of the garage into traffic, she realized that the light rain from earlier in the day had increased to a pounding downpour that made visibility kind of tricky. No matter. This small deterrent couldn't hold her back after everything else she had been through this week.

CHAPTER THIRTY-THREE
Julie

Scrubbing a sink full of dirty baby bottles, Julie wished that she had picked up some bottle brushes to make this task more efficient. Her little boy loved to eat, and keeping up with his demanding eating schedule was becoming quite taxing. If this was easiest to do in your twenties, then Julie was definitely feeling the punch of exhaustion from trying to keep up with a new babe in her late forties.

Thankfully, sweet little Michael was asleep now. An easygoing baby, he was making this so much easier than it could have been. Even after all these years, Julie could remember how demanding Claire had been as an infant. This little guy was easy in comparison. He was currently taking his first nap in Felicity's room, and this made her nervous. Putting the pack 'n play in there had been a test, trying to draw Felicity into this experience, to force her to make a decision one way or another.

When Julie tried to ask Felicity last night about her intentions with the baby, Felicity interrupted her with, "You would understand if you weren't so ancient! What WAS it like to be on the ark with Noah?"

Typical Felicity, but it still stung and questions flooded her mind. Was Julie too old to do this again? And without a husband?

Julie's tired mind wandered to her family's last Christmas with Brad. A pajama-clad family around the breakfast table— they were laughing, joking, and fighting. Claire and Trevor were newlyweds. Felicity was a sweet ten year old. They were a complete family. No holes in the tightly constructed ship, they were a family that stayed intact in both smooth and bumpy waters. Julie stood to the side of the dining room, pausing with her coffee refill and just soaking in the moment. Her eyes took a mental picture of her children mid-laughter. She remembered wanting things to stay like this always. She loved her husband's mockingly stern face as he gave Claire a hard time about the way she picked apart her cinnamon roll layer-by-layer before neatly eating each bite and gave Felicity a hard time about the way she tried to cram the whole roll in her mouth while licking frosting off her cheeks. Joy brimmed from everyone's eyes. Happiness filled each air particle surrounding them. Presents were a mere afterthought to the gift of family Christmas. She missed this fiercely. The togetherness, the feeling of belonging, the unity that came from family bonding over such simple activities as eating cinnamon rolls and drinking coffee. Nothing had been the same ever since Brad died, but especially Christmas had taken a hit. The deep voice of encouragement and loud boisterous laughter upholding their family— it had left a hole impossible to ignore. If Michael stayed here, what would it be like for him to grow up without a father figure? Would Michael ever know that happy Christmas scene? Could they somehow recreate it even without Brad?

She stared unblinking out the window over the kitchen sink while continuously scrubbing formula residue from imaginary corners inside the round bottle. It started as an overcast, gloomy day. Or at least, Julie thought that was this morning. Was it gloomy yesterday morning and sunny this morning with just a slight overcast? The days were all starting to blend into each other inside this sleepless fog of newborn care. However the day had started, now the rain was pounding down onto her front walkway, which started in front of her porch and puddled all the way down to her driveway. At least her plants were getting watered. Goodness knows she hadn't had a chance to go tend to them this week.

Julie kept scrubbing even though she knew the bottle was already clean. Something about the task of working with her hands on simple, repetitive chores helped confusion organize itself in her mind. It centered her. Scrubbing something clean made the world make sense— at least for a moment in time. Normally she would just throw dishes in the dishwasher, but she wanted to be extra careful about the bottles so she was doing it by hand. Strangely therapeutic, this activity went to work mending broken parts inside of her.

Rinsing the bottle and placing it on the bottle rack, she paused, suddenly overwhelmed with thanksgiving for the sweet little bundle who she suddenly missed even though he was just upstairs asleep. No doubt his wrinkly neck needed some kisses while she inhaled his glorious baby fragrance yet again.

"Dear Lord, I cannot thank you enough for baby Michael. You created him so perfectly, and I am in awe of your handiwork. Thank you for sending him to us. Thank you for keeping him so healthy and safe even through the unexpected pregnancy. Please help us get the details sorted out as to whether he will be Felicity's baby or not. But please, please don't take him away from me. Please let me be a mother again. Please. But most importantly, please help me to accept if you say no. Please give me peace about whatever the right decision might be for Michael. If his life would be better in a family with a father figure, please give me the strength to say goodbye."

Tears sprung to her eyes with the earnestness of her prayer. As she was wiping them away and staring transfixed at the powerful rain, she couldn't help but think about the same powerful person who created the rain. How He cared about something so small as her life that He already exquisitely planned out how this situation was going to resolve. And His resolution was in her best interest, for her good— even when all she could see was the flooding of her walkway. The same rain that flooded her front yard was quietly watering the many plants in the backyard.

The same God who made the rain made my troubles. Both have purpose— planned by God for my good. Julie made a mental note: potential cross-stitch pillow material?

It seemed as if she had a lot of rain in her life. Losing her husband so early. Saying goodbye to her parents while still in her twenties. And well, that other thing that she still couldn't say out loud. Once Gordon had asked her why she didn't live life in a constant fetal position. Julie laughed and then shrugged. With so much rain, she had to find a life raft— someone stronger to carry her even when she felt weak.

"Dear Lord, please help Claire to discover her own life raft. Please help her to depend on you during this difficult time. Please grant healing to her baby, but just as importantly, please grant healing to Claire's heart. Help her to trust you in a way she's never trusted before."

As if her prayers summoned her eldest daughter, Julie was surprised to open her eyes and see a drenched figure rushing through the sheets of rain to get up to the covering of her front porch. Wearing the teal shirt that Julie bought for her a few weeks ago, there was no mistaking the identity of the soggy visitor. Claire was here.

What had prompted Claire to break her vigil from her baby and rush here? Julie's heart froze.

Looking down through the kitchen window, Julie noticed that her usually perfect-postured daughter had bent shoulders. Julie felt a twinge of guilt. There was bad news to be told, she sensed, and she hadn't been there for Claire when it went down. Her throat started to close and her stomach clenched. Samuel. It was hard to breathe. Was he— was he—? She couldn't even finish the question to herself.

"Oh dear Lord please don't let it be that. Anything but that. Please don't let my baby feel that pain."

When she heard from Trevor about the possibility of a genetic abnormality, her heart sank, but she pressed on, asking Trevor about health details. She didn't want her grandson to have to struggle to achieve simple things in life, but she was more anxious to hear if he would even have a life in which that would be an issue. She didn't want her daughter to have to bury a child. No one— *no one* should ever have to do that.

She ran out of the kitchen toward the front door to meet her girl.

She knew Claire better than perhaps anybody, and she knew that an intellectual disability would be a bitter pill for a perfectionist like her daughter to swallow. So she prayed. And prayed and prayed and prayed. For God to please let that test come back clear of anything abnormal. But more importantly, she prayed for Claire to accept with a gracious heart if the Lord chose to say "no". If He in His divine sovereignty chose to grace her grandson with an extra chromosome, she prayed that Claire would not become embittered, but would instead take this as an opportunity to lean even more heavily on the strong arm of her Savior. As she told her Sunday School class just last week, "Sometimes the things that we need the most in life are the things that we desperately pray will not happen. God loves us too much to answer those prayers." Julie loved that she had an almighty Savior who was wise enough to always make the right decisions for her good. And she was thankful that He was the strong arm upholding her as she struggled through the learning process.

As she flung the front door open and welcomed in her daughter, she could see pain on Claire's normally calm face.

Her cute little nose was red and dripping, her dark brown eyes were lined with grief, her mouth was twisted as if tasting pain, and her small hands were clenched into tight fists at her side. Her dark curly hair was a wet mess down her back, and her outfit was so muddy and wet it looked like maybe she had slipped and fallen in the driveway in her rush to get inside.

Claire hurried through the door to Julie, wrapped arms around Julie that were so perfect for making the violin come alive and started crying. A rush of emotion packed a punch into Julie's gut and she had to swallow hard before asking.

"Is he— is he still alive?" She whispered into her daughter's dripping hair, praying like anything for the answer would be "yes", but dreading that the answer was "no".

A wet nod on her shoulder answered her question. Her daughter's sobs escalated in intensity until her entire body was shaking.

"Does he— does he have Down syndrome?"

Another nod into her shoulder.

Julie breathed a sigh of relief and silently said, "Thank you, Jesus. Thank you that he is still alive."

She led her little girl over to the dark red couch in the front room that both girls had always claimed was the most comfortable seat in the house. It had some years on it now, but Julie just couldn't bring herself to replace it. This couch was part of the healing force during the worst of the stay-at-home sick days. This couch saw friends bond as they chatted about everything and nothing. This couch was where the family cuddled on family movie night. This couch saw the girls stretch out with a book and enjoy learning in a comfortable spot.

Mother and daughter sat side-by-side on the couch bursting with family history. Julie's arm was draped over Claire's shoulders. Claire continued to cry. Julie prayed for the right words.

"How is he doing physically? Any improvement from the last church email sent out?"

Claire paused and then said with a slight hiccup, "He's about the same. No change."

"Do they know what's causing him to need so much oxygen? Does he have pneumonia?"

"No. They said something about the pressures in his lungs still being really high because of a few holes in his heart that aren't closing on their own."

"And the leukemia? Still resolved? The heart surgery?"

"The leukemia resolved itself within the first twenty-four hours and hasn't been an issue since although they are still watching it. The heart surgery still looks like it's on, but they're hoping that they can close the hole through a catheterization procedure instead of a dramatic open-heart surgery. He will have to be bigger first though."

"That's great news!" Julie said.

"I guess." Claire said.

The effort of giving these explanations seemed to temporarily stop the tears. Sniffling, she stood up to find a tissue. Julie handed her the box from the glass side table, and waited for Claire to be the first to talk. She seemed like she had more on her mind. Replying, "I guess" to good news like a good blood count and a much reduced surgery plan was not the response of a happy mother. After daintily blowing, wiping, and crumbling up the Kleenex, Claire's request became known.

"Do you have any cake?"

"Cake?"

"Yeah— your chocolate cake with three layers and the super fudgy frosting."

"No, but I could make you some if you want." Julie tried to hide her surprise. Cake?

"Oh I would hate for you to go to all that bother." Slender shoulders shrugged just as her face fell in disappointment.

"It's no bother at all. I have to run to the store first, but I needed to go anyway because we need to get more diapers and

206

formula." Julie was exhausted and knew that another sleepless night was ahead of them, but there was nothing she wouldn't do for her little girl.

Claire had her mouth open as if to say something, but as soon as Julie mentioned the ordinary needs of the baby upstairs, she shut her mouth firmly and fell silent with a hardness curtaining her eyes.

Julie mentally kicked herself. What were the rules here? Would it hurt Claire to hear anything about Michael? She couldn't very well ignore Michael because she was all he had right now. But yet she needed to be here for Claire too because her oldest baby was in serious pain.

Claire broke the silence.

"I'm just so tired," she confessed, closing her eyes and sinking back on the couch.

"Why don't you go lie down for a bit in your old room? I think you have some pajamas still here as well. Why don't you change out of your wet clothes and I'll wash them for you while you nap."

"But Samuel—."

"—Is at the hospital being cared for by an amazing team of nurses. You need to take care of yourself right now. You won't be able to help your baby until you get some rest yourself. Just an hour or two. I think it will really help you gain some perspective."

Claire hesitated and then nodded.

"Okay."

"I'll run to the store for the ingredients and then I'll be right back to whip it together. When you wake up we'll all have chocolate cake and we can talk more if you want or we can not talk if you would prefer that."

Julie smiled at her daughter, loving that she could express her love for Claire so tangibly. It was nice to be able to do something to help. Also, she hoped that a nap would help Claire get back onto fighting ground. She had almost the same look in her eyes that she had had in high school when she lost the symphony solo competition and collapsed in her room— crying for a solid four hours at the unfairness of the judges giving her third place instead of first when she was convinced that no solo was ever more perfect than hers. Or so Julie gathered from the wailing of those four hours.

Leading Claire up to her old bedroom which had been kept mostly intact as a guest room, Julie found Claire some clean pajamas, collected her wet clothes, and then helped her lay down on the queen bed, spreading her favorite black and white comforter over her and tucking it around her as if to protect her from the all the pain in the world.

"I'll be right back. You rest."

Claire looked like she might answer, but then Julie realized that she had fallen asleep as soon as her head hit the pillow, thick hair framing her pale face and reminding Julie of the dedicated high school student who used to study herself to sleep each night determined to get that A no matter how hard she had to work.

Julie smiled at this memory. A good nap can begin healing for the most troubling of emotional problems. As a mother to two girls— she knew this to be a fact.

CHAPTER THIRTY-FOUR
Felicity

Awake from her nap, Felicity stared at her suspiciously silent phone, willing it to buzz with a text, a ring, a song, a dance—anything. Why hadn't he called? Was it something she said at the hospital? Backtracking through the entire visit, she tried to think about when she might have appeared too needy, too uncool, or too undesirable. Nothing came to mind other than the obvious—looking like she had just birthed a child while half-naked on a hospital bed. Pretty sure that wasn't ever going to be a centerfold in *Playboy*.

Just when she was about to swallow her very large pride and text Elliot, Mother walked in. Without knocking. Again. Seriously? Not cool.

"MOTHER! It's called knocking!" she yelled.

Immediately following her outburst, a small cry came from the blue baby cage left here earlier. Um. The baby was actually in here? This whole time?

209

Mother rushed across the room and picked up the baby. "Shhhhh it's okay," she said.

"Um, excuse me, why is the baby in my room?" Felicity asked.

"Isn't he yours?"

"Well, yes, but I thought you were going to help me."

"Key word being *help*. In order to help you, you would have to do something as well. It's not a duet if only one person sings."

"Were you downstairs cross-stitching that onto this year's pillow?" Felicity asked sarcastically.

"Maybe." Mother quipped back. "While you were up here selflessly caring for your child."

"Touché."

"The real reason I came up here was to tell you that Claire is resting in her room, and I need to run to the grocery store. Can I trust you to take care of the baby while I step out? I'll be able to get the errand done faster if I leave him here."

Felicity shifted her gaze from the too-still iPhone with the glittery pink case to the little bed that held what was supposed to be her Elliot magnet. Claire was here? Slacker.

"Sure. It's my kid, isn't it?"

Her mom paused. Almost as if she didn't trust her. Well that was just ridiculous.

"We'll be fine. Go." Felicity said.

"Okay. Well, if you need anything don't hesitate to text me. I'm going to Publix just down the street. Michael just finished eating, so he shouldn't really need anything while I'm gone. He should be fine to rest in the pack 'n play. Just watch him and pick him up if he starts really crying. Make sure you support his neck. Michael does have a strong neck for a newborn, but he is still a newborn. It's very important that you support his neck."

"Michael? Who's Michael?" There was a pause as understanding set in, "MICHAEL? You named my baby?" This did not sit well with Felicity.

"Oh sorry. I've just been calling him that in my head. You hadn't named him yet. Did you pick a name?"

"No."

"Ok, well— anyway. The *unnamed child* just finished eating, and I'll be right back."

"Whatever." Ignoring her mother's lame attempt at sarcasm, Felicity turned back to her phone and focused her attention on what was really important. Did he find her unattractive now that she was fat? How fast could she lose this baby weight? Should she try a special cleanse? A juice fast? She absentmindedly saw her mother leave and only then had a panicked moment with the thought that the baby was left with her. Alone. If he cried she didn't have a "help" button to push. If he woke up screaming, what did she do first? If he needed a diaper change, how did she even do that? What if he peed on her while the diaper was off?

This prompted her to yell out, "Hurry back! He promised to make you a special treat in his diaper while you're gone!"

She heard her mother "humph" in the hallway as she walked away. Eh, Claire was here. Felicity's streak of days without having to do a diaper change wouldn't be ending today.

CHAPTER THIRTY-FIVE
Claire

Claire's eyes drifted open from deep sleep and the first thing that she saw was a picture propped up on the nightstand next to the bed. Framed in a solid black frame with delicate silver edging, this particular picture had been picked to print from hundreds of pictures that had been snapped on that day of celebration— the afternoon of her college graduation. She was standing there with her parents with their arms draped around each other, posing for Felicity who had snapped the picture while shouting "Smile if you love Felicity!" All three faces were beaming with pride. Some of the beaming could perhaps be written up to an extra layer of sweat due to the high temps of the day, but pride was definitely in the equation as well. Looking at that picture now, she saw the thrill of a huge accomplishment in her eyes— eyes brimming with raw, naked hope and excitement for life ahead. Three weeks before that picture was taken, she had won her seat in the Charlotte symphony. The graduation-gown-clad arm resting on her Dad's shoulders sported a flashy diamond that Trevor had lovingly placed there during a dream proposal over a romantic dinner before a Beethoven series concert. All her dreams were coming true.

There's something exhilarating about finishing a well-earned degree and looking into the fresh slate ahead of you. Grabbing that diploma and setting off into the world. Thinking that you are unstoppable. Feeling the heady sense of accomplishment overwhelm your senses. Wondering what next will look like while being convinced in your heart that it will be awesome.

The night after her graduation, Claire remembered collapsing on the cool sheets of a hotel room halfway home and declaring that day to be the best day ever. Sure, long boring graduation ceremony in horrendous heat that melted her eyeballs. Plus, she had to pack up her dorm room and move her entire life back home (she did hate the unsettled feeling of having her entire life packed up into boxes)— but it was an awesome day nonetheless. She had accomplished the first step to her dream. Degree finished. 4.0 maintained. A Bachelor of Arts in Violin Performance from Peabody was now part of her resume. She did it.

There were moments in those four years that she didn't think she would make it. Her violin teacher was a notorious jerk who rejoiced when he got students to cry in their lessons. But he was the best. He pushed her further than she thought she could be stretched as a musician. Not satisfied with anything less than brilliance, he taught her not to accept a sound out of her instrument that wasn't pure, spun gold. Every part of each note counted— the beginning, the middle, and the end. And every part of every note had to be perfect, centered, and beautiful. His demands for her to "find her voice" sent her into long nights of crying and tortured practice sessions that made her feel like she was driving blind. It was such an ambiguous task to "find her voice", and it seemed impossible to figure out because it wasn't something black and white in a textbook that she could memorize and simply repeat note for note. But Mr. Henderson kept pushing, pushing, *pushing* until she thought she would break. And then one lesson she showed up with slightly bleeding fingers from a week long of seven hour practice days with her Bach preludes ready to rock his world, and he closed his eyes and moaned a little bit as she finished pouring her very soul into those dramatically leaping notes. "Your voice. Claire. *That* is your voice."

He prepared her for her second violin audition for the Charlotte symphony through hundreds of hours of hard work and dedicated practice. Each of those excerpts became permanently imprinted into her mind. This was her dream job as it would put her geographically close to her parents and Trevor while still allowing her to do what she loved most in the world. Mr. Henderson told her that she was a fool to hang all her hopes on one audition. She was told that there were hundreds of people showing up to audition for just the one spot, he said. People oftentimes took dozens of auditions before they finally landed a job if at all. But he rolled his eyes and pushed her that much harder. "Practice doesn't make perfect— it makes permanent. Perfect practice makes perfect!" She could still hear his gravely voice muttering this to her over and over again as he, with his caustic teaching style, shaped her playing from good enough into professional quality. Earning that degree taught her to work through difficult things, emerging stronger and better suited for her career and life ahead. "I can do hard things. I can do hard things. *I can do hard things.*" became her mantra every step of the way.

Little did she know that the difficult part of life would have nothing to do with her career at all. Could she still do this hard thing?

According to their brief conversation in the hospital cafeteria, Trevor seemed fine with their son's new diagnosis, but to Claire it just all seemed so hopeless. A vaguely spiritual answer from a husband who was always in youth pastor mode didn't satisfy the burning questions, fear, or sense of unfairness on her mind. Without answers, Down syndrome was quickly becoming a weight around her neck that was dragging her to dark places. The fact that she couldn't even talk about how she really felt with her husband made it all so much worse. The brokenness inside of her was quickly growing beyond repair.

Lying on her right side (her favorite side to sleep during pregnancy), she stared at that photo now and felt as though the pink-cheeked, eager young woman proudly grasping the brand new diploma with a decided air of sorrow naiveté in her eyes was a complete stranger. It was hard enough when she had lost her Dad. The man who walked her down the aisle at her wedding with the same tender love and care that he helped raise her with had unexpectedly passed away while she was on a symphony tour in the Midwest. It was hard enough having to say goodbye to the man who shaped her dreams. The one who handed her that tiny 1/8-sized violin and said, "You can do this." The one who hugged her after every recital and told her how proud he was of her. The one who encouraged her to keep working— keep achieving. She thought that losing him would be the hardest thing she would ever have to go through, and when she somehow was able to pick up the pieces and keep going, she thought the hard part would be over. She was wrong.

She reached out a trembling finger and touched the picture, wanting to reach through the photograph to grab that moment of happiness and desperately cling to it. Was this it for her? Would happiness always be only a memory from this point on? Was this framed 8x10 the only thing left that she had of the life that she dreamed would be hers? The one she worked for, sacrificing whatever it took to get there?

As she touched the frame, she could feel the still-lingering rush from when she got that phone call from the concertmaster welcoming her into his section. The strong handshake she got from the President of the University of Peabody when he said, *"Good job, graduate."* The dark red roses a blushing Trevor had handed her after the ceremony. The hug from her parents who both whispered, *"Honey, we are so proud of you"*. She recalled loading up her life into her parent's van with promises from Trevor that they could house hunt as soon as they returned to Charlotte. She had had dinner out with all her favorite people the night before they left campus for the last time— Mother, Dad, Trevor, and Felicity. Conversation was rolling with witty barbs, laughter, and the sense of belonging that was only gotten from family. After dinner, they had enjoyed a family road trip all piled on top of each other with constantly rolling, thought-provoking discussions.

She grabbed the picture and held it tightly against her wobbly, empty middle. The middle that one short week ago was swollen with new life and more hope and excitement than she had ever had before. Sliding back down under the comfortable soft quilt that smelled like fabric softener, she felt like she was falling. Falling, falling, falling from the high point in this picture to— she didn't know where. Closing her eyes as the tears came once more she prayed the only words that would come to her: "Lord, please, *please* make it stop."

CHAPTER THIRTY-SIX
Felicity

Felicity was starting to get majorly ticked. This was just ridiculous. When Elliot visited at the hospital, Felicity had been under the impression that he was planning to come check on them as soon as they were home or at least in a day or two. They were at the end of day two of being home and still no word. Why the heck hadn't he checked on them yet? And why did her entire life consist of sitting on her bed and waiting for her phone to ring? It was like watching paint dry in a rainstorm. Or nail polish dry in the shower. Or— well, something wet dry while being pummeled by something wetter.

Staring at the sleeping baby, she wished that Elliot would somehow know that this moment would be an excellent time in which to call. He could stop by while Mother was out and before Mr. Poopy Pants decided to start screaming again. They could put the baby over in the corner and then maybe fool around a little bit on the bed. They wouldn't go all the way, of course not, she just had a baby after all. Not to mention she had definitely learned her lesson about the dangers of sex. No more mistakes for her! But she had been so very lonely these past months while his schedule picked up speed, and she would appreciate a long hug and maybe some strokes of her hair. She did so love it when he stroked her hair. But really, if he would just *be* here. She was going crazy with no one to talk to. Her mind was starting to turn on itself. She wanted to suggest that he climb up into bed with her at the hospital and just talk for a while, but he hadn't offered, and she was afraid of being turned down. The only thing worse than him not climbing up to be with her would have been for her to ask for it and him to say "no."

Closing her eyes, she leaned back against her headboard and thought about what should happen next. How would this look? Would he ask her to marry him? Would she move in with him and his dad? Or would he want to move in here so that they could have Mother's help with the baby? She knew that they were young, but there was no denying the life they had created. People got married in high school all the time, right?

Michael. She mulled the name over in her head and decided it wasn't horrible. She had been leaning more toward Usher, but then she could imagine her mother asking where she got it from and when she said it was from her favorite performing artists, she could see the frown on Mother's face as she often had when Felicity had her headphones in, turned up too loud, and blocking out the annoying world around her. Michael. Hmmmm.

What would Elliot say about this name for their son? She smiled and felt courage grow. *Their son.*

She was going to do it. Time was up, mister. No matter how horrible and needy it made her look, she was doing this. Pink walls were starting to close in on her. Her social life was desperate to be jump-started, and she was willing to sacrifice a piece of her pride to do so. No more tears, no more weird feelings, she was going to make normal happen for her again.

Grabbing her phone, she typed,

"Where ru? Coming to visit baby?"

218

"Can u talk?" Elliot texted back after a long minute and thirty-six seconds. (Not that she was counting.)

"Sure. Now? Call me."

"I mean in person."

"Oh. U coming over? Felicity added a few emoticon hearts to this and then deleted them, sending the message emoticon free.

"Can't. Working. Meet me here?"

Felicity looked at the baby and texted "With the baby. Can this wait?"

"Come eat dinner. Really need to talk. Only have a few minutes right now. Can't your mom watch him?" *Emoticon kissy lips.*

Kissy lips!

Could she go to him now? Felicity remembered what her mom had said about Claire napping in the other room. Why exactly was Claire here anyway? Lucky Claire didn't have to be tied down by a baby since Felicity was pretty sure she heard Mother say that Claire's baby was still at the hospital. Surely she could listen for her nephew. She wouldn't mind helping out, right? Trevor was always saying to let them know how they could help her. Baby and Claire were both napping and probably would still be asleep when Felicity got back. She could just slip out for a few minutes to talk to Elliot and be back before her mom got back. Or if her mom got back first, really who cares? Baby care was covered either way. This was obviously more important. Her relationship and her little family's future depended on her talking to Elliot while he was ready to talk. This week had taught her that this was a rapidly shrinking window of opportunity She could hold and feed her baby anytime. Michael would always be around.

What to wear? Pulling open her dresser drawer, she was pleased to see a clean and neatly folded purple tank top right on top of her top drawer. Her favorite tattered jeans were nowhere to be found, and Felicity silently promised herself that she would exact her revenge if Mother had thrown them out. Settling with a pair of denim shorts that normally were a little big but for some reason today barely fit up over her hips, she felt ready to face the world.

Pulling out a bright pink post-it note from her desk, she wrote in loose cursive with hearts over her "i"s as if to somehow make the note seem more apologetic and loving than it actually was.

"C- had to step out for a minute.

b right back.

listen for bb in my room.

g8 thanx."

She placed it quietly on the door of Claire's room and then tiptoed away.

It was only when she reached the front door that she realized— how would she get there? The McDonalds where Elliot worked was only a five-minute drive away, but she had no car and didn't feel up to riding her bike or walking. Spying a set of keys with a miniature violin key ring carelessly lying on the entry table, she decided quickly.

Grabbing the keys, she headed out to borrow her sister's car for a quick drive. She had her temporary license and was only going a few blocks. No one had to know. Felicity was an excellent driver, everyone said so— well except for that one mailbox that leaned so far out into the street, but really it had just been asking to be hit. Claire would hate her for borrowing her car, but she hated her anyway. What's one more mark against her?

Getting behind the driver's wheel, she felt semi-normal for the first time in weeks as the opportunity for a breath of freedom filled her lungs and made her feel alive.

CHAPTER THIRTY-SEVEN
Claire

Claire was having the best dream. Snuggled tightly into her childhood bed, everything played out exactly the way it should. Perfect pregnancy, perfect birth, perfect baby. In her dream she was meeting her little boy for the very first time. Pink-cheeked, sparkly eyes, dimpled elbows, round belly— he was so handsome. Joy filling her entire being, she rocked him. Nothing else existed except for this moment. The world stopped spinning around her, all noises ceased, the vibrant colors of movement turned blurry as her focus stayed on the bundle in her lap.

She raised him to her face and put his warm cheek against hers. She felt their souls touch. He was so tiny, and yet he was the biggest thing in her world. All her other accomplishments melted far away compared to growing this human being. He was her everything. She kissed his soft ear and then whispered, "I love you. Oh little boy you have no idea how much I love you."

Suddenly a cry bubbled up into her ear. She turned the light bundle toward her while carefully supporting his head and saw a small poochy lip turn into a whimper which swelled first to a soft cry and then quickly accelerated to gut-wrenching screams.

She couldn't figure out why he was crying. Her insecurities shot to the surface. Was she holding him wrong? Was she not enough for him? Was she not a good enough mommy?

"Shhhhhhhhh," She soothed him just like she had practiced, but her very best soothing only added fuel to his crying fire.

Suddenly she bolted up in bed, forced into wakefulness. The baby's screams were coming from somewhere in the house. Samuel! Her Samuel needed her!

But then it all came back in ugly waves. She must have fallen back asleep. She was dreaming because none of that had actually happened.

Samuel was at the hospital. Samuel was sick. Samuel had *Down syndrome.*

The disappointment hit her all over again like a punch to her still-floppy-from-carrying-a-baby gut. Her happy dream ended. Cold, harsh reality took its place. She stared into the darkness of her old room while it all came screaming back to her, feeling even crueler when surrounded by a sleep haze.

An intense headache was drilling into her forehead. She touched it gingerly, and then swung her feet out of bed. Something fell to the hardwood floor with a crash and a tinkling sound. What did she drop? The room was now bathed in darkness, so she flipped the bedside lamp on. Leaning down she saw it. The picture that showcased her happiness was surrounded by jagged pieces of broken glass.

Sounds about right.

Staring down at the younger version of her face— the happy version of her face, she suddenly felt very old. She couldn't break her gaze. She couldn't blink. Bright dots danced in her vision, but her eyes wouldn't let her look away. The smile on the faces in the picture mocked her.

The newborn crying broke her trance. If it wasn't her baby, then this was obviously Felicity's. Why wasn't Felicity helping him? Was mother not back yet? Were they seriously expecting her to take care of him?

Her chest felt heavy. Painful weight gathered in her breasts, and her whole body was starting to ache. Looking down she saw wet marks drenching the front of her shirt.

Just listening to the healthy, loud cries tightened her heart in a funny way. She couldn't explain it, but the sweet innocent cries made her angry. Furious. Livid. She thought about how her baby couldn't summon the energy for even a peep, let alone a loud, lusty cry. His lungs were so compromised and sick, a cry like this would be a dream come true.

She stepped out of bed and felt something inside her snap. She looked down and idly noticed that she had stepped directly onto the glass. She took a step and saw blood smear on mother's perfect floors. She felt nothing.

Focusing steely eyes forward she slowly made her way out of the room. The note from Felicity on the door caught her attention only for a second as she pieced together the fact that she was alone in the house with Felicity's baby.

Her hands clenched into fists. Her shoulders tightened. Her brain hurt from thinking, so she shut it off. Her heart was pounding, and a thick thud throbbed in her ears to the point she almost didn't hear the baby crying anymore.

Staggering across the hallway to the room her sister had decorated with trashy posters and tacky pictures— she felt herself give in to the dark, emotional storm that had been building inside of her. It was time to make things fair again.

223

CHAPTER THIRTY-EIGHT
Julie

Pushing the cart quickly, Julie hurried to gather the items on her scribbled list so that she could get back home. It's not that she didn't trust Felicity with the baby. After all, it was her baby. It's just that— she totally didn't trust her.

An additional item was niggling at the back of her mind. What did she need to get? While she was here and baby free, what was it that she sat up in the middle of last night and swore to remember to buy?

Felicity had never even wanted to babysit before let alone for a newborn this young. At the hospital Felicity had gladly given over all care to the nurses and to Julie. As she drove the ten minutes to the grocery store, she couldn't remember if Felicity had even held the baby yet. In the hospital— when they got home— during any of his many feedings? Had she ever even held her baby?

Always pleading exhaustion, Felicity seemed to have no qualms about putting Julie in charge. Julie bit her lip thinking about this. Felicity was alone with the baby now. Julie left quickly, so eager to help Claire that she didn't really think this through. What if Felicity didn't support his neck? What if she dropped him? What if he started to choke but she didn't know how to help him? What if he cried and cried but she just ignored him? The potential consequences were too horrible to imagine. They weren't dealing with a houseplant, a pet, or a family consumer science project. This was an actual, live baby.

Flour, some brown sugar, 8 ounces of bittersweet chocolate— Julie swept the listed items into her cart without even thinking. Quickening her step, she almost ran to the formula aisle as she started to rethink her decision to leave the baby with Felicity. Michael would be okay for these few minutes she was gone, right? He would most likely sleep the whole time, right? But what if he didn't?

Bottle brush! That was it! Seeing the bottles next to the formula reminded her that she needed a brush for more efficient cleaning of the many bottles now filling a drawer in her kitchen. Julie dropped the first one she saw into the cart next to ingredients that she usually kept on hand, but had gotten low on thanks to an early baby delivery and the inability to do her weekly shopping trip this week.

Julie got a nervous feeling in the pit of her stomach. Something was wrong. She just knew it. She remembered the extra item that she forgot to write down, so she knew now that it wasn't forgetfulness unease— this was something more. She needed to get back home. *Now.* Grabbing a pack of size one diapers and a carton of formula, she rushed to checkout. Hurry, hurry, hurry. Sweet Michael needed her. Why did she leave him in the care of Felicity so soon? Felicity wasn't ready for this. They both knew it.

She started picturing her sweet boy waking up in a panic, tears streaming down his cheeks and sweet mouth opened in panic— gasping for air between sobs. Finishing her self-checkout in record time, she ran crazy-person style with surprising agility out to her car. And the running had nothing to do with the pelting rain.

CHAPTER THIRTY-NINE
Claire

She knew what she had to do.

In spite of her many flaws, Claire never thought she would be the type of person to commit murder, and yet right now it was the only thing that she could think about.

Stepping slowly into the room, she stopped for a moment in the doorway, holding out a trembling arm to steady herself against the tall dresser. Closing her eyes, she could feel the smooth and slightly sticky bumps of duct tape and remembered the weekend her sister insisted that they all help wrap the entire surface of the dresser in hot pink duct tape, changing it from a dull brown to a pink that could be seen from outer space. "Why don't you just paint it?" They all asked. But Felicity had just rolled her eyes, refusing to change her mind and pushing the project stubbornly forward no matter the opinions from the people that she referred to as "the peanut gallery".

Claire could hear the whirling of the ceiling fan adding its voice to the almost silent air conditioner, attempting to ward off the intense heat that she had been almost oblivious to this week. All winter long she looked forward to this heat. She longed for the days that her body would immediately bead up with sweat just going from the car into the house. She lived for the long days, the bright sunshine, the picnics, and the beach trips. The sticky, don't-turn-on-the-oven, blasting heat of July seemed to take forever to get here this year. She had been counting down, and for a while there between March and April she could have sworn that time stood still. It's as if nature knew what would be coming her way and wanted to delay the inevitable as long as possible. If only she had known, she would have thanked that blessed clock for its speed of mercy.

A crack of thunder interrupted her musings and the pattering of the rain on the roof picked up speed. But even the storm wasn't breaking the muggy heat of today.

Forcing herself to keep going, she lifted her bare foot to take a heavy step forward, feeling almost as it there were duct tape on the floor as well, giving just enough resistance to make her question what she was about to do. Looking down at her feet, she saw another painful reminder. The room was dark, but the light from the hallway allowed her to see her toenails painted a perfect dark red. She remembered her pedicure appointment last week, blissfully preparing for her perfect day of delivery. She wished she could get that happiness back— the hope— the expectation of joy. If only she had known that there was a timer on those emotions, she would have squeezed every last drop out of them while she could.

A soft gray cat brushed against her leg, whining for attention. She ignored it.

Dragging one beautifully pedicured foot in front of the other through the quiet room, her body moved more slowly than she wanted it to due to this week's events. She wanted to do this quickly— to get it over with, but her legs, just like everything else in her life right now, refused to cooperate.

Once she was close enough, she smelled it. The ripe smell of a diaper gone horribly wrong wafted up to her. Perhaps she should have done something about this. Perhaps she should have cared. But really, all she could think about was the fact that no one had to weigh that diaper and meticulously record it with exuberant high fives and extra baby kisses for this huge achievement! It was a dirty diaper, not a Pulitzer Prize. Success in this area was assumed for human survival. It was not an achievement. This was just one more expectation in life that had been shaken, turned upside down, and then cut into tiny, insignificant pieces.

Only a few steps away now. Shuffling the last few steps, she tried not to think about what she was about to do. Nestled in the blue pack 'n play lay the baby that should have been hers. He was no longer crying. Up and down his tiny chest fell, no effort given to drawing each breath. No wheezing, no machines to help, no beeping of an additional machine tracking the job of the first machines— just gentle, natural breathing. His cheeks were wet from his tears and flushed in sleep, not taped up with tubing and wires. Perfectly shaped eyes lined with long eyelashes were closed for now, but she knew all too well the look of intelligence this baby had thanks to the new album on Facebook proclaiming his arrival. His entire body, down to the little fingers balled up into tiny fists, was plump and strong, just like a baby should be.

It wasn't fair. This was so unbelievably unfair that she could barely breathe. Every time she remembered the unfairness her heart started skipping beats and streams of tears sprung unbidden to her eyes. She simply couldn't keep going knowing that life had dealt her splinters instead of diamonds and that the diamonds that she had earned were flaunted in front of her daily, hung shining and beautiful around someone else's neck while she stood to the side crying over the pain of these giant, ragged, horrible splinters.

She wanted to love this baby who easily blew out his diaper and magically breathed on his own. She wanted to be okay with this, but she could barely even look at him. He was too perfect. An effortless perfect. His very existence mocked the sick baby fighting for his life at the hospital. Every time she saw his round face of baby flawlessness, she could only think about what had been taken from her, and she was nauseous at this constant reminder. How could God be a good God and still let this happen? Didn't he promise to reward her for her obedience to him?

She obeyed. She had gone above and beyond and yet her heart was still torn into painful splinters. She deserved better than this. She deserved— she heard a soft sleep moan and looked back down. She deserved this baby.

No thinking no thinking, she silently chided herself. Only one thing would make this fair. Only one thing would right the wrong spin of the motherhood wheel. No one had to know.

She picked up the baby's light blue blanket carelessly thrown on the bed. The blanket was so soft— nothing like the coarse threads provided by the hospital NICU. No one would question what had happened. With a mother who abandons the baby, leaving her only babysitting request on a post-it-note to an unknowing babysitter, accidents happen. They happen all the time.

Staring at the almost unrecognizable arm holding the fleece blanket with satin edges, she felt the oddest sensation of floating out of her body to watch this all from above. Aghast, she couldn't believe what she was seeing let alone comprehend that she was capable of this. But there it was happening. Right before her eyes. A distraught woman stood weeping over the baby while moving his blanket. Moving it so slowly and yet deliberately. Moving it, over the baby's head.

CHAPTER FORTY
Julie

Julie forced herself to walk slowly up the walk through the pounding rain to her house. Her paranoia had been in full swing while shopping, but all those doubts about Felicity really had been ridiculous. Anxiety strikes again! She didn't hear a baby screaming from the house, so clearly Felicity was keeping things under control. But then again, would she hear a baby screaming through the sound of the rain?

Falling in smooth sheets around her, the rain was a constant of today.

Huddled under her umbrella, she glanced back at her driveway and wondered where Claire's car was? Did Trevor drop her off earlier? Julie thought Claire had driven, but now she felt like her mind was playing tricks on her. The lack of sleep was really starting to mess with her. She hoped Claire hadn't gotten a call from the hospital and needed to leave.

Carrying two grocery bags holding all the things missing from her pantry to make Claire's chocolate cake along with more diapers and food for sweet little Michael, Julie wanted to pause and think about how truly blessed she was. Two beautiful daughters and two grandsons— her nest and her heart were full. She had spent most of the ride home praying for little Samuel. Praying for peace for Claire. Praying for the future of their family traveling this unknown path. Her mind then naturally led into praying for Felicity. For strength to make the right decision, for the maturity to take the next step, for the graciousness to carry out whatever path the Lord might have for Michael— Julie had had a hard time not praying what she really wanted to say, *"Lord, please help Felicity realize that she should let me adopt Michael and call him mine"*. She tried to keep a loose grip on this baby— to be open to the Lord's leading for whatever might be truly best for the baby.

But the desire of her heart was strong. Her question was— was this a bad desire? Or a good one?

Her mind preoccupied with heavy matters, she didn't notice that the house was unusually dark when she stepped inside. She almost didn't hear the muffled sobs combined with soft whines. Pausing in the darkened entryway, she felt all her senses stand on edge.

"Felicity?" She called out— feeling her previous wave of panic return tsunami style when only silence greeted her.

"Claire? Are you awake?"

Silence. A few more whimpers. A few more muffled sobs. Her senses were standing alert, screaming for help.

Her heart started to pound hard enough to shake off any excess rain that managed to fall on her. The silence was full of the wrong kind of assurance.

Something was wrong. Something was horribly, horribly wrong. She could smell it, feel it, and see it through the darkness. Abandoning her dripping umbrella on the floor, she subconsciously took on a cover of fear.

"Felicity??? Claire???" more urgency accompanied her voice.

She dropped her grocery bags and ran toward the stairs. She heard one of the paper bags tear as it fell and the sound of groceries falling onto the floor. She didn't stop to pick them up. She hurried up the stairs with a speed she didn't know that she possessed.

Once in the hallway, she stood still for a moment to figure out where the noises were coming from and to catch her breath. Glancing into Claire's room which was directly on the left, she saw only rumpled sheets and a folded over quilt. Her mind worked to piece this together. If Claire was no longer sleeping, was she still here? Where was she?

Glancing down onto the hardwood floor, she saw a large smear of blood making a trail from the guest room to the loudly pink room across the hall.

Felicity's room. *The baby.*

Dread overtook her. Her feet all of a sudden seemed leaden as she found herself shuffling towards the room where unmistakable crying took center stage.

Julie saw Claire, collapsed on the floor next to the baby's pack 'n play. She was shaking with sobs. Julie looked toward the baby's bed and whispered, "Oh Claire. What did you do?"

CHAPTER FORTY-ONE
Felicity

Felicity fidgeted with her second fudge sundae while waiting for Elliot to finish up with this last line of customers so that he could join her. It was time to talk. She looked at the time on her phone— 4:15. She had been gone only twenty minutes. Traffic had been light and the drive over gave her no problems in spite of the intense rain, but Elliot wasn't ready to join her when she got there so she ate a quick snack by herself. Now she was just waiting. Was the baby still asleep? Was it a mistake to come here? She poised her finger over her text app— thinking that maybe she should shoot Claire a text to make sure she saw the post-it-note.

But she didn't. Who was she kidding? Claire no doubt had things completely under control back at Casa de Felicity. Felicity had the unfortunate experience of hearing the baby cry red-faced with copious tears a few times at the hospital before someone got a bottle into that big ol' mouth. If he cried, there was no way Claire wouldn't hear him. That kid had some volume on him. (It was hard to tell where his extreme dramatics came from since she was so level-headed and all.) No doubt Super Mom Claire would not fail to get that kid whipped into shape in no time.

Forcing the baby from her mind, Felicity set her mind on more important issues— her relationship with Elliot. Clearly he had something to tell her, or else he wouldn't have texted back. Maybe he was ready to commit? Perhaps he was going to propose? Okay, admittedly maybe that one was a little farfetched, but she did just have his baby. They could skip a few steps and get to the happily-ever-after faster. Perhaps they were bit young to get married, but they could work it out. She did just turn fifteen, after all. She wasn't a child anymore.

There was plenty room for Elliot to move into Felicity's room after they got married. They could put in a big bed with a huge canopy just like Mother had in her room. She had wanted a new bed now for a while and this seemed like the perfect time for her to upgrade.

If they lived with Mother, she could help with the baby so Felicity could continue her life as it was meant to be. Having the entire responsibility of the baby was not something Felicity was willing to take on right now. An extra roommate who would remind Elliot why they belonged together at hotel de la madre? She could really get on board with that.

She glanced at the time on her phone again. What was taking so long? She didn't want Mother to get home and see that she had left the baby. Most likely she would use extreme words like "abandon" and "too immature for a baby". No need for name calling here. There was no reason to place mistrust in Mother's mind about whether Felicity was able to handle her own baby. Well, more mistrust than was already there. Felicity was no fool. She could see the look in Mother's eyes. It was just like her famous "Okay I'll trust you with a real china plate from Grandma Eugenia's collection but I really want to give clumsy you a paper plate instead because this china is absolutely irreplaceable and your fingers are slicked with oil and soap" look. Mother would only let Felicity eat off of

Grandma's china once a year because Christmas dinner would look ridiculous with one paper plate on the beautifully laden table.

Just as Felicity was about to go visit the little girl's room, she saw him ambling towards her table. Felicity beamed. And then blushed. Gaw he was cute. The endearing tilt of his long face toward her made this last half hour of waiting feel like nothing. She was so lucky that he had chosen her. She would lose this extra weight as soon as possible to help him be attracted to her even more. To help his eyes sizzle as he stared only at her. She would be the perfect girlfriend and not nag and whine like he claimed that she used to do. A new chapter of Felicity starts right now. Pushing away the rest of the fudge sundae, she almost laughed at the memory of the last time Eliot saw her— at least she wasn't wearing a gown with breast slits this time.

One part gentlemen two parts handsome devil sat down across from her, staring down at his hands. She squirmed remembering the things his thick yet smooth hands had done to her.

Felicity wanted to stare at his stunningly long fingers too, but instead she immediately started talking as quickly as possible, trying to show him that she was different now. More grown up.

"So I was thinking of getting a bigger bed. I've been needing a new bed for a while, and I think it's time— so why not go bigger? More comfortable, you know? And then if you were to move in—"

He cut her off with, "I think we should break up."

Stunned, she stopped right before she was about to explain about the canopy and how it signified their entrance into adulthood together as hopefully married parents.

Her mouth gaped open, fat tears of rejection sprung uninvited into her love-struck green eyes, and she could have sworn that her heart stopped beating for just a second.

"Break up? But— what— why—?" She wanted to ask the question to completion, but there seemed to be a communication problem between her brain and her tongue. Did he really just say *break up*?

"I just can't do this." He had yet to look her in the eye since sitting down at her table. Why wouldn't he look her in the eye? Glancing everywhere but at her, he took off his hat and ran his hands through his ponytail and then put his decidedly moist-looking hat back on.

"The baby—", She trailed off.

"I'm sorry about the baby— truly, but I can't help you. I'm making $8.50 an hour, and I need every penny of that for college or a new car or an apartment. I haven't really decided yet which direction I'm going to go, but I hear that they're all expensive. The point is— I can't be a dad. I just can't."

"But I thought you said—."

"I know. I tried. I really did. But then I got super overwhelmed thinking about having to do this with you, and just realized I'm not ready to settle down. You have a baby! I'm not ready for that. No. Just no. Danielle says that I have to focus on me right now. I really have high hopes for our band to go places. That's not going to happen if I play the Daddy game. Danielle suggested—"

"Danielle? Wait, who's Danielle?"

His lips betrayed himself as they accidentally spread into a dreamy smile. He quickly stifled it and said, " I've been meaning to tell you. She's my girlfriend."

Felicity felt the hot tears start to multiply as she had the sudden urge to grab his ponytail and either pull his face to hers or yank it as hard as she could. Raising a hand, she tried to wipe tears away before he noticed them flooding her cheeks.

"You said you wanted a family. We can be that for you. We can be your family!" she whispered.

"My parents split when I was four. I don't even know how to be a family. I think that was just wishful thinking."

"We could learn together! I'm sure my Mother would help us. We can—"

"No. I said no. Okay?" His voice was harsh— almost meanly so. He stuffed his hat back on his head and stood back up.

He softened his voice and said, "Sorry, it's nothing personal. Now I have to get back to work. I wasn't supposed to get a break tonight anyway. I can't talk anymore."

"Can we talk later? I feel like we could still work this out."

"No. No we can't. I'm sorry, but I don't want to talk any more about this. My mind is made up. Go get your new bed and figure this out yourself. I'm out. Don't call me."

He turned and sauntered back to the employee entrance to the kitchen smirking at the girl spilling out of her unbuttoned work shirt who she could only assume was the boyfriend-stealing Danielle.

Felicity looked down at the fudge dripping down into the melting ice cream and wondered how it was possible to hurt this much. She willed herself not to cry, but it was too late. She let her tears fall into the sundae as she pulled it back towards her, mingling her tears with a few more bites of the melting ice cream. So this was rock bottom.

CHAPTER FORTY-TWO
Claire

"I can't believe what I just did. I can't believe what I just did." Claire's mind was spinning, whirling, exploding with confusion and hurt. She looked down. Her foot was covered in blood. She suddenly realized that it hurt. Badly.

"What did you do?" Claire would know that voice anywhere. Mother's soft voice came at her elbow. Where had she come from? Had she been here this whole time? Claire jerked her head over and saw Mother kneeling next to her. She hadn't heard her return. Was Felicity back too? How was she going to explain this to Felicity?

All her life Claire had watched other people make horrible, awful, life-ruining mistakes, thinking, "Well, I would never do THAT." But here she was— on the floor of her sister's room, shaking from the intensity, holding an innocent baby, a baby who she actually wanted to hurt. *HURT a baby.* What was wrong with her? Did motherhood turn her into a monster? She was a good person! A Christian! A youth pastor's wife! What was wrong with her?

She felt the gentle pulls, looked down, and stared in amazement where the baby was latched onto her. She thought back to a few minutes ago when she was poised to do— she didn't even know what, when her breasts started leaking. The hardness was painful in a way she had never experienced before. The intensity of this pain got her attention and somehow snapped her out of her angry haze. She put down the blanket, picked up the baby and held him in position without even thinking about it.

His little mouth pulled at her, desperately seeking for food, and she saw white milk bubble around his mouth as he greedily swallowed and hungrily sucked for more with his tiny, strong lips.

The tears started falling once more. This was supposed to be her baby. If she could ignore the bright red hair clearly stamping him as Felicity's, she could close her eyes and pretend. *This is how it was supposed to be.*

He was soft yet heavy in her arms— tiny yet an undeniable presence. He smelled like the first flowers of spring, the anticipation of Christmas morning, the slight breeze wafting down from falls' golden hues, the perfect summer morning.

Wrapping her shaking arms around him, she didn't stop him. She held him tightly and let him eat, desperately clinging to the warm body in her arms and wishing just as desperately that this was the baby that she had grown. This is just how she dreamed the sensations of nursing would be. And yet, this was nothing at all like she had dreamed.

"Mother, I think something is wrong with me." She sniffed through the tears, not having a hand free to reach up and wipe her running nose.

Mother moved closer and put an arm around her shoulder.

"I just can't do this. I can't. It makes absolutely no sense, and it just can't be right. I don't deserve this. *I don't deserve to have a baby with Down syndrome.* I can't do this. I can't be his mother."

"What do you think you deserve?" Mother asked quietly and calmly, her voice low and soothing.

"A healthy baby. A baby with a future. A baby who isn't broken. A baby who is the result of all of the work I put into him— all of the prayers— all of the tears. I deserve a perfect baby. Not Felicity. She didn't even want a baby. And yet, here her baby is well enough to nurse, and my baby is at the hospital with tubes stuffed down his throat. I can't even hold him. *He is too sick to hold.* This isn't fair. This so isn't fair." She had started with a whisper, but her voice rose as did her emotions as she said aloud the thoughts she had been holding onto ever since she got the news.

It felt wrong to put that negativity into the air. It was okay to think it, but to actually say it out loud? Maybe she should've just faked it until she made it. Maybe if she had just pretended forever, she could convince herself that everything was okay. If she posted all over social media— "We feel so blessed that God entrusted us with such a special child" and testify in church— "How amazing that the Lord chose US to be his parents" and tell her friends— "I've always secretly wanted a child with special needs. How cool!" Maybe then she could force herself to believe it. If her mouth said the right things, perhaps her heart would follow suit.

But she just couldn't do this for another minute. And after what she just almost did, she didn't trust herself to leave this all bottled up inside. She had to say it out loud. She had to release all the excess pressure or else she would explode. Arms grasped the velvety warm baby and her stomach sank as she thought about how she almost directed that pressure.

A hand stroked her neck with light tickles like Mother used to when Claire was a little girl. It had an almost immediate stilling effect on her. Sitting there, nursing her nephew and crying, Claire waited for what Mother would say.

"Sweetie. I think it's time I told you something. Something I swore I could never tell you girls because it was simply too painful to share. But I think perhaps my journey could be of help to you, so here goes."

Claire's hand brushed the soft whispers of hair on the baby's head, and she listened intently. Maybe she had some miraculous way to make this all better like when she used to add spices to Claire's bland dishes in order to transform them into masterpieces. Or like when she fixed a few wrong stitches on Claire's blanket project in junior high and made it beautiful. Maybe she could somehow fix this.

CHAPTER FORTY-THREE
Julie

Julie's heart was thudding. How did she tell Claire about this? After all these years? The deeply buried secret was painful to retrieve.

Seeing the look of desperation on Claire's sweet face, she knew that it was time. Claire's normally calm face was etched with overwhelming amounts of anger. Her beautiful dark eyes that normally danced and sparkled looked pierced through with pain, desperate to find relief and peace.

Dreading actually having to say the words, tears began to drip down her cheeks and a lump in her throat suddenly swelled to a suffocating size. Decisively giving her cheeks a quick wipe and awkwardly clearing her throat, Julie opened her mouth to begin telling her daughter the one thing she had been keeping from her all these years. She had always hoped that Brad would be by her side when she had to talk about this again.

Silently begging for wisdom from her Heavenly Father, she started to tell her story.

"Twenty-eight years ago, I was pregnant. Your father and I prayed for this baby, and we were so excited."

She paused, swallowed, and prayed for strength to continue.

"At the end of the pregnancy, I gave birth to the most beautiful baby boy— Adam Thomas Reagan." A smile broke out on her face through the tears. "Seriously he was gorgeous, and I immediately fell in love with him."

Claire's eyebrows rose to new heights as Julie saw her try to process this and figure out where this information fit into her formerly neat little life.

"The first few days of his life were heaven. I wanted to be a mother so badly, and he was even more amazing than my wildest dreams. He loved to nurse and would cuddle up to me so close with his eyes squeezed tightly shut and his body sighing in contentment. When his eyes were open they held a twinkle as if he was already so wise. His small hands would wrap around my fingers as if possessively claiming me as his.

Her smile faded.

"But then after those first three days of bliss, he started sleeping a lot and not really wanting to eat. It was when his fever spiked and his breathing became labored that we knew something was wrong. We rushed him to the Emergency Room thinking that perhaps they needed to just monitor his breathing and fever for a bit."

"They hooked him up to all kinds of machines and he fought to live for twelve hours. I remember how the ER room filled with so many doctors we were crowded out. They all fought for him, and he fought hard for himself. But he— he never came home."

Julie found it difficult to continue.

"After he died, I was holding his little hand, and it started to grow cold. I tried to warm him up– tried to get him to respond to me. The pastor came– read some verses. I just kept thinking– this is not for us, this is not for us, this is happening to somebody else. His hand just got colder and colder until they told me that the social worker needed to take him away. There was nothing that they could do. I would have done anything to get his tiny hand to warm back up– for his eyes to blink at me again– for his lips to curve into a smile. What I wouldn't have given to believe what my heart was telling me– it was one big shocking joke. That it wasn't real. But nothing I thought or did could bring him back. His life was over before it even really started.

"I felt like I was living a nightmare. We stumbled out of the emergency room that night with empty arms. We went home to where all of his things where. They still smelled like him, but he was never going to return to them— or us again. I felt like I was walking in a fog. I couldn't believe that he was really gone.

"I will never forget how his casket was so tiny and white. And I just knew he was going to be cold all alone in the ground. *Don't!* I wanted to cry out. *Don't take my baby away from me!* But I couldn't say the words. Because he was already gone. There's no way that little casket could protect him from the cold and rain. Who would keep him warm? Who would keep him dry? My baby would be all alone, and there was nothing I could do about it. This couldn't be real. This broke me.

"I had to say goodbye to the baby that I put to my breast— the baby that I carried for nine months— the baby who claimed my entire heart. I touched his white little casket with my finger and thought about how wrong this was. How unfair. Why? Why did he have to die? We would have given him an incredible life. We were a family. We were whole. But then all of a sudden without warning, we were broken beyond repair.

"On our last day together, I wish I had known that that was the last time that I would hold him alive. I wish I would have realized it was the last night that I would have been up all night nursing him. It was the last morning that we would have nothing to do but cuddle and eat. If I had known, I would have enjoyed every second of our last hours together. I would have let my lips linger on his warm forehead that much longer. I would have held tighter to his soft body. I would have never put him down for a minute. I would have told him how much I loved him, how much he would be missed, and how nothing in the world would ever fill the hole he left.

"Claire, I just kept asking why? Why did he have to die? I would have done anything for him to live. *Anything.* I was prepared to sacrifice my entire life for him— for his health. Whatever he needed. But I never even got the chance."

Julie stopped talking to swallow and catch her breath. Her eyes had turned into faucets that rivaled the storm outside. Her arm around Claire was trembling. This was so hard.

Claire was listening intently. At first she looked curious about Julie's story. By the end, Claire was crying with her.

"I am so sorry." Claire said quietly. "I had no idea you lost a baby, Mother. I am so sorry you had to go through that."

"It was a long time ago, but sometimes it still feels like it happened just yesterday."

"What was wrong with him? What happened?"

"A rare strain of pneumonia. Something so simple, yet so deadly for the newborn immune system. The doctors promised us that it was nothing that we did. They said that nothing that we could have done that would have saved him. It's just one of those things, but it certainly didn't make it any easier."

"So twenty-eight years? Was this before you had me? Did you get pregnant again right away?"

"Sort of."

Julie sighed and then continued. "You see, a few weeks after we buried our little boy, our pastor was contacted about a pregnant mother. She was struggling with a cocaine addiction, and she was looking for a Christian home for her little girl due in a few months. He asked us if we would be interested in helping out, and we decided that we weren't ready to give up on our dream of being parents. Since it had taken us a few years to become pregnant in the first place and my body had taken quite the beating during the pregnancy and birth, my doctor told me that my chances of conceiving again were almost nonexistent. We prayed about it and decided that this was the next step that we should take. During the next several months we completed paperwork to become foster parents and to eventually be adoptive parents once all of the requirements were met. All of that took some time. By the time the baby was born, she came home with us. And she was— you were so beautiful." The tears that were glistening on her cheeks were now happy tears as she remembered that marvelous day when they met their daughter for the first time.

"You mean— *wait*— you mean, I'm not really your daughter?" Disbelief and surprise etched themselves onto Claire's expressive face. Julie had always loved what an open book Claire was.

Julie leaned over to Claire and said earnestly, "Oh my dear love— *no one* has ever been more my daughter than you. Did I give birth to you? No, no I did not. But from the very start, you have been the best daughter I could have ever asked for. There was never a time that I didn't feel 100% your mother. Family isn't always about always genetics. Family is about choosing love. And we chose to love you. You are our family. And honestly I think that you saved my life. There was a time after losing sweet Adam that I didn't think that I could keep living or that I had a reason to get out of bed in the morning. And then suddenly I had this beautiful baby girl who needed me so badly. You gave me hope and a purpose. You gave me a reason to live. You helped me through the darkest time in my life.

Julie took a big breath and then tentatively asked, "Are you mad that I didn't tell you this before? Are you angry?"

CHAPTER FORTY-FOUR
Claire

"No, I'm not mad." At least she didn't think she was. At this point it was hard for her to tell.

The room seemed to suddenly be bathed in a different sort of light. Claire could see dust particles floating in the air in front of her. Suddenly it seemed extremely important to focus on these aimlessly drifting pieces of dirty fluff. She recalled her mother retelling with a warm smile how three-year-old Claire pointed at similar floating pieces of dust and yelled "Bubbles!" and how crushed she had been to learn that these were not, in fact, bubbles at all.

"So, you replaced your baby— with me?" Claire ventured.

"No. No one replaced anyone. We lost a baby and we had a baby. These were two separate events. The timing was really a God thing because our hearts were so broken and this beautiful baby girl born with a head full of curly brown hair desperately needed a home. When you looked at me that first time with your big brown eyes, I fell deeply in love. And I have thanked the Lord for the miracle of your life every day since."

"I'm adopted." Claire had grown very still. She was barely breathing next to Julie as she took in this news. The dust settled on the carpet in front of her. Claire wondered when it would ever get vacuumed with a caretaker like Felicity in charge of the responsibility. This caused her to remember her parents' references to Felicity as their "miracle baby" in addition to her being the spitting image of their father. The sister's extreme differences suddenly made sense to her.

"Yes." Her mother's gentle voice answered her.

"Why didn't you tell me this before?" Claire asked.

"When this all happened we were living in Vermont. When we moved here to Charlotte, you were only two. With our family's fresh start, we didn't want to tell our new church because we didn't want the pity. Plus, you were so much our daughter; we didn't feel the need to announce how you came to be our child. As you grew, we didn't find a good moment to bring it up."

"Until now."

Julie looked apologetic. "Until now."

"Wait— is this why you took so many vacations to Vermont? Is he buried there? I mean— how many times do we need to walk the same nature trails?"

"Yeah. We tried to get back at least once a year to his grave."

Claire could feel her Mother tightening her grip around her shoulders, and Claire remembered the countless times Mother had held her this same way hundreds of times before through disappointments, times of learning, or just a Friday night girl's movie night side-by-side on the couch. Never had Claire questioned her presence in these arms. She belonged here.

"But you must have been so angry. How did you get over it? Why did God take your baby? *Why* did you have to go through that?"

248

Julie sighed. "I was angry. Extremely. It blinded me with its intensity. It crushed me with its strength. It strangled me in its grasp. For a long time I didn't know if I would ever let go of it or if I even could. *It wasn't fair.* Eventually as I got lost in the busyness of raising you, I somehow tucked the anger beneath some secondary emotions, but it stayed there, hidden below the surface at all times. Of course, I wasn't angry with you. You were the breath of fresh air that kept me waking up every morning. No, I was angry with God. Having to say goodbye to my precious, beautiful boy who would never grow past his first week of life— it broke me. Losing a child took part of me I never even knew existed. I felt dead inside— beyond revival For a while I didn't know if I would ever feel again. And I never got over it. Over the years I eventually learned to live with the pain— the loss. I knew that I was a daughter of the Heavenly Father. I trusted that this was all part of his plan for me even though I didn't understand it, and I definitely didn't agree with it. I just did the next right thing, and step-by-step He taught me how to be happy again, eventually extracting the last bit of anger from my clenched fist and leaving behind only a beautiful memory of my baby boy. God took my broken, angry pieces and rebuilt something stronger— so much stronger."

Claire felt her mother trembling beside her. Julie withdrew her arm and sat back up, using both hands now to grab a tissue from her pocket and blow her nose.

"But WHY? Why would God let your baby die while letting a cocaine addict's baby live? That makes no sense."

"Honey, *you* were the cocaine addict's baby. Do you think it's unfair that you have life? That you're so smart, motivated, and passionate? Do you think it's unfair that God gave you this incredible gift for music? You're so talented. *God made you that way.* God gave you this chance at life. Is that unfair? You had to detox from cocaine addiction when you came home from the hospital as a newborn. And your first year was definitely rough because of your rocky start to life. But God protected you from your birth mother's mistakes and has given you an awesome life. *Is that unfair?* I remember the first time you smiled— really smiled at me. The first time you crawled. Your first step. Your first word. All of these things were such miracles because at the beginning we didn't know what effect your birth mother's mistakes would have on you. And then you kept growing and amazing us, and we were daily reminded of what a strong, good God we have who made you, protected you, and put a light in you to shine his goodness even in the face of sin."

"Something that I have learned is that life rarely makes sense. And it certainly isn't always fair. In fact, life can be downright cruel at times. But God— God is always good. His character is one of goodness even when circumstances seem as opposite from good as you can get. God's goodness sometimes allows difficulty, loss, pain, and sorrow. His goodness and grace abounds both when He spares life and when He takes it. His goodness is all around us when life seems good and equally so when life seems bad. His goodness is not defined by our perceptions or our hopes. His goodness has a plan far beyond what we can even fathom. And as much as this includes blessings and happiness, this goodness equally includes loss, pain, and sorrow. He knows us better than we know ourselves. He wants the best for us, and He provides it for us through his goodness and grace— even when it seems like he is making the biggest mistake ever.

You know the verse, *"He made all of my inner parts and knit me together in my mother's womb"?* God is the Creator who makes no mistakes. He knit Samuel together in your womb— perfectly. Samuel didn't catch a disease called Down syndrome. God *designed* Samuel to have Down syndrome and sovereignly allowed of these health problems. He also knit Adam perfectly together in my womb— this included life and death at four days old. He knit you together perfectly in your birth mommy's womb. We aren't in control of our babies. No matter how carefully we do this, we are not in control. But the good thing is, someone else *is* in control. This is His plan for you. His perfect plan for you. His *good* plan for you. You may not understand why God gave you a baby with Down syndrome, but can I say something without you getting upset with me?"

"Okay." Claire braced herself. There was something worse than all of that?

"Be thankful that you have a baby to love. You haven't lost your baby. You still have a warm forehead to press your lips against, a soft body to hold, a life to mold, and moments to cherish. You still have a future ahead of you with your little man. Be grateful. Whisper praise. Let your heart burst with the wonder of the life that has been entrusted to you— even if the specifics of this life aren't what you expected. So he has Down syndrome. So what? *He is your son.* Motherhood doesn't deliver on order. Motherhood isn't about giving us our dreams. Motherhood really isn't about you at all. It's about your baby. Motherhood is about accepting your child for exactly who he was meant to be and loving him fiercely. Giving him every opportunity to be his best, celebrating his best, and being content in whatever that best that best may be. Motherhood is about sacrifice. It's about finding joy in serving others. Being flexible. Pouring your entire self into another being. Your job is to give your all to your child. Give him a life, a home, *a heart.* This isn't easy. No one ever said that this would be easy. It isn't easy for any child. You don't get to pick and choose the glamorous parts of motherhood that you feel like doing and discard the rest. It's a complete package. Either you want to be a mother or you don't. You can't send back the product that God perfectly created and chose for you while asking for a different model because your imagination produced motherhood differently than your reality. God is good. He has *your good* in mind. It is only your job to accept it. And trust. He has gifted this child to you. He will provide the grace for you to be the mother that little Samuel deserves. So your baby isn't what you expected? Join the club. I don't think any baby turns out exactly like we envision in our heads, but that's the beauty of a

Creator who knows better than we do. Just because something is unexpected doesn't mean that it can't still be breathtakingly beautiful.

Everything in your life up until this point has prepared you for this. All of your talents and abilities were given to you with the knowledge that you would use them in motherhood— this exact motherhood. None of this was happenstance or not fair. This is how it was meant to be. This is your perfect plan."

Claire was silent. The shadows of a stormy late afternoon hid her face as she bent over the baby. Her mother was trembling beside her. While her words made sense, there was something that Claire just couldn't let go.

"But God *owes* me a normal baby," she said

"Why would you think that?" Mother said.

"Because I did everything right." The words popped out before she realized she said them.

"So you think that you can control your child's genetic makeup— his future— his very life based off of your actions? You think that you can create something *better* than an almighty, all-knowing Creator who created the entire universe from beginning to the end? Do you believe that He finished with the intricate design of the beauty in nature all around us, but then He made his very first mistake making *your child*? I love you dearly Claire, but I have tell you— that sounds kind of arrogant.

God is the Creator. He chooses life and death. He saves us from everlasting judgment. Think about it— what do you really deserve? Think about your salvation. You can "do everything right" and still not be putting your faith and trust in God. You can "do everything right" and still be condemned for all eternity because your heart isn't in the right place. Our actions don't control God. God isn't a puppet, a vending machine, or a short order cook. Yes we should make good choices, and yes oftentimes bad choices have certain consequences. But God "owing you" because of the good that you have done? Do you really think that you are the one in

252

control? That your requests and actions should trump whatever He has decided is ultimately for your good? That your prayers and plans overwrite his?"

Claire sighed and said, "No."

As if remembering for the first time since this conversation began, Claire looked down at the baby in her arms. Soft, beautiful, perfect. He had stopped sucking a while back and a lot of the hardness that was in her breasts from not pumping these last few hours had eased up a bit. He appeared to be asleep with her nipple still firmly held in his mouth. Breastfeeding a baby who wasn't hers was the least confusing thing on her mind right now.

Adopted. Bio mom was one of those drug users she totally judged in the NICU. Mother buried a baby. Mother challenged her view on God answering her prayers. Mother claimed that God was good even in the midst of hard times. That perhaps this wasn't a Band-Aid statement on top of an amputated arm, but maybe it was source of strength to lean into through the amputation. It was going to take a long time to sort all of this out in her head. She had never before felt this before— a mix of surprise, sorrow, hope and strange anger.

"But what about losing Dad? Was *that* good? Don't you feel like God owes you a husband? What did you do to deserve to have him taken away so soon?"

"Nowhere in the Bible does it promise us a spouse or a healthy child. If you read it extensively, in fact, you will find quite the opposite. Death, sickness– it is everywhere. All of it is used to bring God's people closer to him. There's a sort of triumph when you face suffering, knowing that it is bringing you closer to your Heavenly Father. No, it doesn't make sense and no it doesn't always feel good, but I trust in His almighty provision, and I rejoice in the years that he gave your father and I together. I don't know why God chose to take your father home so early. I miss him every day. But even though I don't understand it in this life, I will someday understand when I join him in heaven. I like to think that Daddy is up there taking care of our sweet Adam. They have each other now. As hard as it was to say goodbye, I know that God didn't make a mistake. I know that he wasn't surprised by your Daddy's death. He has numbered all of our days. God planned it specifically from the beginning of time. He even planned for you to have a child with Down syndrome before you were born yourself. He makes no mistakes, dear. And I think if you truly embrace your calling, you will find much joy in a place where you can only see shadows right now. Will it be easy? No. But life never is– no matter what your story, and no matter which chapter you are on."

Julie changed the subject suddenly. "You know how much I love to cross-stitch?"

"A new favorite pillow every Christmas." Claire dutifully replied.

"Yes, well, you are welcome." Julie said with deliberate syllables— pretty close cousin to sarcasm. Mother and daughter smiled at each other even while tears were still wet on their cheeks.

"Have you ever seen the back of one of my cross stitch projects?"

"The back? No. Why?"

"If you ever look at the back of a cross stitch project, you see random bits of strings. Chaotic, colorful, disorganized string tangled every which way. It's rather disconcerting how horrible the back looks. Even with a beautifully smooth, organized, brilliantly stitched picture in the front, the strings in the back will be a mess. In fact, if you look only at the back, the picture makes absolutely no sense. If you look only at the back, you would have to wonder at my sanity as the artist. Have I started to go senile?"

"I think we saw that start to happen years ago." Claire quipped with almost a gleam in her eye.

"Ha. You are hilarious," Julie said.

"I guess my point is," Julie continued, "Life is like that, too. Sometimes we see only the beautifully perfected front picture. Sometimes we see only the tangled mess behind the scenes picture.

But the truth is, both are valuable parts of the same picture. The tangled, messy parts create the beautiful picture, but the beautiful picture wouldn't exist without the tangled side. When it comes to hard things in life, God uses them to purge away ugly parts of us to make us more beautiful to him. Hard things will happen for no discernable reason. But the artist? He has this all planned so carefully. What seems like a tangled mess to you right now is the beginning of the most glorious picture that you can even imagine."

"But what will people think? What will they say? All they will be able to see is that we have a disabled child. To them it will look like we've failed at parenting before we've even started."

"Honey, something I've learned in life is that people tend to criticize and judge those things that they don't understand. When someone else's style is totally different from what you would choose, you call it tacky. If an event is not exactly your cup of tea, you say it wasn't planned very well. Should you attend a charity that you have absolutely no interest in supporting, you say it's a waste of time and energy. The thing is– people may judge from afar. People may treat your family and Samuel differently at times, but the biggest reason why is because they don't understand. You will have this amazing secret. It will be a revelation that you get to live with every day while the average person might have to live a long time to learn it."

"A secret? Like what?"

"You will know the value of a human life— all life. You have in your grasp the opportunity to truly understand the selfless sacrifice of serving your child, the importance of loving unconditionally, and the knowledge that God's creation is a beautiful thing— all of it. Every last person was crafted perfectly and brilliantly even when we don't always understand. I can't help but think of the Special Olympics. I've been volunteering with them for several years now with Uncle Gordon— he's on their board of directors. Have you ever been to one of their games?"

Claire shook her head feeling that her wet curls dried enough to bounce just a touch with the movement. Uncle Gordon was on the board at Special Olympics? How did she not know this?

"Those events are just the coolest, most amazing things I have ever been to," Julie said. "At first, it was strange seeing so many people competing on a level so foreign to what I was used to seeing. During the Olympics, the participants were achieving simple things and people were cheering so loud— I mean, *so loud*. But Gordon convinced me to stick around and give it a try, and I'm so glad that I did. Getting to know some of those athletes, seeing their drive to achieve things that I took for granted, and witnessing their happiness over their successes was such a joy. It was awesome to see the support of their families and watch their families love them fiercely for exactly who they are. They were there applauding for their athletes and watching them beam with pride over simple achievements that we often ignore– a short dash, a passing of flags– all of it representing years of physical victories. The Special Olympics gives an opportunity to celebrate every ability that God has given– the big and the small. This might be a different world than what you are used to, but it is a beautiful world. It is a world full of hope and promise, a world of happiness and joy, and a world that I think you could really learn something from."

Learn something? Claire pondered this. She had a thriving career and had maintained a 4.0 GPA throughout her entire schooling experience. While she appreciated the picture her mom painted for her, she had a hard time understanding what she could learn from someone who gave awkward hugs at Wal-Mart.

"But…" Claire tried, "It's horrible and awful to have a child with Down syndrome."

"How do you know? Have you done it before?"

"Well, no but—"

"It's your *perception* that it's a horrible and awful thing to have a child with Down syndrome. That doesn't mean that that is reality. It's like you've been studying a set of flashcards your whole life where one side says *child with Down syndrome* and the other side says *BAD*, and you memorized it that way. But what if your handmade flashcards got it wrong? Like your tenth grade history test where you got a B- because you copied half of the answers down wrong on your study cards?"

Claire remembered that dark day all too well.

"You don't have to passionately love your baby today. It's okay. You're allowed to process this however you need to. There is no right or wrong way to do this. But show up. Show up for your baby. Be there for him. He needs you. Go through the mundane motions of day-to-day and allow him to show you who *he* is— not his diagnosis, not his health problems— him. Because God gave him a personality all his own that you are not going to want to miss. Give your baby a chance. Don't judge him based on a label. He could change your life in a really wonderful way. But it's up to you if you will let him. Open up your heart and let him in."

Claire paused for a long while, her mother's words sinking into her heart slowly. She had one final protest. "But— but what if he's deaf?" She whispered.

"Then you learn sign language. Whatever it takes."

Suddenly a new voice erupted through the room. "Oh.my.gosh. Gross! What are you doing to my baby?"

Felicity was home. Suddenly painfully aware that her nephew was attached to her breast without permission, Claire blushed at her sister's greeting but didn't try to move him away from her as she stayed on the floor next to Mother.

So she merely owned it and said, "Welcome to the party, sister dear."

CHAPTER FORTY-FIVE
Felicity

Felicity strode into her room indignantly. It seemed different somehow. Strange. First there was the baby. Then there were her sister's naked boobs exposed to the entire world. No, she didn't want that baby sucking the life out of her one boob at a time, but even more than that she didn't want to see her sister's boob stuffed in the baby's face. Disgusting! Nobody wants to see that!

"Relax, dear. No one is hurting your baby. Breastfeeding is a very natural and beautiful thing. It is extremely beneficial to both your sister and Michael. No one is forcing you to watch," Mother said.

"Um, hello! You're in my room! Where else am I supposed to go?"

"Clearly you've already figured that out. Where have you been? I thought you promised to watch him while I stepped out?" Mother said.

Now it was Felicity's turn to blush.

"Yeah, well, I left a note. I figured Claire wouldn't mind helping her sis out in a pinch."

Claire said nothing, head bent over the baby. The look of adoration on her face ticked Felicity off. But there was something else too— a look Felicity recognized well from years of sibling competition. Jealousy? Why in the world would Claire be jealous? There was nothing special about her baby. It was just a baby! An over enthusiastic pooper at that. Literally, he was a poop.

"What kind of pinch, exactly?" Mother pressed, nosey as ever.

"I had to go see Elliot, okay? He finally texted me and this was my chance." Felicity followed this up with a kind of deep sigh that would discourage probing.

"Chance to do what?"

Clearly, her passive aggressive sigh didn't do its job. She followed it up with an eye roll and a slight stomp of her foot.

"UGH you just don't get it! I'm sorry I left the baby. Really, I am. But he's fine. Everything is fine." Felicity tried to keep her voice calm, but she clipped the last "fine" with a bit of a throat squeeze, dramatically gesturing around her room to demonstrate all of the fineness that surrounded her.

"Everything okay with Elliot?"

"Well if you must know, he broke up with me. Okay? Are you happy now? Of course you are. You've wanted me to break up with him since the beginning. You never liked him. And this is so not fair. Please, can I just have my room back to take a nap? I am exhausted. I don't think you guys can even comprehend what a horrible day I've had."

Mother and Claire exchanged a look that Felicity didn't understand, but it ticked her off even more. Rude.

"How about it, dear. Should we go make that cake so that Felicity can recover from her tragic day?" Mother patted Claire's knee and stood up with noticeable creaks coming from her old lady bones as she did so.

Felicity could have sworn they were laughing at her. And also— cake?

"Yeah, that sounds good." Claire took the sleeping baby and lifted him gently back into the pack 'n play. "I thought he had a messy diaper, but it looks like maybe it was just gas."

"Are you sure it was the baby's?" Felicity smirked at her older sister.

"Oh right, it was just a lingering odor wafting out of your closet. My bad," Claire said.

"Why, did you hang out there earlier?" Felicity said.

Mother put an end to the banter. "Felicity, go ahead and take a nap. We'll hear the baby if he wakes up." Mother said, ever the peacemaker, pointing to the baby monitor on the nightstand.

A baby monitor? Her room was bugged? What the— how long has that been there? Is that even legal? No matter. Tiredness grabbed ahold of her annoyance and told her it wasn't worth fighting any more battles today. She didn't have the energy to deal with this startling breech of her privacy right now. She would pitch a hissy fit over that later.

"Felicity?"

"What?" Mothers never knew when to let things go. What now.

"I just wanted to say that I'm sorry. I know you really liked Elliot."

"Whatever."

"I want you to always remember that you are beautiful. And strong. Your relationship with Elliot failing or succeeding doesn't define your worth in life. You are an amazing person with or without a boyfriend. One day you will become more comfortable in your own skin, and hopefully then you will finally be thankful for the unique person that the Lord has made you to be. You are so much like your dad sometimes it's unreal. You got his brains…and his red hair. What more could a girl want in life?" Felicity could hear the smile in her Mother's voice as Felicity turned away to hide the sudden tear that popped into her eye. *Traitor*, she thought angrily.

Felicity paused before clearing her throat and saying very quietly, "Do you think he would still think I'm beautiful? I mean, I've changed a lot since he left." She gestured toward her lumpy middle, which was somehow still popping out from underneath her longest, most favorite tank top. Had it shrunk too?

"Oh my goodness, yes. You are gorgeous. Beauty isn't defined by Hollywood or magazines or social media. Beauty comes from within, and it is there for you whenever you are ready to see it."

Felicity was soaking in her mother's words like a dry sponge thrown out into the rainstorm when an unexpected source jumped into the conversation.

"I've always been jealous of your hair, you know." Claire admitted.

Felicity whipped around to face her sister. "You? Of my hair?" What? For years she had lusted after her sister's stylish brown curls.

"Yeah. Your hair always has this sheen to it that makes it look like it was just straightened by a professional. I could never get my hair to look like that in a million years. Plus, the color is so fun. Brown seems to boring to me if I spend too much time around you."

"Boring? You?" The idea of Claire ever wanting to be more like Felicity was news to Felicity.

"Yeah. I've made my peace with it. But when I was your age, I remember hating everything about my body and hair. Now I've come to a point where it is what it is and I stand up tall and proud with what I've got. What was boring to me as a teen are all of Trevor's dreams come true. Now I wouldn't change myself for the world."

Mother and Claire left the room, and Felicity collapsed back on her beautiful, beautiful bed.

Driving home, she had been overcome with sadness. She couldn't believe that her relationship was over. Done. Something inside of her felt dead, betrayed, depressed.

But now she felt something— she wasn't entirely sure what— growing in the midst of the ashes. Something strong.

What should she do about the baby? Now that Elliot didn't want her for the baby, what was she doing thinking that she could be a mother right now? Her mind went back to her default. What would Daddy say? Felicity thought back to when she was signed up for basketball last year because she was tall and logic suggested that this sport might be a good fit for her. But somehow her coordination failed to get the memo that she was meant to do well and she ended up in the Emergency Room with her second concussion of the season (how did such a flat floor keep tripping her?) Mother had told her that it was okay not to do basketball anymore.

"But I would be quitting! Daddy said never to quit," Felicity protested.

"Daddy was absolutely right. But if he were here, I think he would tell you that sometimes there are things that you are naturally good at and things that you aren't. It's up to us to decide whether we want to work to become better, or move on to other interests. That's part of the joy in life— discovering the things that we love to do."

Felicity remembered this conversation now as she lay in her bed. Would it be quitting to give up on the baby? Did this same rule apply?

Thinking of her brief stint in basketball reminded her of meeting Elliot at one of her games. Well, *after* the game in the Emergency Room. He was waiting to get some stitches due to an unfortunate incident with a glass bottle and they shyly exchanged numbers before Mother invited him to their youth group activity that weekend. He showed up for the movie night and the rest was history.

When she was finally ready to once again leave her bed sanctuary, she would need to look extra fabulous to show Elliot what he was missing. She needed to get super awesome grades to show all those people who said she was so dumb for getting pregnant how smart she really was. Daddy had always said she was brilliant. Who was right– him or the rest of the world? Maybe it wouldn't kill her to focus and make some life goals. Mother was always hinting for her to "make plans for life" (like a hammer hints to the nail to go into the wall). Mother had said a baby would be a "wake up call," and while Felicity didn't appreciate the overly dramatic way Mother said this, maybe she was right.

Oh goodness, just those words made Felicity's skin crawl, *Mother was right.* But mother also said that Elliot wasn't good enough for her, and clearly she had been right about that. What a jerk he was. He was— words that she couldn't say without getting her mouth washed out with soap.

But even more than proving it to Elliot and all the others, Felicity wanted to prove it to herself. That she was more than this mistake. That she was more than the girl who got dumped over a fudge sundae. That she was more than the bad sister— the daughter who made poor choices.

She thought about the look of disgust that Elliot had given her, the look of disappointment on Mother's face, the look of disapproval on her sister's. Felicity missed the look that her Dad used to give her. One that she never had to earn or fight for, a look of pure love and acceptance.

Could she be beautiful? Could she be happy in her own skin? Could she really make something of her life that would make Daddy proud? It was time to care about something real. She was tired of all the looks of shame. The question was— what?

A thought was tickling at the back of her mind, but she was afraid to say it out loud. Maybe a nap would provide her the strength she needed.

She was suddenly hit with the enormity of what she had done, at how far she had strayed from truth and obedience to that truth. The baby was the least of it all. The lying, sneaking around, and giving things to Elliot that weren't his to take were a pretty big deal. The weight of her selfishness crushed her in a way that it hadn't in a very long time. Tears popped into her eyes, and she didn't move to wipe them away even as they slid slowly down her cheeks.

Closing her eyes, she did something she hadn't done in a year.

"Dear Lord, I'm so sorry. I don't even know what to say or how best to say it because 'I'm so sorry' doesn't seem strong enough somehow.

"I know I've changed— or as mother would say "strayed from the path." Please help me figure out what I'm supposed to do next— how I can make this right. Please forgive me for the mistakes I've made, and thank you for helping me through these last few weeks. Thank you for helping my baby to be healthy. And thank you that Mother has taken care of him for me. Please—"

But somewhere in there she fell fast asleep, sleeping more peacefully than she'd slept in a long time. And while she slept, she dreamed of her Daddy. They were playing chess together again, and when she was stumped as to what that next move should be? He gave her a suggestion.

CHAPTER FORTY-SIX
Julie

Julie would always remember this day. Leaving Felicity's room, they first bandaged up Claire's foot, but now they were ignoring the heat of the day and baking a cake. She was enjoying measuring ingredients, stirring, beating, pouring chocolate goodness into a pan, baking, frosting, praying for wisdom— all the while sharing a new kind of openness with Claire that they had never shared before.

Claire turned on some Baroque music for some ambiance and even though baking a cake is normally a one-person job, an extra cook in her kitchen had never been more welcome and fun.

Wearing matching ruffled aprons and washing each dish the other had just used, they worked together as the perfect team.

Julie was relieved to finally share the truth with Claire about her adoption. Claire had all kinds of questions that peppered throughout their baking hour at random moments.

"What was she like?" Measure two and a half cups of flour.

"Well, she had beautiful curly hair like yours only she wore hers short above the shoulder. She was very sweet and very hopeful that her daughter could have a good life. She cried when she handed you to me. It was hard for her to say goodbye." One teaspoon of baking soda.

"Then why did she give me up?" Sprinkle in some salt. Pour in melted chocolate.

"She told me that she didn't feel like she could give you the life that you deserve. The dad was no longer in the picture, and she struggled with many different types of addiction. She wanted you to have a chance to have a family who would love and care for you. I think it was so brave of her to make this decision, and I have been so thankful for her every day since." Add flour to the sugar/butter mixture with some buttermilk.

"Do you think a lot about the baby that you lost?" Turn off mixer for a moment of silence.

"Every day. But in my mind when I see him, I see him as my third child growing up alongside you and Felicity. I wouldn't trade you for the world, but truth be told I probably would have never met you if he hadn't died. God was good to bring us together. I can't even imagine life without you. I am so proud of you— every day." Pour batter into carefully prepared round pans with wax paper lining the bottoms.

"Whose idea was it to adopt me— yours or Dad's?" Pop three evenly filled pans into the oven, lean against the counter, and grab now-lukewarm cups of coffee.

"He actually came to me with the idea first. It took me a few weeks to be won over, but he was so excited to help this new little babe that he convinced me. When he met you for the first time…I have never seen him more in love. I think you completely stole the thunder from our wedding day! From the very start you were his little girl."

As the lovingly prepared batter rose and baked in the oven, their conversation continued to follow questions about the adoption

266

and then into their usual everything and nothing. Claire loved that her mother was her best friend and that they could talk about anything together. Knowing now that she was adopted and knowing that this familiar dynamic between them would never change made Claire's heart swell with love anew. She was so thankful for the childhood that she had been given. She was thankful for the mother who was brave enough to give her up and the mother who was brave enough to love her so fiercely all these years.

The last of the delectable fudge frosting was just being swirled onto the top of the stunning chocolate cake when a yawning stretching Felicity came walking slowly down the stairs.

"Mother." She said. "I have made a decision."

Julie froze with frosting-covered fingers and a slight dusting of flour on her forehead.

"I have decided that I don't want to be a mom. Like not at all. Not even a little bit. Nope. Big no. Absolutely not."

"Okay," Julie said slowly.

"I think we should give the baby up for adoption."

Pregnant pause.

"Honey, how would you feel if I adopted him?"

"Do you really want to? Or are you just saying that because you feel guilty or something. I mean, no offense, but you're kinda old."

Deep breaths. Julie steadied herself.

"I would really, truly love to adopt him. I would love to do the baby thing again. I feel young enough at heart to do this again. We could keep him in the family, and although you wouldn't be functioning as his mother, you would be able to watch him grow up. Would you be up for that?"

"Okay, cool. Well, yeah, sure, if you really want him, he's all yours. I would audition you for the role of mother, but that feels rather ironic. I guess it wouldn't be the worst thing in the world to have him kicking around here. He is kind of cute. As long as I don't have to change any diapers!" Felicity's facial expression held a dozen conflicting emotions.

"But will you care in ten years when you're ready to start a family of your own?"

"Trust me. I ain't going through that again. I mean it when I say— I don't want to be a mother ever."

"You'll change your mind."

"No, I won't."

"Yes you will," Claire whispered.

Felicity shook her head no.

"What *do* you want to do with your life?"

"Well, I've been thinking a lot about that doctor who was so cool getting the baby out. It might be fun to do that someday."

"Deliver babies?"

"Well maybe. Some kind of doctor thing. Because it was just neat how he helped me to get through that horrible, no-good, very bad day. I was in so much pain and kind of panicked. He kept calm and coached me through it. It was kinda awesome. I would like to do that for someone someday."

Julie said, "If you want to be a doctor you're going to need to step up your game. Study harder. Goof off less. In order to go to med school, your academics have to be spotless."

"*Mother*. I know. I can do that. Hey— cake! Is it ready? Can I have some?"

Julie shot Claire another "oh Felicity" look. And then they cut up the sinfully chocolate tower of goodness, sat around the kitchen island, and ate cake.

After two large bites, Felicity went from cold to warm.

"Hey mom?"

"Yes?"

"I just wanted to say...thanks. Thanks for being so cool about all of this."

The magic 't' word. Chills went up and down Julie's spine.

"You're welcome dear. I love you very much."

The "love you too" was quiet and was muffled by bite number three of cake as Felicity quickly averted her eyes. But Julie heard it.

She really needed to make this cake more often.

It was only after several minutes of lively conversation between the three with just the normal touch of loving sarcastic twist that Julie asked, "Claire, are you going to go back to see Samuel again today?"

Claire nodded, swallowing her last bite of cake as if refueled by an unseen resolve. "Yes, yes I am."

CHAPTER FORTY-SEVEN
Claire

"So what's the deal? Why is he still at the hospital?" Felicity asked.

"He, um, he's pretty sick." Claire said quietly.

"But why? Why is he sick?" Felicity pressed, focusing on scooping a large bite of moist goodness onto her fork.

"He— well really, um, he, well, Samuel has, um, Down syndrome" This sentence by far was the hardest sentence Claire had ever spoken to her sister.

"Down syndrome? Really? Hey there's a kid in my class who has Down syndrome— Jenna. She is super sweet and everyone at school loves her."

"Jenna? What's Jenna's last name? How come I've never met her?"

"Jenna Brickman. She isn't really involved in the music program at school so she doesn't go down your classroom hallway at all. But she is super into art. Her stuff is almost always on display on one of the front bulletin boards. Hasn't Trevor mentioned her?

He is always stopping her in the hallway to ask about her latest creation."

"He is?" Claire could totally picture this happening.

"Oh yeah. He calls her 'Jenna The Master Artist'. She gets a big kick out of it. I'm surprised he hasn't ever mentioned her to you," Felicity said.

"Do the other kids ever— you know— make fun of her for being different?"

"Well, sure, once someone did. But then that person was found beaten to death in the back alley. Figuratively, of course. Everyone loves Jenna. There's no pressure around her to pretend to be something we're not. We can all just be ourselves and she loves us exactly for that. I think it's cool that your baby will be like her."

"Well, not just like her. He will still be his own person," Claire corrected.

"Yeah, sure. Well, he could do a lot worse than be just like her."

"Like be the pregnant teenager dropout?"

"Who's dropping out? I'm going to be a doctor, haven't you heard?" Felicity protested.

"I did, in fact. But then I figured *The Onion* probably wasn't the best source for my news," Claire smirked.

"Hardy har har. Are you going to finish your cake?"

Claire pushed the rest of her piece toward her sister. "It's all yours. I have someplace I need to be. And sis?

"Yeah?" Felicity paused, fork mid-air.

"Thanks."

"For what?"

"Just, you know, for being you. I love you, and I'm really glad that you're my sister. I think you're going to be an amazing doctor."

Felicity blushed and studied the refrigerator magnets as if her life depended on it.

"Yeah, well, no need to get all mushy. A romantic comedy called— they want their final scene back."

Claire grinned and gave her sister the thing that she loved the most— having the last word.

CHAPTER FORTY-EIGHT
Claire

Grabbing her keys and giving Mother a peck on the cheek, Claire left, having slid back into her once again dry clothes while she waited for the cake to finish baking.

It was no longer storming outside. The rain was exchanged for a sodden landscape; the air was heavy but clear. Her car was carelessly parked on the opposite side of the driveway where she normally parked it. Claire shrugged. It had been an emotional ride over from the hospital.

It was a thoughtful drive back. Even with the late hour, the sun was still up as the summer sun refused to hide itself until the very last. Claire loved the light evenings of the summer. The air that almost started to cool down. The slight stickiness that promised long walks on the beach, ice cream cones, and campfire smores. Tonight the extra light seemed to promise even more to her than usual. Tonight the light brought with it *hope*.

The thought that she had been adopted was new information and challenged her perception of this situation in every way.

Was she disappointed that her birth mother didn't show up for her? That she didn't try to accept her even though she wasn't wanted? No, not at all— although she did have about a hundred questions for her and wondered if meeting her was a horrible idea. Claire had the best childhood and parents a girl could ask for. She was thankful for her birth mother's strength to offer her a chance at life because she was guessing that it wasn't easy to sign over her baby to a complete stranger.

Claire wondered what that was like— putting the baby's needs so selflessly in front of your own that you were willing to give her to a different mother just to ensure that your baby got a good life like she just watched Felicity step up and do for Mother. It made her ruminate on the question— could she give Samuel a good life?

Traffic was clear, and the roads were free for her to make excellent time back to where her boy was still fighting at Grace Hospital NICU. It was 8:30pm. It occurred to her that she hadn't been keeping in contact with Trevor today. No love texts, no info as to where she was— silence. After parking in the surprisingly empty parking garage, she reached for her phone and realized that it was dead. When did that happen?

Walking up to the NICU, she felt a stab of guilt that she wasn't there for Samuel today. What were the nurses thinking about her abandoning her baby all day like that? But in the next instance she pushed the guilt away. She needed today. She needed to take time for herself and to talk to her mother. She took the guilt, mentally packed it into a little box, and then crushed it with a conceptual hammer. Guilt was not going to control her. Not today.

Arriving at the now familiar solid door where she had to wait to be buzzed in, she was thankful that the NICU didn't have visiting hours, rules that dictated the hours in which she could or couldn't see her son. Walking into the room holding the NICU reception desk, she heard the same noises; she smelled the same smells; she felt the same level of panic in the air; but she didn't feel like the same person who had left here earlier today.

A tall figure stood next to her baby's bed. Even the back of his head was handsome. Her footsteps on the hard tile must have caught his attention, because he turned, saw her, and flashed her the stunning smile that she fell in love with those many years ago.

"One of the holes in his heart closed." He excitedly blurted out.

"What?"

"His heart. They did an Echo this afternoon, and the biggest hole closed on its own. Surgery is off the books."

He was beaming.

"What? Nobody called me!"

"They tried. I tried. We couldn't get ahold of you. Did you turn your phone off?"

"Oh yeah, it died. I'm not sure when."

He studied her for a minute. She blushed under his scrutiny and looked down.

Trevor said, "You look better than the last time that I saw you. Not that you looked bad before— you could never look bad, it's just that—" He said.

"Stop. It's okay. I feel better. I went to Mother's and took a nap," Claire said.

"Good. I'm glad you were able to get some rest. Are you ready for the second part of the good news?"

"There's more?"

Claire looked down at her little guy and much looked the same— and yet entirely different. The yellow pallor was gone. His face actually looked pink. The cpap hiding most of his face had been replaced by a clear tube that ran up each of his cheeks and into his nose. She could really see his face for the first time. Catching her breath, her first thought was, "oh my, he is handsome."

"His oxygen numbers have improved so much that they're letting us hold him."

"What? Really?"

"The nurse left to get some more pillows to help keep him still and steady in our arms, but yes, the doctors said it's now okay to move him enough for a hold."

"Can I...do you mind? Would it be okay—?"

"Of course you can hold him first. I was going to do it when you weren't here, but now that you are here, you should definitely get first turn. And Sweet?"

"Yes?" She broke her gaze from her little boy to look back up at her husband.

"I'm so proud of you. You did such a great job getting our little bub here."

She blushed at the intensity of his look and was embarrassed to admit how much she needed to hear him say those very words.

Ending the moment, the smiling night nurse returned holding two large pillows.

"Are you ready to hold your son?" The nurse asked.

Was she?

Claire sank into the large easy chair that had been pushed into the room apparently for this very reason. The nurse put a pillow into her arms, and then carefully— oh so carefully— lifted him onto the pillow. It was tricky getting all the wires out of the bed untangled and still plugged in, but this nurse knew what she was doing. Claire just sat with arms open and ready to receive the most precious bundle ever gifted to her.

One arm held the pillow possessively while the other snaked up to his face. Brushing the skin that she was just seeing for the first time, she smiled.

Almond-shaped eyes squeezed tightly shut. Puffy cheeks lay still under the tubing. A long forehead rested under something that she was finally able to see for the first time— a head full of curly brown hair. Shiny curls lopped into each other with playful familiarity. He lay still in her arms. His chest rose and fell with the breath of life.

Trevor knelt down next to her and reached out a hand to stroke Samuel's little cheek. "Isn't he beautiful?" he said.

"He sure is," she whispered.

Staring at his tiny face so full of miraculous life, it suddenly clicked with her that this wasn't about her at all. This wasn't about her dreams, ambitions, or goals in motherhood. This wasn't about her birth story being messed up or her plans going awry. This was about *him*— his life— his story. This was about the many moments in front of this tiny new person and the life— however long or short— that had been gifted to him. This was exactly how he was meant to be. There was no mistake here. No judgment from God. Samuel was created perfectly just for her. She just didn't realize that she had been defining "perfectly" with misinformed perceptions until now. Who was she to tell the Creator what was and wasn't perfect and good? She didn't know what this would look like or how she would do the long term, but she knew what she had to do today— right now.

"Dear Lord," she prayed silently, "Please forgive me for my selfishness— for somehow thinking that this was about me. Thank you for sending me this beautiful baby. Thank you for healing his heart and his transient leukemia issues. Please help me to be the mother that he deserves. Please help me to be able to daily die of myself in order to be there fully for him and provide whatever he might need to navigate this life. I choose happiness. I choose joy. *I choose love.* I choose to embrace this calling that you have for me with all the talents that you have gifted me. Thank you for sparing his life and for sending him to us. Even though I don't understand why he has Down syndrome, please help me to graciously accept it as part of who he is. Please give me the strength and wisdom to be the best mom possible to my sweet boy. Amen."

Staring at her son, she realized that he didn't need to *achieve* to be great. He was already great, simply by being him.

"He's such a gift to us," Trevor said, breaking the silence
"A gift?"

"Yeah. I mean, there will be hard times— like now when
he's so sick. But I think that's part of the gift. The Lord uses hard
times to bring us closer to him to try us in fire and purify us further.
He's choosing us for this because He wants us to become more like
Him. He wants us to change even further into His image. Samuel's
diagnosis is a gift. It's a chance to serve, to grow, and to love. I
mean— look at him; the boy's got spirit! The nurse told me that he
pulled his feeding tube out twice today. He's a fighter. I think he
gets that from you."

Trevor grinned at her before continuing. "I don't think that
God could have sent us a more amazing child, and I don't think the
hard times will be as frequent as we think now. I think we're going
to have a good life with our little bub, and I think he will surprise us
every step of the way. I know this because he told me that he has
big plans for life in Morse Code with his wire yanking antics."

Claire nodded with a smile toward her husband, strangely
enough no longer annoyed with his perspective toward Down
syndrome. She then grabbed the chubby hand with the adorably
short fingers, still wearing the bracelet that said that he was hers.
Taking a deep breath full of promise and love, she said,

"Hello, Samuel Lewis Bailey. It's nice to finally meet you.
Mommy's here."

She had said that before— met him already. But this time,
she really meant it.

EPILOGUE
(five years later)
Claire

Claire jumped. Holding two small hands and feeling the air rush around her, she jumped on that trampoline with abandon and yet care. The little boy in front of her couldn't keep his balance if she jumped too high, and they were jumping together. So she gave it her all in spirit while holding back physically, a smile owning her face.

He grasped her hands tightly, lifted his feet slightly off of the tightly stretched surface of the trampoline, and grinned up at her before shouting, "Bounce!"

"Good job! Good jumping!" She gushed as he did it again, his sturdy legs decidedly getting a workout. Looking up at her with the adoring look that small boys reserve only for their mothers, his grin turned into a completely dazzling smile that she would never tire of, paired with an infectious giggle.

There was a time that he had fought to walk. And now he walked, ran, climbed, swam, and jumped like no one's business. He was so strong. Perhaps the strongest little boy she had ever had the privilege of knowing.

Mother and Felicity were watching on the sidelines. Felicity was home on a break from school. She had just finished her first year of her undergrad at Duke University studying premed. Surprising them all with her determination to become a doctor, Felicity had changed dramatically from that teenager who had left a post-it note as her child's babysitter.

Michael was on the play set next to the trampoline. Climbing, sliding, swinging, running— this boy was constantly on the move as well.

Looking around at the yard that any daycare would be proud to claim, Claire smiled. Trust Mother to go all out in making a yard for Michael and Samuel. A play set, a trampoline, three push cars, two tricycles, a sandbox. What happened to Mother's beautifully manicured lawn?

Michael ran over to the trampoline to talk to his cousin.

"Samuel, come on! Come swing with me!"

"Okay! Swing!" Samuel enthusiastically said in his sweet voice that Claire would never tire of hearing before he jumped down to join his cousin. Claire had been abandoned, but she didn't care. Smiling as her son ran the short distance to the swings, she couldn't help but remember.

She remembered those long ago NICU days. She remembered the fear. She remembered the countless doctors appointments and the hundreds of hours of therapy. She remembered the many gracious people that fought with them on Team Samuel. She remembered the first time that he smiled at her, an eye-squinting smile that engulfed his entire face. She remembered the first day she could carry him around without the oxygen machines. She remembered his first step at twenty-seven months. His first word at thirty months. She remembered the first time he called her Mama. She remembered his first day of preschool. She remembered when he made his first friend. She remembered when he drew a circle, colored a picture for her, wrote his name.

But most of all she remembered his first violin lesson. His learning curve was definitely slower than that of her other students, but he was getting it. He worked tirelessly on Mississippi Hot Dog, and she knew that he would get it in his own time. He grabbed his tiny 1/16 case and ran to her every time she practiced, desperate to play his "ioin, IOIN" too. She remembered when she first realized that he loved music— that first time he danced with epic moves— that first time he clapped along in almost-perfect rhythm. She remembered the first time she realized that Down syndrome wasn't stealing his ability to enjoy music. If anything it seemed to enhance it. He enjoyed music with a reckless abandon that she never seemed to have, with an ability to really feel the music on a secret level that she had never reached. She envied him for this. She herself had grown as a musician in ways she hadn't seen coming as she mothered her music-loving boy.

And as she remembered, joy and thanksgiving flooded her heart until it was overflowing. This was not a new pastime, this remembering. She did it often. But never once did she want to take for granted the miracle of life that she had been given. She was so proud of her son. Heart-clenchingly, all-consumingly proud of him. He was the most amazing person that she knew. Being his mother was the happiest she had ever been in life.

Five years ago she was terrified of Down syndrome. Now, she couldn't remember why.

Because as she showed up for Samuel, as she worked alongside him, and as she cheered for his accomplishments, she learned that her flashcards had been wrong. Oh so very wrong. It wasn't: one side: Down syndrome, flip side: BAD. It was: one side: Down syndrome, flip side: a little boy. A valuable, perfectly created, one-of-a-kind little boy. Having a child with Down syndrome was what she made it to be. And as she put all of herself into parenting this little boy, got to know him, and learned many things about life along the way, she discovered that this was very, very good. Parenting Samuel was an experience she wouldn't change for the world.

The list that listed the physical and mental things to expect with Down syndrome that absolutely terrified her? Yeah, she rewrote it for herself. She now knew that there was so much more to that list than the coldness the medical brochure claimed.*

She thought often of the greeter in Wal-Mart who had so annoyed her while pregnant, and on this side of things imagined how that mother must feel about her son. *Happiness* that he found a job that made him happy. *Pride* that he could speak and walk so well. *Love* that he was out in the world making his mark. *Hope* that people could see him through the lenses of acceptance instead of through the blindness of prejudice as Claire had done. She had learned that when it comes to individuals with a disability, there was more to them than what first impressions might offer. There was a deep well of love and hope and happiness and pride and *personhood* underneath the outer shell of difference. When this comes across as something to be feared— it is not the person with disability's fault. It is the fault of the mind too narrow to comprehend a life beyond what might be perceived as normal. This she had learned. Samuel taught her this.

She read on a blog somewhere "I have learned that parenting is not about who we make our children to be, but rather about how we respond to who they fundamentally are." Claire immediately requested it to be on her cross-stitched pillow for Christmas this year. Mother had complained that it was too long. Felicity then requested an entire page from a medical journal on her pillow so that she could learn through osmosis as she slept, and Mother decided that Claire's request wasn't that ridiculous after all.

Claire jumped down off the trampoline and went to join Felicity and Mother at the patio table. They were discussing Felicity's latest boyfriend— a fellow pre-med student who wanted to study podiatry.

"No, he doesn't have a foot fetish. He is just really interested in studying the bones of the feet."

"Does he give you foot rubs?" Mother asked curiously.

"Well, maybe. But doesn't everyone do that?"

"Um…sounds like a foot fetish to me." Claire added with a gleam in her eye. They so loved to tease Felicity. Especially since she could give it back so well.

"Oh brother. You're just jealous because your husband is only a Vice Principal." Felicity said.

"Actually— you can take away the 'Vice' in front of that. He just got word that he will be the new #1 around Edgewood Charter School." Speaking of Trevor, Claire thought again about how their marriage had changed since they added in a child with a disability. Claire was deeply thankful that the experience had drawn them even closer together as they joined forces to fight together for their son.

"Really? Oh so exciting! The boys will be thrilled to know that Daddy/Uncle Trevor is the one in charge of their new kindergarten experiences next month," Mother said.

"It will be nice to know that they are in good hands. Felicity, have you decided on a focus yet?" Claire asked.

"To be honest I've known for a while now. Just waiting to see if I could actually do this thing before announcing it to the world."

"Really? What? You can tell us."

"So you can tell me I have a fetish too?" Felicity grinned.

"Of course I won't! Spill!"

"Cardiology. I want to study the heart so that I can help other ten-year-old girls avoid losing their Daddies like I did. And I know that cardiology is ridiculously hard. I know this. But I am going to work my butt off to get there. For Dad."

There was a moment of silence while they all blinked back something that looked a lot like tears.

"That is amazing. You will be an awesome cardiologist." Claire beamed at her sister while reaching over to give her hand a quick squeeze.

"Tea?" Her mother asked, clearing a suspiciously tearful sounding voice. "Do you want some tea, dear?"

"Oh yes, thank you." Claire replied.

Holding out her arms, her Mother surrendered back the pink frilly bundle she had been bouncing on her lap so that she could grab the pitcher and pour another glass of sweet tea. The condensation on the outside of the pitcher promised ice cold goodness in Claire's glass for this warm afternoon play date.

"Hey baby girl." Claire smiled into the dimpled face of her beautiful daughter with bouncing curly brown hair to match her brother's. "How was your time with Grandma?" The chubby cheeked seven-month-old cooed in response while trying to grab the glass of tea for her own.

"Oh our Elizabeth just gets cuter and cuter every day!" Mother gushed. Being thrown into new motherhood again with Michael, Mother had never looked better or had more energy. Something about having a babe in her life seemed to be keeping her young.

Claire was about to quip back "Of course!" when she noticed the action on the playground. Samuel was climbing toward the slide; Michael was holding out a hand and helping steady Samuel during the worst of the climb. Samuel was much shorter than his cousin, but the boys could almost pass as brothers. Handsome brothers. Even though she knew they didn't actually share genes, she still didn't think that they would ever be able to deny each other.

She watched him slide confidently down by himself, and she loved the normalcy of the moment. A normalcy she never thought she would have. And yet— life had never been better or sweeter. Every moment and every accomplishment no matter how small brought a new kind of appreciation. Was that because of

Down syndrome or just motherhood in general? It was hard for her to differentiate between the two.

Looking around, she whispered a prayer of thanksgiving. She took in the beautiful day of sunshine and leafy green, the family with which to smile and banter with, her son's enthusiasm and ability to play like any other boy, and the way that she had changed and grown because of Down syndrome. She was thankful. Down syndrome was her God's good for her. God planned this life for her— this amazing, fantastic life, this life that she fought and cried against. And yet little did she realize while fighting, this was gifted to her by the God who never failed in his goodness even when she doubted Him. All things do work together for good.

The first year of his life, she continued to struggle with his diagnosis as his health issues took center stage. She needed to rediscover peace and acceptance more than once. But with her family's support, she buckled down into the hard and found beauty. Inspired by how hard he worked to achieve things, she found a new hero in life. Getting to know him through the thick of some rather pressing health issues, she learned how to love, *really love*. Down syndrome didn't ruin her life— it brought her new perspective. Perspective because of her son who was growing her along with him— opening her heart, widening her eyes, and teaching her ultimate trust in a God who is always in control and who is always good.

Thankful, she whispered a prayer of love in her heart for her little family. This wasn't what she planned for her family. It was so much better.

©2015 deannajsmith.com

*Claire's Rewritten LIST:

Like most new parents who receive a Down syndrome diagnosis for my child, I was given a list. A list of potential features/problems to expert.

This list is cold, emotionless, and almost comes across as grotesque if you are reading it with fear already in your heart. The sharply angled words on this list tore apart my motherhood dream and became almost like a "side effects" commercial gone wrong.

Now the list has become a part of my life, and I think that whoever made these lists didn't capture the spirit of their assignment. Kind of like if someone was told to describe a Christmas celebration and they said only "Might include an evergreen tree and extreme cold *the end*."

Down syndrome is no longer just a list. It has become a part of my heart beating outside my body. And as I was thinking on this list the other day, I decided to rewrite it for myself— with the spirit put back in.

Those **"short fingers and small hands"** are to me those sweet, warm hands that reach for mine and fold so perfectly into my awkwardly large hands. These tiny hands hold a crayon so perfectly, dress himself with such finesse, and tenderly hold onto his favorite toys as he goes throughout his day.

The **"simian crease"** is the line in the palm of his hands that tells me where to lightly stroke as he lays his head against my shoulder and we watch a movie together.

"Flattened facial features" describes the most delicately beautiful face that fills my entire world with joy. Those cheeks are the ones that curve upward into the most gleeful smile imaginable. The extra flatness across his eyes and nose, adds a sort of exotic beauty— an air of mystery— a unique kind of charm.

"Small nose" is the tiny hill in the middle of his face that decorates it perfectly. It's the exact same nose that his sister has.

"Gap between toes" is just a feature of the tiny feet that staccato through my house as if performing a song of victory with every confident step. The feet that run into school full of independence and pride. The feet that walk toward me tired with a "good job well done" theme when school is done. The feet that climb, jump, and run. The feet that keep up with his very active cousin every step of the way.

"Short neck." I have discovered that this is the perfect spot for kisses. A ticklish spot— his neck is guaranteed to get belly laughs that will put a smile on any face. This neck holds high a head full of brown curls. This neck turns quickly as soon as he hears the smallest sound of chocolate being eaten in the farthest corner of the house.

"Small, abnormally shaped ears." This is the place where I gently tuck his hair. The ears that hear me say "I love you". The ears that take in the world around him and then he responds accordingly. The ears with which he appreciates music.

"Upward, slanting eyes" are the almond shaped windows into my son's soul. The most beautiful soul housed in the most beautiful of eyes— this unique shape only adds to the beauty that is Samuel.

"Poor muscle tone" means that when he wraps himself around me for a hug, his entire body melts into mine with a warm grasp that makes all other hugs suddenly seem lacking in comparison. When I pick him up in the morning, there is something very cool about the way he melts into my arms, rag doll fashion. His arms reach up to hold onto my neck, and his face presses into me. Never do I feel needed and loved more than when he lets me carry and hold him.

"Excessive flexibility" means that he does splits and awesome gymnastics tricks like nobody's business. Someday we will find a place for him to channel this skill. But for now? He wowed the socks off of his swim class teacher last week as he did the splits in the water…while swimming.

"Tiny white spots on the colored part of eyes" describes to me blue eyes flecked with extra goodness and love. It's like he has bits of cloud floating in his blue eye skies.

"Short height" means he stays in each size a little bit longer which makes is so much cheaper to dress him handsomely. As he needs more help with certain things, it makes it so much easier that he is smaller and lighter to carry around.

"Extra large, protruding tongue" Honestly he has never once had his tongue protrude. But if he did, I'm guessing it would be to stick his tongue out at me with the sass that I have come to associate with his personality. He does struggle with speech, and I think this does go back to having an extra large tongue (with extra small mouth). But he works so hard, and he has seen huge success in this area. This tongue is the one who says "Mommy" and "Baby" and "Michael" and "Gwama" and "Daddy". This tongue is the one who tells us what Samuel wants. This tongue is the one that tastes his food and has told him that he definitely likes chocolate the best.

"Intellectual disability, mental retardation" He knows the list says this, and he uses this knowledge to always pretend that he doesn't understand instructions (he does)— while he then does whatever he wants, grinning at pulling yet another fast one over on me. #evilgenius There is a difference between developmental delay and "stupid". Samuel is the farthest thing from stupid. In fact, I would venture to say that oftentimes he is way smarter than both of his degree holding parents. Oftentimes things take him longer to learn, but he gets there. In his own time he gets there and then he makes us all wonder why we were in such a hurry.

"Possible heart defects" He ended up having one heart surgery but no actual heart defect. His surgery (at six months old) in fact ended up just being an umbrella shaped object put into his thigh and carried up a vein to his heart. He came away from "surgery" with only a bandaid. A BANDAID. His last heart checkup included perfection and "AHHHHH he's so cute!" from all involved.

"Possible vision problem or crossed eyes" He does wear glasses (just like many others in our family), and they turn him into a mini profession/model/intellectual faster than you can say "cute baby". His ophthalmologist says that because of his flattened features, it makes the eyes look even more crossed than they are. A sort of "crossing mirage" if you will. He has had surgery for crossing. But I will say— these eyes— crossed or not, bespeckled or not— they miss nothing. His favorite activity is learning to read. He works on this all of the time.

I think when doctors hand over the list to new parents shocked with a new diagnosis; they should include all the facts. Like— this list really means nothing. Except to tell you— you are about to have a baby. A super cute, amazing baby. A baby who will rock your world in unexpected ways. A baby who will have struggles and strengths. A baby who will steal your heart and make you wonder how your life even existed before this baby came into your life. A baby who might have some extra health problems but who was paired perfectly with a fighting spirit to overcome and thrive.

So there you go. My Christmas includes more than a stark evergreen tree and extreme cold. It includes twinkly lights, presents, sugar loaded baked goods, a spirit of happiness, plenty of snow, Christmas movie marathons, a story of hope, and so many more awesome things.

Love,
Claire

ACKNOWLEDGEMENTS

So many people made this book possible. First of all, I could not have done this without my three wonderful children who gave me the time and inspiration to write. Second, thank you to my awesome editor, Andrea Huerta who worked tirelessly and patiently with me to get the manuscript ready for publication. I so appreciate her lending me expertise and skill in this area. Then there are all of those who encouraged, read, and helped me along the way— Jennifer Naselli, Sandra Savage, Ruth Sanford, Arielle Hanudel, Sarah Fabrizio, Lydia Bixby, Elizabeth Newton, and Patti Rice. I very much appreciate all of their gracious encouragement and support along the way. Thank you also to Sarah Fabrizio for introducing herself to me in the NICU five years ago and for her encouragement during last year's conversation of "I think I might write a book in which the special needs mom is the villain" (and for not laughing at me when I said this). Patti Rice, thank you for letting me glimpse inside the mind of a mom with teenage girls. A huge thank you to my sister Rebekah Slepitis who not only read and encouraged, but who also gave me insight into the pain of losing a child. John William will forever be in our hearts. Thank you to Kimberly Pratt for discussing with me the goodness of God in the face of loss. Thank you to Wes Pastor for the same conversation involving disability. Thank you to Becky Harris who shared this wisdom with me— "God gave you your talents to prepare you for this motherhood". Thank you to my husband who so graciously put up with a much more stressed-out version of me this past year. Thank you to my wonderful blog readers. Your support and encouragement of Everything and Nothing from Essex (www.deannajsmith.com) means the world to me. It's because of you that I found the courage to write this book. And last but certainly not least— I am so very thankful to God, who in His goodness gave me a child with Down syndrome.

19651630R00167

Made in the USA
Middletown, DE
02 May 2015